An Irresistible Pursuit

REBECCA ROBBINS

AVON BOOKS NEW YORK

AN IRRESISTIBLE PURSUIT is an original publication of Avon Books. This work has never before appeared in book form. This work is a novel. Any similarity to actual persons or events is purely coincidental.

AVON BOOKS
A division of
The Hearst Corporation
1350 Avenue of the Americas
New York, New York 10019

Copyright © 1995 by Robin Hacking
Published by arrangement with the author
Library of Congress Catalog Card Number: 94-96866
ISBN: 0-380-77671-5

First Avon Books Printing: August 1995

AVON TRADEMARK REG. U.S. PAT. OFF. AND IN OTHER COUNTRIES, MARCA REGIS-TRADA, HECHO EN U.S.A.

Printed in the U.S.A.

RA 10 9 8 7 6 5 4 3 2 1

AN IRRESISTIBLE PURSUIT

He loomed over her, seeming almost over-whelmingly large. It occurred to her that Sir Malcolm was in superb physical condition.

Her heart fluttered strangely. When she looked at his face, she found that he was gazing down at her with an expression that seemed as peculiar as the way she was feeling.

"What do we do now?" she asked in a breathy whisper.

For a long moment Sir Malcolm said nothing. Then one corner of his mouth lifted in the crooked grin Phoebe found so engaging.

"My dear girl," he said softly. "Given the circumstances, there can only be one answer to that question."

Phoebe gasped with surprise as he leaned toward her.

Boy meets girl ~~story~~ *How they get together*

Praise for Rebecca Robbins'
AN UNUSUAL INHERITANCE

Sealty Pursuits

"Delightful . . . It will keep you laughing to the very last page."

only in a book

excitment   *Affaire de Coeur*   *suspense could it happen*

"A sparkling tale . . . chock full of amusing touches to charm a growing readership."

Romantic Times

Other Regency Romances by
Rebecca Robbins

Lucky in Love
The Mischievous Maid
An Unusual Inheritance

Other **Regency Romances**
from Avon Books

The Black Duke's Prize *by Suzanne Enoch*
Dear Deceiver *by Elizabeth Lynch*
The Fictitious Marquis *by Alina Adams*
Lacy's Dilemma *by Barbara Reeves*
My Lord Lion *by Rebecca Ward*

Coming Soon

Famous Miss Feversham *by Christie Kennard*

This book is for my mother, Susan Hacking—a woman even more impuslive than Phoebe Lawton. I love you, Mom.

Author's Note

The London Metropolitan Museum, much to the author's dismay, exists solely in her imagination. There is, however, a superb museum in London known as the British Museum.

An
Irresistible
Pursuit

1

Miss Phoebe Lawton pressed her nose close to the glass display box in the London Metropolitan Museum's Egyptian Room, just as she had for the last five mornings and would very likely continue to do as long as her companion and cousin, Mathilde Stoat, was amenable. From the irritated grunts on the bench behind Phoebe, however, she doubted her cousin's goodwill would extend for much more than a few minutes.

Feeling wholly unsympathetic to Matty's groans and mutterings, Phoebe scowled and continued her study of the artifact in the case. She had no patience for those without an appreciation for ancient treasures. Matty's idea of an enjoyable morning was remaining in bed with a sumptuous breakfast and a good book.

While ordinarily Phoebe would not have forced her own desires upon the older woman, just now she was utterly enthralled by the Egyptian amulet in front of her. Thus, she was prepared to hold out against her cousin's displeasure for as long as possible.

She was vaguely aware that the bun into which she'd hastily arrayed her hair that morning had loosened from its pins and lay lopsidedly above one ear. This was no reflection on Tribble, her maid. Phoebe frequently dressed both her hair and her body, since she was not fond of waiting for Tribble's excellent but slow ministrations—or, for that matter, waiting for anyone to do something she could do faster or more successfully herself.

This was especially true when it involved something she desired. She had learned long ago that, if she wanted something, the quickest way of obtaining the desired item was to pursue it herself. When she saw something she wanted, she went after it wholeheartedly and without reservation.

She knew that some people would, undoubtedly, have called this trait impulsiveness. Matty, for example, frequently bemoaned Phoebe's reckless nature, saying that no gentleman in his right mind would ever take such an unrestrained female to wife. After hearing the same argument for the last six years, Phoebe no longer bothered to remind her cousin that seven gentlemen had already tried to do just that—and had been summarily, though politely, refused.

Being self-sufficient was far better, in Phoebe's opinion, than waiting for a gallant knight to sweep one off one's feet and carry one away on a snow-white stallion to his castle on the hill. If a woman did that, Phoebe reasoned privately, she was more likely to step in something unpleasant that the horse left behind, than to live happily ever after.

And who wanted to live in a castle, anyway? Phoebe's own townhouse was comfortable and cozy, and she had everything she needed without depending upon a man to give it to her. Though her preference for living without a man was considered eccentric, that was the way she liked it and she saw no reason to change just to suit society's mores.

Despite Matty's conviction that a husband was a panacea for all of a woman's ills, Phoebe knew otherwise. Her own parents had been a prime example. No one could have observed her father and mother and still come away believing that marriage was the most sublime situation in which a woman could find herself.

Stephen and Lucretia Lawton, with their only child,

Phoebe, had lived on the Lawton ancestral estate in Dorset. It had been no secret to anyone in the neighborhood that Stephen had made Lucretia's life almost unbearable. Phoebe had always known that her mother, who had fallen ill and died of a consumptive ailment when Phoebe was ten years old, had been more relieved by dying than recovering.

It was not that Stephen Lawton was physically abusive. It was, rather, that he, like most men, had always considered his own wants and desires before anyone else's. Especially those of a mere wife. Everyone in the neighborhood had known, when Lucretia Lawton died, that her cause of death had not been the illness that had wasted away her vitals. She had, quite simply, died as a result of too many disappointments.

Lucretia, for example, had always longed to go to London. Each year, Stephen had promised. Each year, something had inevitably arisen to make the trip impossible.

Along with his unreliability, Stephen had had an unfortunate propensity for gambling. Thus, whenever something was needed on the estate or there were bills to be paid, there was never enough money to cover them. It never failed that, when the moneylenders inevitably came banging on the door, Stephen was always away from home, leaving his poor wife to deal with the unpleasantness.

The neighbors had shaken their heads and sighed behind their hands. Poor Lucretia, dying so young. Such a pretty woman. So unfortunate in her marriage. So sad.

Phoebe's father had lived for another seven years after his wife's death, during which time Phoebe was shunted from private school to private school. Her father had made no secret of the fact that, the very day she turned seventeen, she was to be sent to London to find a husband. Fortunately for Phoebe, he had died before fulfilling this dire promise.

By the time Stephen Lawton died, he had gambled away every shilling, as well as the ancestral estate in Dorset, leaving his daughter in unfortunate straits. Phoebe, however, was fortunate to have an adored maiden aunt,

Lucretia's older sister Hepsibah Snood, who lived in London. Thus, Phoebe did indeed go to London, and did indeed have the Season her father had insisted upon.

However, the four offers of matrimony she received in that time were all turned down flat—with Aunt Hepsibah's blessing. By the fourth refused proposal, Phoebe was quite sure her father must have been twirling in his grave.

Aunt Hepsibah was wealthy in her own right. Lucretia had also been wealthy but had, as perforce happened to women the moment they completed their marriage vows, handed her fortune into her new husband's hands for safe-keeping, since everyone knew that women had no financial or business sense. Stephen Lawton, one of those wise, financially shrewd men whom society trusted to handle their wives' dowries, had spent every shilling within three years.

When Aunt Hepsibah died, Phoebe inherited everything, including the London townhouse she now shared with Matty, and she was determined to maintain control over their futures.

While she found men interesting to talk to, she simply did not trust them. Furthermore, even at the furthest reaches of her imagination, she could think of no situation in which she ever would. So it was that, being unconcerned with whether or not the gentlemen at the museum thought her attractive enough to warrant their attention or their future offers of marriage, Phoebe gave her untidy coiffure little more than a passing thought.

Pressing still closer to the display case, she sighed wistfully, like a hungry street child gazing at steaming currant buns in a bakery store window. Squinting, she read aloud softly from the embossed white card that lay in front of the amulet.

"The Eye of Horus. Egyptian. Fourth dynasty. From the burial tomb of Pharaoh Setet II. Discovered in the year of our Lord eighteen hundred and sixteen, by Sir Malcolm Forbes, explorer and adventurer; an Englishman."

She gave a faint nod, recalling the *Times* article about that esteemed gentleman.

Sir Malcolm, who had received his baronetcy from the regent three years before in thanks for all his contributions to the national museums, as well as a few bounteous gifts to the prince of Wales's personal artifact collection, had discovered the magnificent Egyptian burial site approximately a year and a half ago.

The newspaper reported that Sir Malcolm had, prior to the discovery, searched for Setet II's tomb for two years. Then, one fateful afternoon, the baronet lost a lens from his eyeglasses. He bent down to retrieve it and found, instead, the edge of a partially revealed step against the side of the hill. That small happenchance had led to the most incredible archaeological discovery in recent history.

When the Egyptian diggers uncovered the tomb door, the first thing they'd seen was a human skeleton. It had probably belonged to a gravedigger, who had broken into the freshly made tomb intending to loot. In one bony hand he had clutched a small, glittering, solid gold amulet. The Eye of Horus.

Further study of the amulet had uncovered a particularly hideous curse inscribed on its back—a curse which had sent nearly all Sir Malcolm's Egyptian workers scampering.

No doubt, Phoebe thought with grudging sympathy. She felt a chill as she recalled the exact words of the curse—words that, although she'd never expected to see the actual Eye of Horus until finding it at the London Metropolitan Museum, had remained embedded in her mind from the first moment she'd read them.

The curse ran thus: "Woe to him who disturbs the sleep of the pharaoh and steals the sacred Eye of Horus. May his eyes be bored out by dung beetles. May he be trampled by a hundred bull elephants. May he die a painful death and be found wanting on the scales of Anubis. May he be pitched into eternal blackness."

It had been necessary to put the excavation on hold for four weeks while the deserters were replaced.

Phoebe could not fathom how Sir Malcolm had waited those long weeks instead of battering down the tomb door with his bare hands. *She* would have gone crazy at such an obstacle. But then she had always been a bit restive, headstrong if you will, or, as Matty insisted, foolhardy. Sir Malcolm, on the other hand, must be a very patient, deliberate, restrained sort of man.

Considering the reason behind the diggers' flight, Phoebe brushed an errant strand of golden hair out of her eyes and gave a superior sniff. Curses. How utterly ridiculous. Egyptian pharaohs always put curses on their treasures. Everyone knew that. Just as everyone knew the curses never amounted to anything.

Of course, she had to admit that the occurrences surrounding the tomb's opening—once a new digging crew had been found—*had* been a trifle strange. Just as Sir Malcolm had split the seal on the heavy outer door, a large boulder had fallen from the cliffs above and crushed three workmen standing nearby. Sir Malcolm had barely escaped with his life and was said to have walked with a cane ever since.

Phoebe sniffed again. The incident had been strange yes, and most unfortunate. But it had definitely, positively, unequivocally *not* been due to an ancient curse.

Laying her gloved hands against the sides of the display box, she continued studying the amulet with single-minded scrutiny. About three inches wide and two and one half inches long, the Eye was made of solid gold and was suspended from a fine chain of the same precious metal. A large ruby teardrop hung from its right inner corner. The iris was one enormous midnight-blue sapphire, and the pupil appeared to be a rare black diamond.

Wrapped around the amulet's top eyelid was a wide band of lapis-lazuli, the color of the English Channel on a sunny day. A narrower band of lapis ran along the Eye's bottom lid. The inlay work was superb. It was impossible to tell where the blue stone ended and the gold setting began.

Phoebe sighed blissfully. It was splendid workmanship. Simply splendid.

Suddenly another, much louder groan than those which

had come before made Phoebe turn to look at her cousin. "Are you all right, Matty?"

The older woman emitted a sigh not unlike a monsoon wind. Her angular, horsey face creased with displeasure. Her cheeks were flushed the same purplish hue as her gown. She glared balefully.

"No, I am not," she snapped. "Nor would you be if someone had dragged you out of your bed and onto the town with no breakfast."

"We had breakfast," Phoebe replied, keeping a careful rein on her temper. "And we did not leave the house until just before the museum opened, which was shortly after eleven."

Though Matty was seated now, when standing she towered above Phoebe's five feet, two inches. At nigh on six feet, the older woman was a large, raw-boned creature with prematurely gray hair and a nose like a falcon's beak. She was thirty-two, seven years older than Phoebe.

Upon Matty's father's death six years earlier, Matty, penniless and alone, had gratefully agreed to come to London to live with Phoebe. Each quarter Phoebe deposited a generous sum in Matty's bank account, insisting that if Matty were not living with her, she would have to pay a companion anyway.

Although possessed of plenty of money thanks to this generous wage, Matty never wore any colors other than purple or gray, neither of which did anything to improve her sallow complexion. Long ago an admirer had told her that she looked charming in those colors. Phoebe, despite strenuous arguments, had never managed to convince her cousin that the gentleman had obviously not meant Matty to cast off every other hue for the rest of eternity.

The little purple feather in Matty's bonnet swayed back and forth as she shook her head. "No, I am not 'all right,' Phoebe," she repeated. "We have been at the museum for nearly an hour. My backside is beginning to ache from sitting, and, even though you insist we had breakfast—although I do not remember it—I am certain we have missed tea, for my stomach is complaining loudly.

"If you have not heard it, it is merely because you are once again indulging your unladylike worship of ancient gew-gaws. I do not know how you expect to catch a husband if you refuse to give a man as much attention as you do these dusty piles of mostly broken memorabilia. This behavior simply will not do."

Phoebe's cheeks warmed. She glanced around the room to see if any of the other museum patrons had overheard her cousin's remark. It appeared that no one had.

"You know I do not wish to marry, Matty," she remonstrated quietly. "So I do not know why you persist with the suggestion. My fortune is large enough that I may live quite comfortably without the aid of any man, and, since I have no father, brothers, or other extraneous male relatives to force me into an alliance, I need have no fear of becoming any man's chattel, which is precisely what happens once a man gets a ring on a woman's finger.

"As for being hungry," she said with forced cheer, "would you like an apple?" She held up her pistachio silk handbag. Its jonquil drawstring matched the silk piping on the hem of her pomona-green walking dress, as well as her perky yellow bonnet. "Suspecting that you might get peckish before we left the museum, I put two of them in my reticule this morning before we left the house."

"No," Matty retorted. "I do not want an apple. I want tea, and possibly a few scones with butter and raspberry preserves. I do not mean to be sharp with you, Phoebe, but you know how my disposition suffers when I do not get enough to eat."

Phoebe's temperature began rising despite her good intentions. "You could not possibly be hungry," she said tartly. "It is not yet twelve o'clock. And we *did* eat breakfast less than two hours ago. But I shan't coax you to eat one of my apples. I shall merely enjoy them both myself."

Removing one of the fruits from her reticule she polished it vigorously with a handkerchief she extracted from one lacy green sleeve, until the apple's surface shone like a rich, red garnet. Then she tucked the cloth back into her cuff and bit into the fruit. It made a loud crunch that caused several museum patrons to glance in her direction. "Mmm," she said thickly. "Delicious."

Matty sighed mournfully, but held out one gloved hand for the remaining apple. Phoebe handed it to her. The older woman devoured the fruit in four huge bites and tossed the core in a refuse pail beside the bench. Then she pinned Phoebe with an unrelenting stare.

"You know," Matty said pointedly, "your attitude concerning marriage was all fine and good while you were still a young woman. But it will not serve for much longer. At twenty-five you are nearing your last prayers. This Season—your eighth, I feel duty-bound to observe—will soon be over and all eligible males will have left for their country estates. You must marry, Phoebe, before you no longer have that option."

Phoebe did not reply.

"At least attach someone before this Season is finished," Matty pleaded fervently. "I fail to see why you fight nature. Marriage is a woman's lot in life. Women are incomplete without men, and vice versa. A woman has no greater calling than to care for her husband and children, to make her household a heaven on earth."

Goaded, Phoebe retorted, "Do you not remember how miserable my mother was with my father, Matty? How do you know, you who have never married, that holy wedlock is not more like the fiery pits of hell than the cloud-filled realms of heaven?"

She immediately wished she could call the words back. Matty had always been inordinately sensitive about her failure to make a suitable match despite not missing a Season since her come-out fifteen years earlier. She sighed. "I did not mean that. It was uncalled for, and I humbly beg your forgiveness."

Matty's face seemed to crumple. Her eyes glittered with unshed tears. "It is precisely *because* I never married that I realize the need for a man in a woman's life," she said brokenly. "I do not wish you to be as lonely as I have been. Therefore, I insist you cease coming to the museum day after day, and turn your attention to more genteel pursuits.'' She moved toward the door. ''Now, do come along. I am tired and hungry and want nothing so much as to return home and find something more satisfying to eat than a bit of fruit.''

Tossing her own apple core into the refuse pail, Phoebe shrugged. It was no use trying to force someone to appreciate the museum's ancient treasures. She allowed herself to be led out of the building.

She was so wrapped up in her own thoughts that, on the museum doorstep, she collided full force with a tall, well-formed gentleman with sandy-brown hair visible beneath a worn hat, and wire-rimmed spectacles behind which glinted lustrous hazel eyes. In his right hand he clutched an ebony, gold-tipped cane with a handle shaped like a cobra's head. His clothing looked faintly dusty, and was obviously several years out of fashion.

He gave a small grunt of pain as Phoebe's slippered foot came down hard on his instep. Without a word he hooked his cane over his arm, reached out, lifted her effortlessly into the air, set her back down well out of his way, and continued on into the building as if he'd not even been aware of her presence.

''Well!'' Phoebe said breathlessly, feeling as if she had run into a solid rock wall instead of another human being. There was a tickling sensation in the pit of her stomach that reminded her of the time she'd dragged Matty to a balloon ascension and actually been borne aloft like a leaf on a summer breeze. Quite exhilarating. ''Well.''

As Matty chattered on about nothing at all, Phoebe soon forgot about the gentleman. Her thoughts drifted back to the Eye of Horus. If only it belonged to her. If only she could add it to her collection. Surely it would be the most magnificent piece she would ever possess. There had to be a way to obtain it.

Suddenly she smiled. Turning, she hurried back up the museum steps and paused beside a young guard posted outside the building. ''Pardon me,'' she said eagerly, ''but can you tell me where I might find the curator's office?''

"Yes, miss. Take the staircase on your right just before you enter the main hall. Two floors up, and it's the last door on your right."

Sir Malcolm Forbes decided that he would far rather be sitting in his perennial garden than here at the Metropolitan Museum. The flowers in his garden were blooming, and he was eager to transplant a particularly lovely clump of bright blue forget-me-nots—precisely his favorite color—that he had pilfered from a friend's country estate.

Instead, he settled himself in one of the hard chairs lining the museum's boardroom wall, leaned his cane against his chair, removed his hat and gloves, and rubbed his right knee, which had been damaged in the excavation of Pharaoh Setet II's tomb. Because of England's cool humidity, it seemed as if the joint ached constantly.

One by one, other men entered the room until the twelve chairs surrounding a circular mahogany table were filled. A wooden podium sat between two of the chairs. To the right of the podium sat Mr. Jacob Grundle, the museum curator. Mr. Grundle was almost completely round, and must surely weigh twenty or thirty stone. The curator's head, too, seemed quite spherical. He constantly swiped at his florid cheeks and totally bald head with a dingy white handkerchief.

When everyone had been seated, Mr. Grundle cleared his throat. "Ahem. We have assembled this afternoon at the request of our good friend and benefactor, Sir Malcolm Forbes, baronet, who has donated numerous artifacts to our beloved museum over the years."

A murmur of anticipation rippled through the other eleven men like soft waves shushing against a pebbly shore. Twenty-four eyes glittered greedily as if in anticipation of some new treasure Malcolm had brought them. For, they seemed to be thinking, what other reason could the baronet have for calling them all together? What other reason, indeed.

"Without further adieu," Mr. Grundle concluded, "we will turn the floor over to Sir Malcolm."

2

Malcolm stood slowly. Clasping his ebony and gold cane tightly in one hand and his hat and gloves in the other, he moved with a slight limp to stand at the podium. He deposited his burdens on the table and pushed his spectacles firmly up onto the bridge of his nose. Then he gripped the podium tightly with both hands.

"I fear," he said hesitantly, "that I am going to disappoint a great many of you this afternoon. I can see by your expressions that you are under the mistaken impression that I have brought you a new piece to exhibit."

The board members' brows, raised expectantly, now lowered uncertainly as if they were all connected by a single string.

Malcolm cleared his throat and gripped the podium even tighter. "Actually," he managed past dry lips, "I have not come to give you something. I have, rather, come to take something away."

The murmur of voices rose once again, this time in consternation. They sounded rough and harsh, like a stiff breeze blowing through a stand of scraggly Scotch pines.

"What's that?" Mr. Grundle exclaimed, scowling. He wriggled in his chair, which creaked beneath his vast bulk as loudly as if it were about to be reduced to a pile of toothpicks. He mopped his brow. "What's that? Take something away? What can you mean, Sir Malcolm?"

Malcolm pushed his glasses up again, as *he* had begun sweating now, and they had slid down to the tip of his nose. He held up one hand, indicating a desire for silence. "Please, hear me out. I know each of you personally, and trust that you believe me to be a logical, honest, forthright individual.

"However, I fear that what I am about to say will come as a shock to all of you. I can only hope you will remember my sterling reputation as a scholar and a man of extensive education. Therefore, when I explain my reasons for desiring to remand the Eye of Horus, I trust you will listen with open ears and not judge my decision before you have heard my reasoning."

The room buzzed anew.

Mr. Grundle glowered. "Surely, Sir Malcolm, you cannot expect us to hand over our best museum piece to you just like that." He snapped his fingers. As they were slippery with perspiration, they made no sound. "I am surprised at you, sir. What you are suggesting is the outside of enough."

"Naturally I intend to reimburse you quite generously," Malcolm assured the curator. "I promise that you will come out much to the good for this transaction. I will pay whatever you ask."

Mr. Grundle's scowl lessened. His bald pate gleamed as if covered in gold leaf. Malcolm was momentarily distracted by seeing his own reflection swimming blearily on its shiny surface. He blinked and looked away in order to focus his thoughts.

"Just think of all you could do to the museum with the money," he pressed. "Just think of the new exhibits you could purchase."

"T'would be an appealing prospect, to be sure, were there not so many wealthy men on this board, Sir Malcolm," Mr. Grundle answered drily. "Men, I might add, who would give their eyeteeth and half their fortunes to possess the Eye of Horus. Why, only last week Mr. Montgomery Milhouse inquired as to that matter. As did the earl of Bumstead and Lord Deauville, a few weeks before. All three gentlemen, as you know, are collectors as well as members of this esteemed board. And all three were prepared to pay hefty sums.''

Malcolm gripped the podium so fiercely that his knuckles turned white. His heart seemed to block his throat, making it difficult to breathe. ''None of those gentlemen were allowed to touch the amulet, I trust?'' he said hoarsely.

Mr. Grundle frowned and tipped his head up as if searching the office eaves for his memory. ''No. Not that I recall. To the best of my knowledge, only I—and you, of course—have had that honor.''

''Thank God,'' Malcolm said quietly. His heart settled back into his chest.

Mr. Grundle continued. ''I trust you are willing, at the very least, to match their offers?''

''Naturally. I will readily double the highest offer submitted.''

The curator brightened. ''Well, I suppose it is only right, under those conditions, that we seriously consider returning the Eye of Horus to its donor.''

Malcolm bowed slightly. ''I appreciate your willingness to accommodate me, Mr. Grundle.''

''But before we come to any final decision,'' the curator persisted, ''you must explain your sudden desire to take the amulet away from us, Sir Malcolm. Just for the record, you understand.'' He wiped his brow yet again, then fanned his face with the dingy handkerchief. ''To that end, say what you have to say, and let us get out of here. This room is like an oven.''

''Gladly.'' Malcolm straightened. ''You may remember the stories about the pharaoh's curse that surrounded the discovery of Setet II's tomb, wherein the Eye of Horus was found. And perhaps you, Mr. Grundle, have even read the inscription on the back of the Eye itself, proclaiming the fate of any who touched it to be certain death.''

''Indeed,'' the curator admitted. He waved a hand dismissively. "But what has that ridiculous fantasy to do with anything?"

Malcolm swallowed a sudden shudder of nervousness, painfully aware that his entire scholastic reputation was at stake here. If the members of the board did not believe what he was about to say, his character would be tarnished forever. But he had to speak up. He had no choice.

"The curse has everything to do with this matter, gentlemen," he said firmly. "I wish to purchase the amulet from the museum because it has come to my attention that the curse of Setet II was not quite so ridiculous as we all assumed. It is, instead, hard fact. Therefore, the Eye of Horus must be destroyed."

The boardroom erupted in a cacophony of outraged male voices.

Malcolm spoke above the din. "The amulet is well and truly cursed. Everyone who has ever touched it, except thus far myself, and Mr. Grundle, has died. Twelve men, and one woman, have perished."

The din became a roar.

"That is quite enough, Sir Malcolm!" Mr. Grundle shouted above the other board members' angry voices. "I cannot credit what you are saying. You have donated many fine artifacts to this museum, sir, but surely you must have contracted some exotic foreign disease on your travels that makes you speak so foolishly."

"I assure you, I speak only the truth!" Malcolm's heart pounded frantically in his chest. "We must destroy the amulet before it claims any more victims." He could scarcely hear his own voice above the board members' outraged babble.

Mr. Grundle surged to his feet, looming over the circular table like a warship in full sail. His florid face had turned a deep fuschia.

"I know I speak for the rest of the board, Sir Malcolm," he bellowed, "when I assure you that I will never, ever, for any amount of money, consider releasing as fine an artifact as the Eye of Horus into hands that would destroy it. I will thank you, sir, to leave this establishment at once.''

Abruptly the room became as silent and still as a mountain lake. All twelve board members glared down the length of the table as if daring the baronet to utter another word.

"Mr. Grundle," Malcolm tried one final time, "I—"

"Enough, sirrah!" Mr. Grundle's voice softened as he sank back into his chair. He waved one pale hand, weakly. "Go home. Go to the country. Take a holiday. Once you have recovered your senses we shall forget all about this madness and be more than happy to welcome you back."

Malcolm studied the implacable stares of the men seated around the table. At last a sigh, dredged up from the depths of his soul, slipped between his lips. Picking up his hat, gloves, and ebony cane, he straightened his shoulders and limped from the room.

As she passed him in the museum hall, Phoebe instantly recognized the tall, bespectacled, unfashionable gentleman she had collided with outside. Once again, however, he did not appear to see her. She stepped out of his way just in time to avoid being trampled.

Moving on, she came to the chamber to which the young museum guard had directed her. No one answered her summons, but she heard a group of male voices at the end of the hall. Following the sound, she walked toward an open door. Twelve men, seated around a circular table, were deep in discussion.

Sticking her head into the room, Phoebe said pleasantly, "Good afternoon, gentlemen. I hate to disturb you, but I would like to purchase an item from one of your exhibits, and need to speak to whomever is in charge of this fine establishment.''

A huge, red-faced, profusely sweating man who looked very crabby, glared in her direction. "And which item would that be?" he grumbled.

Phoebe turned her most winning smile in his direction.

"The Eye of Horus, my good man. Just name your price and, if it is within my power, I will be happy to meet it."

Seconds later she found herself propelled out of the museum and standing alone on the sidewalk. It took no great leap of understanding to comprehend that her request to purchase the amulet had been rejected. Undaunted, she climbed into her carriage and sat down beside the long-suffering Matty.

One way or another, she resolved with typical determination, the Eye of Horus would be hers. Whether she had to beg, borrow, or . . . Her spirits rose.

Or *steal*.

The following evening just before five, Phoebe dumped a svelte, ecstatically purring brown tabby cat from her lap, rose from the chair beside her dressing table, and picked up an oversized, bulging reticule.

She had hastily dressed her hair in a Grecian knot, and was wearing a walking dress of Mexican blue muslin (a steely blue color she frequently favored), gray kidskin gloves and slippers, and a new French gray sarsenet pelisse. She very much liked this new French ankle-length cape, and considered its unusual shade of white with ivory, black, and Chinese blue threads particularly attractive with her golden hair. To its credit, the pelisse also had very deep pockets, which Phoebe hoped would come in handy during this night's adventure.

After several unsuccessful attempts at fitting the oversized reticule into the pelisse's right pocket, she lifted the brim of her wide French bonnet and deftly tucked the reticule under the hat. Then she turned from side to side before her looking glass, considering. Yes. It would do nicely. Though large, the reticule was not so heavy as to be uncomfortable, and the hat's fashionable rear pouf and the riband around its middle would keep the bag from sliding out at an inconvenient moment.

She left her bedchamber and moved furtively down the hall, managing to reach the front door without alerting Mames, her ever-vigilant butler who guarded the townhouse like Cerberus at the gates of Perdition. She did not have to evade Matty, as her cousin had developed a headache, taken a powder, and gone to bed. Since the headache powders inevitably made Matty very drowsy, the older woman would undoubtedly be flat on her back until well into the following afternoon.

Phoebe slipped outside and ran down her front steps. A few blocks away she hailed a cab and climbed inside. When the vehicle reached the London Metropolitan Museum, she climbed out, tipped the driver generously, and made her way toward the multicolumned building.

She climbed the museum's circular steps and bowed her head so the same young guard who had given her directions to the curator's office the day before would not see her face. Threading through the mass of people thronging the building's main hall, she moved swiftly toward the stairs leading to the next floor.

When she reached the Egyptian Room she was careful not even to glance in the direction of the glass case containing the Eye of Horus, but walked instead toward a low settee. Adjusting her hat so that the reticule on top of her head was well-centered, she sat down to wait until six o'clock—at which time the museum evicted its patrons and closed its doors until the following morning.

Taking a deep breath, she passed the next half hour studying her surroundings.

The Egyptian Room was a large chamber that stretched upward for two floors. High above, in the center of the ceiling, a thirty-foot stained-glass cupola with a scene of hippopotami, lotus blossoms, reeds, and crocodiles let the afternoon sunlight stream into the room. A clear glass circle, three feet in diameter, was set in the center of the colored glass. This was surrounded by a wide band of metal. Along with three-inch-wide, spokelike shafts radiating out from the central metal circle, the metal circle served as a brace for the entire domelike structure.

One of the walls was decorated with a mock-Egyptian frieze, a scene of the Nile with a low, flat boat drifting among the reeds and lotus blossoms. Standing in the vessel's prow, a hunter in a short white skirt held a bow in one hand and a fistful of dead waterfowl in the other. A partially naked woman with one arm wrapped about the hunter's waist gazed at him admiringly, while a girl-child clung to his knee. On the distant shore stood the pyramids of Giza, gleaming as if covered with diamond dust.

Numerous bits of tile and sherds of pottery were placed on shelves and in display cases in the center of the other three walls. The light from the window on the eastern side of the building, as well as that shining in through the stained-glass dome, coaxed the sherds' pale, delicate patterns into view. As Phoebe had several perfect pottery specimens in her collection, these held no great interest for her.

Statues of various Egyptian gods and goddesses—the jackal-god, Anubis, the cow-goddess, Hathor, and the cat-goddess, Bastet (for whom Phoebe had named her own puss, whom she'd rescued at great peril to herself from a gang of street boys intent upon torturing the poor creature), among others—punctuated the areas between numerous low settees where the museum's guests rested when they grew fatigued or merely wished to contemplate their surroundings.

Though she enjoyed everything in the room, Phoebe's favorite part of the exhibit was the ancient jewelry. Whenever she looked at the dainty strands of carnelian or agate or lapis-lazuli or coral, strung with tiny golden beads or bells or flowers, her fingertips itched to lay them gently over her fingers, arms, and neck.

But despite the jewelry's magnificence, despite the way she felt when looking at pieces either exquisitely delicate or strikingly bold, nothing had ever affected her like the Eye of Horus. She felt no qualms whatsoever about what she intended to do this night. In her mind, the amulet already hung about her neck.

Suddenly the other half of the long settee cushion dipped as someone sat down beside Phoebe. She looked up to see the very gentleman she had collided with the day before. He still wore the same dusty brown coat, and he still looked oddly distracted and dishevelled as if he seldom gave any thought to his appearance. Phoebe felt an immediate, mysterious kinship with him.

Grimacing, the gentleman removed his hat and gloves and laid them and his ebony cobra-handled cane, decorated with hieroglyphics picked out in gold leaf, on the floor beneath the settee. Running a hand down his right leg, he massaged the area just above his knee. Behind his spectacles, his eyes surveyed the Egyptian Room and its occupants.

If Matty were here, Phoebe knew, she would point out that the gentleman was obviously eligible—that he appeared unkempt because he had no wife to take proper care of him. To her surprise, Phoebe, who had never felt a burning desire to mother anyone or anything but her cat, felt a sudden, piercing inclination to take this gentleman under her wing. Narrowing her eyes, she looked askance at the man, trying to understand what had caused the sensation.

He seemed familiar, somehow. Though she could not remember when, Phoebe could have sworn she had seen his face somewhere even before their two brief meetings, although she could not put her finger on exactly where.

Then the man turned and glanced at her. His eyes, which at first appeared hazy, as if he were not truly seeing her, abruptly cleared and took on a sparkle that seemed to light up his face like the fireworks that illuminated Vauxhall Gardens. He stared at Phoebe with an expression of such unabashed delight that she felt her cheeks turn rosy.

"I say," he said raptly. "Do you know that your eyes are exactly the color of a bouquet of forget-me-nots? Precisely my favorite shade of blue."

3

Phoebe's mouth dropped open. She blinked, uncertain whether his comments were innocent or if she had misread his boyish innocuousness for something far more sinister. "Er, no," she stammered. "I was not aware of that."

"Well, they are." Abruptly his expression sobered and his cheeks flushed as if he realized how outrageously forward his comment had been. "Ahem. Amazing exhibit, is it not?" he said, gruffly. He tugged at his cravat. It, like the rest of his clothes, looked at least five or six years old.

Seeing his discomfort, Phoebe decided that he must indeed be quite harmless, and that his first, dreadfully personal comment had been due to genuine surprise rather than from a desire to be intimate. She stopped gaping at him like a wide-mouthed bass, and was again struck by his boyishly guileless demeanor.

She smiled, eager to relieve his discomfiture. "Yes," she agreed. "Everything is quite, quite magnificent. Whenever I come to the museum I spend a great deal of time in this room."

"Do you indeed?" His hazel eyes became frankly curious.

"Oh, yes. I am a great lover of Egyptian artifacts. I find those kept here far superior to those at Picadilly's

Egyptian Hall, although the Hall has better artifacts from
the Americas and Africa, as well as a marvelous preserved
small animal and insect collection. I only wish the Metropolitan Museum had hieroglyphics carved on its front like
the Egyptian Hall does.''

"That would be spectacular," the gentleman concurred.
"I, also, enjoy passing the time in this chamber when I
am in London. Of all the museum exhibits, this is my
favorite. Take that frieze for example." Bending down, he
picked up his cane and pointed with it. "I can almost
imagine being in Egypt when I look at that."

Phoebe reluctantly tore her attention from his face and
directed it obediently to the indicated wall on which the
hunter, his wife, and child floated by on the Nile.

"Except for the extreme temperature difference, that
is," the gentleman continued, putting the cane back down.
"It feels wildly peculiar to be chilly while surrounded
with antiquities from a hot, arid land. Not to mention that
the dampness here in England makes old wounds ache
abominably. My knee, which I wounded over a year ago,
has not stopped throbbing since I stepped off the ship
from Egypt."

Phoebe gasped as her memory, as in an abruptly remembered dream, flashed the image of a *Times* portrait before
her eyes.

"You are Sir Malcolm!" she cried. "Sir Malcolm
Forbes! The man who discovered the Eye of Horus! I saw
your portrait in the newspaper, many months ago. Oh, it
is a pleasure to meet you, sir. I *am* sorry I ran into you
yesterday. I do hope it did not hurt your leg excessively."
She flushed then, realizing she was gushing like a green
girl.

The gentleman looked absurdly pleased by her recogni-
tion. He smiled crookedly. "I am he." He did not inquire
about her identity since, despite his imprudent remark
about her eye color, he seemed nonetheless well acquainted with propriety's demand that a young woman
must be introduced to a gentleman by a mutual acquaintance in order to give her name.

Phoebe, however, deciding that she had already broken several of society's mandates by striking up a conversation with the baronet, thrust down her sense of decorum and held out her hand. Sir Malcolm took it uncertainly, and looked taken aback as she shook his fingers briskly.

"I am Phoebe Lawton," she said. "I am interested in history, especially that of ancient Egypt, and collect artifacts from that country when I can find them. How thrilling it must have been for you to have found Pharaoh Setet II's tomb."

Sir Malcolm inclined his head. "It was." Then he flushed again. "I must apologize for not stopping to see if you were all right after our collision yesterday. I was in rather a large hurry, you see."

"Oh, do not trouble yourself. A man like you must be forever dashing off to interesting places and doing exciting things. One can hardly expect you to stand about apologizing for something that was not even your fault, when there are so many things waiting to be discovered." Phoebe sighed wistfully. "I have often wished that ladies could have such grand adventures as you men do but, alas, it is not so."

Gazing at the unruly cowlick that drew a lock of Sir Malcolm's sandy-brown hair just to the left of his forehead straight up into the air almost like an exclamation mark, and the way his hazel eyes sparkled with humor behind his wire-rimmed spectacles, Phoebe found herself thinking that he was quite the most appealing man she had ever met. While he was not classically handsome, there was something about Sir Malcolm Forbes, some *je ne sais quoi*, that lent him an appeal all his own. Also, because of their mutual interest in archaeology, she felt as if she had known him for years.

Yet, while he was appealingly youthful, Phoebe could not deny the aura of power that surrounded him, as was evident in the visible strength of his broad shoulders and his large, well-shaped hands. The mix of boyishness and supreme masculinity was a powerful combination, and Phoebe experienced the odd sensation of being unable to catch her breath.

"Unfortunately you are correct," Sir Malcolm agreed, offering his engagingly crooked smile once again. "Our world does not allow women the same freedoms it does men. But do not feel too badly, ma'am. I'm sure you realize that women have their own very important niche in the structure of society."

Phoebe's lips twisted wryly. She had heard the same argument from every man with whom she'd ever had this discussion. What it all boiled down to was a masculine desire to keep women safe and sound—and out of the way. "Oh, do you think so?" she inquired politely.

"Of course." He nudged his glasses higher on the bridge of his nose and smoothed his cowlick in a manner that seemed more habitual than necessary. "But you are correct. It is true that the world is filled with marvelous things. Perhaps your husband will take you on a tour of the continent, or even beyond, someday when your children are grown."

"Oh, I am not married," Phoebe answered blithely. "And I have no children."

"Not married?" Sir Malcolm looked perplexed. "I assumed, yesterday, when I passed you on the museum stairs, that you were the wife of one of the board members."

"No."

Phoebe was surprised to hear that he had noticed her on the stairs, given his air of preoccupation. He looked at her quizzically as if wondering why she had been headed for the offices if not to seek her husband in an office there. Due to her reasons for being in the museum today, however, she felt it wiser to keep her own counsel.

Frowning, the baronet suddenly glanced around the treasure-filled chamber as if taken aback at speaking so freely to a young, unmarried lady rather than the experienced matron he had assumed her to be.

"Where is your companion, miss?" he inquired. "I have been out of England for some time, but doubt the proprieties have changed so drastically that it is proper for you to be sitting here alone. You do have a companion, do you not?''

"Of course. She is merely in the next room," Phoebe replied hastily, experiencing a twinge of guilt at lying to the man who had been her hero for years. She had read every article he had ever written about archaeology. Much of what she had learned about the subject had come directly from his pen. She had never dreamed she would have the opportunity to meet him. "She wanted to see the African exhibit, but I prefer the Egyptian Room. Do not concern yourself; she will return momentarily.''

Sir Malcolm nodded, but he still looked uncomfortable.

"As I was saying," Phoebe continued daringly, certain that Sir Malcolm, as a man of the world, would understand and agree with her views on men and women and their places in life, "I am not married. You see, I am particularly lucky in that I have no male relatives. Or, rather, not lucky, as it was unfortunate for them that they all died so precipitously. It is just that, if one of them had remained alive, I am sure he would have insisted upon my forming an alliance simply because men always consider marriage a woman's main lot in life.''

"Very true," Sir Malcolm said, gazing at her with an even stronger air of concern.

"My father," she pressed on, "was of such a mind. I cannot think why; the very idea that women are helpless creatures is utterly absurd. Women are quite capable of looking after themselves, and thus, surely of having adventures. It is just," she finished mournfully, "that adventures do not seem used to making themselves available to women.''

"You have no male relatives?" Sir Malcolm asked agitatedly. "You poor child. What a dreadful state of affairs. Who watches over you, protects you from the difficulties of daily life? Surely not your errant companion. You may rest assured that if you did have a male kinsman she would not behave so badly or she would be turned off without a reference, immediately.''

"Oh, pooh," Phoebe said. "You sound just like every other man I have told about my liberty. You all seem to feel that a free woman is an abomination to humanity."

Sir Malcolm waved her comment aside. "But who takes care of your business matters? Your banking? Surely you need a man's strong intellect for such difficult endeavors."

Phoebe gave a trill of laughter. "Certainly not. I take care of them myself. It was confusing at first, but I learned quickly. I am really quite intelligent. And of course I have a very good solicitor, who keeps me informed of the state of my affairs. I inherited my fortune from a maiden aunt, you see. 'Twas from Aunt Hepsibah that I learned about independence, and that a woman is equally as intelligent as a man, and thus quite able to take charge of her own life."

"Good God," Sir Malcolm said faintly. He shook his head as if he could not comprehend what she was saying. "Well, I am sure you will change your mind about marriage at some future date. Unless you want to become an ape-leader. No woman willingly suffers that awful fate." He shifted, half rising. "I think it might be wise for me to locate your companion."

Phoebe felt a burst of panic. "Oh, please do not. Truly, Matty is a dragon and I am not eager to have her returned to me so soon." She squelched a quiver of remorse at maligning her cousin, but rushed on, too intent to explain why women did not need a married title before their names to survive, to stop.

For some reason it had become vitally important to earn this man's goodwill, his good opinion. She had to make the baronet understand that her reasoning, though unusual in their stratum of society, was not flawed. This must, she mused dimly, have something to do with wanting to appear as a logical, rational thinker to a fellow scientist.

"I do not see why marriage is my only option," she went on. "My finances are such that I have no requirement for a man's support, I enjoy my freedom far too much to encumber myself with a lord and master, and, at the risk of sounding self-serving, I believe myself smarter than almost every man I have ever met. Not to mention that I frequently find men, with their ridiculous posturing and utterly absurd ideas about females' lack of intelligence, to be rather apelike themselves. So to respond to your statement, give me a gorilla over a man any day.''

Sir Malcolm's lips parted slightly and he blinked several times in quick succession. The light from the eastern window glinted on his spectacle lenses. ''I—I beg your pardon?''

Phoebe bit her lip and dropped her gaze. ''Oh, dear. Although Matty constantly tells me to mind my tongue, it nevertheless often runs away with my good sense. I have offended you.'' She looked up again.

Sir Malcolm lowered his brows. Phoebe was sorry to see his placid countenance turn stormy. Despite his dusty, careworn appearance, the baronet was obviously a man used to having his words heeded and obeyed. The boyishness that had made his face so appealing moments before vanished, leaving in its wake something wholly mature and authoritative.

She felt her respect for Sir Malcolm rise several notches. Though his bedraggled appearance led her to believe him a single man, instinctively she knew that if he ever *did* marry he would always be king in his own castle. Suddenly, the thought of being carried away on a white stallion did not seem quite so repulsive as it always had in the past.

''I think perhaps you have suffered more than you realize by not having male guidance,'' Sir Malcolm remarked firmly. He glanced away.

Phoebe opened her mouth, but just as she prepared to reply she noticed that Sir Malcolm's attention had shifted. Instead of looking at her, he was staring fixedly at a museum guard who was holding a gold-brimmed hat in one hand and slowly making his way around the room.

Sir Malcolm's hazel eyes narrowed behind his spectacles. As the guard neared, the baronet rose. Without looking at Phoebe again, he said swiftly, ''It has been a pleasure, ma'am. But I must be going. Enjoy the exhibit.''

Picking up his cobra-handled cane, his gloves, and his dusty hat, he moved with a slight limp toward the other side of the room.

As the guard paused beside Phoebe's settee, and she recalled her own reason for being at the museum, she fought down a wave of terror. She gasped when he addressed her directly.

"Are you all right, miss? You look a bit pale."

"Y-yes, thank you," she stammered. "I am fine. Just resting. I was feeling a bit faint."

"Would you like me to procure a glass of water?"

"No, thank you very much. I am feeling much better."

The guard nodded and continued on his way.

Sir Malcolm had disappeared. Phoebe gazed toward the Egyptian Room door, cheeks burning. How could she have said all those things to him? What must he have thought? He would never believe her anything but an unruly, brash, outrageous hoyden after this encounter. Why, oh why could she not have kept her views about marriage to herself?

Her heart felt heavy in her chest, and she sat still for some time, feeling utterly despondent. Then, through the eastern window, she heard a clock chime six times from the direction of the tower. One by one the museum's patrons wandered out into the hall, their footsteps fading away as they walked toward the exit.

When the last person had exited the Egyptian Room, Phoebe pushed her disappointment about her encounter with Sir Malcolm to the back of her mind and rose. Moving as rapidly and quietly as possible, she headed toward a gaudily painted imitation sarcophagus.

The wood coffin leaned upright against the wall, only five feet from the glass box holding the Eye of Horus. Its door hung slightly ajar, giving the eerie appearance of its mummy having stepped out for a short turn about the museum. Phoebe managed to squeeze through the narrow opening and into the darkness within. She pulled the lid almost closed.

As footsteps (the guard's, no doubt, making certain all

the museum patrons had gone) rang out on the marble floors, she held her breath and pressed herself against the back of the coffin. Through its narrow opening, she could see the Eye of Horus's display case. When the guard passed that area, she should be able to see him as well.

In her mind, Phoebe went over her plan.

As soon as the guard continued on his rounds, she would sneak out of the sarcophagus, go to the glass box, break a small hole in the side, and remove the Eye. Then she would replace the amulet with the reticule hidden beneath her bonnet. Surely she would be doing nothing wrong. She wouldn't be stealing the artifact; she would be purchasing it.

The breath she was holding threatened to burst her lungs by the time the sound of the guard's footsteps neared the sarcophagus. A sudden, horrifying speculation threatened to shatter her pounding heart. What if opening the coffin, to make certain no one was hidden inside, was part of the guard's nightly duty? Would she be captured and hauled off to Newgate?

She prayed the guard would move on past the sarcophagus. The footsteps drew ever closer. When they reached the area just beyond the coffin, they stopped altogether. Phoebe was sure that, at any moment, the guard would hear her heart slamming wildly against her chest.

When, after several minutes, the guard neither moved away nor opened the sarcophagus lid to expose her, Phoebe hesitantly peeped through the narrow crack and out into the Egyptian Room. What she saw nearly made her plummet out onto the floor from sheer astonishment.

Not five feet away, visible in the late-evening light that shone in through the eastern window, Sir Malcolm Forbes placed his hat and gloves and his ebony and gold cane on the top of the Eye of Horus's display case. His sandy-brown hair gleamed as he bent and pressed a shiny silver device against one side of the glass box. He made a circular motion, pushed, and then stepped back with a satisfied murmur. A round bit of glass fell silently inward, settling on the box's white satin cushion.

Sir Malcolm was also trying to steal the amulet!

Phoebe's fear rapidly transformed into rage. Just as she prepared to leap from the coffin and give the baronet a piece of her mind about exactly who had thought of stealing the artifact first and, thus, who was entitled to it, she heard more footsteps nearing the chamber. This time, she was certain, they must belong to the guard.

Sir Malcolm's head shot up and he turned in the direction of the sound. Seizing his gloves, hat, and cane, he whirled about, his gaze searching wildly for a place of concealment. Seeing the sarcophagus, he dashed forward and wrenched the coffin door wide open.

For a moment he looked as if he were about to drop dead from the shock of seeing Phoebe standing where no living thing should have been. Then he leaped into the sarcophagus and pressed Phoebe backward, dropping his gloves and hat between their bodies.

Phoebe's head smacked into the back of the sarcophagus, knocking off her French tulle bonnet, pulling her hair loose from its hastily twisted Grecian knot, and scattering hairpins, apples and cheese, and hundred-pound notes—as the strings of her reticule, dislodged from its place beneath her hat, had become unclasped in the scuffle—over the floor of the coffin. One of the apples rolled out the sarcophagus door and over the museum floor, coming to rest beside the same settee on which both she and Sir Malcolm had sat not long ago.

Cursing softly, Sir Malcolm reached behind himself and wildly flailed his hand. With the tips of his fingers he yanked the sarcophagus lid toward them, caught the tip of his ebony walking stick in the door, and finally managed to pull the cane inside and close the coffin door. As Phoebe opened her mouth to protest, the baronet clamped his hand over her lips only moments before the air was pierced by a shrill whistle followed by the sound of rapidly retreating footsteps.

The attempted burglary had been discovered.

4

The inside of the coffin was not pitch-black. Pin-sized holes in the outer decorations penetrated the lid and allowed tiny streams of light to illuminate the interior cavity. Also, the painted mummy's eyes were not solid, but two small holes.

Phoebe glared up at Sir Malcolm. Pulling back her lips, she sank her teeth deeply into the soft flesh of his palm.

Rage, pain, and obvious frustration because he could not cry out flashed across the baronet's face. He jerked his hand away from her mouth, then raised it menacingly. Phoebe clenched her eyes shut and braced herself for his blow. When it did not fall, she opened first one eye, and then the other, and finally blinked up at him with both.

"I'm not going to strike you, Miss Lawton," Sir Malcolm hissed, having observed her fear. He peered at his wound. "Though I could not be blamed if I did. God's blood, but you have sharp teeth."

"You remembered my name," Phoebe whispered inconsequentially.

"It is not every day a woman likens me and all other men in the world to apes. How could I forget the deliverer of such a flattering comment?" the baronet murmured wryly without looking at her. He lowered his hand.

"You're very lucky you did not break my skin, or I might have changed my mind about flaying you alive."

Phoebe felt a rush of white-hot anger. "You got what you deserved. You were smothering me. What are you doing here, anyway? And who do you think you are, barging into my sarcophagus? I demand you find yourself another hiding place. This one is much too small for two."

"Shut up," Sir Malcolm snarled. "That guard will be back any minute, and he'll be bringing the entire London police force with him. We'd better be gone when they arrive, or we're going to be far more uncomfortable than we already are. Have you ever spent a night in gaol, Miss Lawton?"

Phoebe shuddered. She tried to make her reply nonchalant, but her words came out in a high-pitched squeak. "Of course not. Do not be ridiculous."

"I assure you it is not pleasant. I also assure you that, if I leave this coffin now and get caught because you insisted I try to find another place of concealment, I will not be enjoying Newgate's pleasures alone."

"You would turn me in?" she exclaimed. "How totally ungallant."

"I fail to see why I should be gracious to a woman who bit me and called me an ape." Bending, he appeared to run his fingertips over the edges of the wood. "Come on, darling, open for me."

"I beg your pardon?"

Sir Malcolm did not reply. He worked in silence for several more moments. Finally he straightened. "I can't get the damned lid open. Looks as if we've got one-way tickets to prison, my dear."

Phoebe trembled at the thought of being sent to gaol with this rude baronet. "Get out of the way and let me try. You men always think you're the only ones who can do anything right—and you're usually wrong."

Blatantly ignoring her demand, Sir Malcolm worked at the lid for a while longer. He pushed. And shoved. And muttered again. "It's no use," he said at last. He glanced at her over his shoulder. "See here?" He pointed to a spot just above their waists.

"Where the paint is chipped?"

"It's not paint. It's a metal hasp. We are locked in."

"What do you mean, 'locked in'?" Phoebe demanded in a shrill whisper. "Whoever heard of a locking mechanism on a coffin? You must be mistaken."

"All right, Miss Lawton," he retorted, "if you're so much smarter than I, a mere man, you have a go at it."

"Certainly." Phoebe gave a superior sniff. "I already said I would get us out if you would just get out of the way."

Sir Malcolm gave her a darkly amused glance. Muttering obscure foreign words that could only be curses, he managed to slide around so that Phoebe faced the front of the sarcophagus.

Angling her body until she was at eye level with the locking mechanism, Phoebe studied the lock, but was unable to ignore the fact that her buttocks were pressed squarely against Sir Malcolm's lean hips. Face burning, she tried to shift sideways.

The baronet gave an odd groan and she asked quickly, "Are you all right? Did I hurt you?"

"No." His voice sounded as muffled as if he'd swallowed a hive of bees. "Just hurry."

She studied the lock for a moment longer, then turned to peer over her shoulder. "Give me your cane."

He handed the ebony walking stick forward. Using its golden tip, Phoebe pried at the joined lids. When this failed to open the coffin, she shook her head. "You were right. We are locked in. I offer my sincerest apologies for disbelieving you."

"What did you think?" Sir Malcolm asked tightly, still sounding smothered. "That I was delighted with the prospect of being trapped with you in a two-foot space? But of course. The things we could do in here boggle the mind."

"Oh, do be quiet." Phoebe used the ebony cane to heft herself back to a fully upright position. She managed this feat only by forcing her body hard against Sir Malcolm's solid male physique.

Then, nearly erect, she turned and raised the walking stick speedily. Sir Malcolm's withheld breath came out in a loud "whoosh." He bent over so abruptly their foreheads smacked together.

"Oof! Damn and blast!" he wheezed. "Bloody hell, woman! Be careful!"

Phoebe rubbed her brow and glared at him. His lips had drawn together in a tight line and he looked like he was in severe pain. Since she did not think their heads had bumped with enough force for such a display of agony, she was preparing to ask what was wrong when footsteps thundered up the hall and into the room. Turning abruptly, she stamped hard on his toes.

Sir Malcolm made a choking sound. "God preserve me from plagues and women! Get off my feet, you wretched female!"

"If they were not so big they would not get in the way," Phoebe returned. "Be quiet. The guard will hear you if you keep going on like that." A second later she peered over her shoulder up at his face. "Now what are you doing? Grinding your teeth? Really, Sir Malcolm, you must be quiet!"

Though he sent her a glare that could have burned the hair off of Lucifer himself, Sir Malcolm obeyed.

"Over 'ere," called a young-sounding voice with a thick cockney accent. "The museum 'ad been closed only a short time, and I was making my rounds. That's when I saw the 'ole. The burglar must 'ave 'eard me coming and made a run for it. Luckily, though, 'e didn't get the Eye of 'Orus."

"Thank God." This was Mr. Grundle. "I'll just take the amulet up to my safe and then I'll be right back." A gasp. "Where is it? Didn't you say he hadn't gotten it?"

" 'Ere 'tis. I grabbed it and put it in my pocket when I saw the 'ole in the case."

Beside Phoebe, Sir Malcolm's body suddenly felt as if it had been replaced by a marble statue.

"Excellent. I'll be right back. Go on with your investigation, gentlemen. I want the blackguard caught."

Phoebe could hear the policemen wandering about the chamber in search of clues.

" 'Ere, Inspector," said the same guard. "It's the device 'e used to cut a circle in the glass."

"Good work, O'Hara." More shuffling. "What's that in your hand?"

"An apple. I found it on the floor over by that bench."

"Let me see." Silence. "Doesn't appear suspicious." There was a loud crunching sound and the inspector said thickly, "Not bad. Find anything else?"

"Not yet," O'Hara said. "I 'ave to wonder, though, 'ow 'e got out. I mean, the doors are locked. I suppose 'e could 'ave gone through a window. We should check them to see if any are open."

"Get on it."

O'Hara's footsteps exited the room. Another set entered.

"Find anything, Inspector Morse?" Mr. Grundle demanded, puffing, no doubt from running up and down the museum stairs to his office. "I put the amulet in my safe. It'll be well protected there, if the thief comes back."

"There's the device he used to cut open the display case." A pause as if the inspector were pointing. "The guard, O'Hara, was wondering how the burglar got out of the building. I have the men looking for open windows."

Momentarily, more footsteps heralded the guards' return.

"Well?" the inspector demanded.

O'Hara spoke up. "All the windows are still locked from inside. 'E didn't get out that way."

When a pair of footsteps approached the sarcophagus, the blood rushed to Phoebe's head. She was certain she was going to faint—was almost hopeful that she would so that she would not have to experience any more of the bone-chilling terror that held her in its icy grip. She also hoped that if she lost consciousness her head didn't bump into the front of the coffin and expose them. She really didn't want to know if gaol was as terrible as the baronet had implied.

The footsteps came ever nearer. Shaking, Phoebe pressed herself back against Sir Malcolm's hard, warm chest. The baronet wrapped his arms around her, holding her close.

"What's this thing, Mr. Grundle?"

"A model of an Egyptian sarcophagus, Inspector."

"Sarcopha-what?"

"Sarcophagus. An Egyptian coffin."

"Anything inside?"

"No. Though it was made in Egypt, and is itself quite over a hundred years old, it's just a copy so it never contained a mummy."

"Huh. I've always wondered what the Egyptians do with all those mummies they keep digging up," the inspector mused. "Seems to me they'd be better off leaving them in the ground."

"There is a large market for ground mummy powder. Some men put it in their food, or in wine, to make themselves more sexually potent—like powdered rhinoceros horn. It's also supposed to be a cure for gout."

"You don't say. Does it work?"

"Wouldn't imagine so," Mr. Grundle replied doubtfully.

"Can we open this thing? Burglar might well be hiding inside."

Phoebe trembled so hard she was certain the two men would see the sarcophagus shuddering. Sir Malcolm squeezed tighter, lifting her slightly against his chest. This was not particularly comforting, however, as it raised her just enough to see through the coffin's small eyeholes, and she found herself staring directly into Inspector Morse's face. The inspector was leaning close to the sarcophagus, an intent expression in his eyes. He lifted one hand and knocked sharply on the wooden coffin, as if testing to see if it were hollow or solid.

Phoebe's heart slammed into her throat and she nearly gagged with fear.

Mr. Grundle moved forward. "Nonsense. Nobody could get in there. The coffin probably hasn't been opened since it was brought to the museum. Leastways, I can't remember that it ever was. It was here when I became curator, and I can't seem to recall if it was ever opened. I do remember, however, from my initial study of the museum's record books, the sarcophagus's documentation stating that it was empty upon arrival."

"I'd still like to have a look."

"All right. Let's see if we can find the release mechanism."

Their fingertips made little skritching noises against the outside of the sarcophagus.

Phoebe turned her face toward Sir Malcolm's neck. He smelled of soap and fresh air, and he felt scratchy, like her cat, Bastet's, tongue. The baronet tucked his chin over her head, pulling her still closer. After what seemed an eternity, the curator and inspector ceased their probing and stepped away. Phoebe slumped in Sir Malcolm's arms, and felt a similar relief in his muscles.

"Damn," said the inspector. "Lid won't budge."

"Doesn't matter. I didn't think he could be in there, anyway," said Mr. Grundle. "If he'd forced it open he would have scratched it dreadfully. Antiquities," he said, sounding as proud as a new father, "even those only a hundred or so years old, are hideously fragile."

"Can we force it ourselves?" Inspector Morse asked hopefully.

"Certainly not! I will not have this exhibit damaged just to salve your curiosity, Inspector. Besides, do you really imagine anyone could be so quiet we wouldn't hear him in there?"

"Hmph. I suppose not."

Both Phoebe and Sir Malcolm tensed again as the sound of the guards's steps signaled that they had reentered the chamber.

"Anything?" Inspector Morse demanded.

"Nothing. Bloke must've gotten away. Can't see 'ow, but 'e's definitely not inside the museum anymore."

"All right. Well, there doesn't seem to be anything else we can do here tonight," the inspector said. "Let's go home and come back early in the morning. Crandall? I want you to help Penrod guard out front tonight. Walk around the building every twenty minutes."

"Yes, sir."

Their voices faded as the men left the room and moved on down the hall. Sir Malcolm released Phoebe, who slid down his chest until she was again standing on her own two feet. Or rather, she amended hurriedly as Sir Malcolm muttered, the baronet's. She moved so that her feet were placed inside his.

"Lean to the left," the baronet ordered in a voice just above a whisper. Phoebe complied and he bent forward to peer out of the sarcophagus's eyes. "I don't see anyone. They must really be gone."

He moved back and Phoebe straightened. Squeezing her arms close to her sides, she shimmied around to face him. He loomed over her, seeming almost overwhelmingly large. It occurred to her that, despite being forced to walk with a cane, Sir Malcolm was nonetheless in superb physical condition.

Her heart fluttered strangely. When she looked at his face, she found that he was gazing down at her with an expression that seemed as peculiar as the way she was feeling. His spectacles glinted faintly, and his sandy hair was tousled. She fought to keep her hands from rising to smooth his cowlick.

"What do we do now?" she asked in a breathy whisper.

For a long moment Sir Malcolm said nothing. Then one corner of his mouth lifted in the crooked grin Phoebe had found so engaging that afternoon.

"My dear girl," he said softly, "Given the circumstances, there can be only one answer to that question."

Phoebe gasped with surprise as he leaned toward her.

Sir Malcolm raised his hands and ran his fingers through her loosened coiffure and over her scalp. His grip was firm, his touch warm and strong.

Phoebe's entire body tingled. She was seized by a delicious sweeping sensation, akin to what she'd felt when she'd run into the baronet the day before and he'd lifted her into the air as if she'd been as light as a feather. For a split second she felt terrified, but when Sir Malcolm's arms dropped and closed around her waist, instinct banished confusion.

Her eyelids fluttered closed, and she tilted her head back in preparation for his embrace.

5

After several moments Phoebe opened her eyes and blinked, feeling embarrassed and annoyed. "Sir Malcolm?"

Though his arms were still stretched around her waist, the baronet seemed entirely unaware of her presence. His attention seemed focused, rather, on something just beyond her.

"Sir Malcolm!" she said again, louder and more sharply.

The gentleman turned away from whatever had caught his eye. "What is it? I'm trying to concentrate."

Cocking an eyebrow, Phoebe tilted her head to one side and awaited an explanation. When none was forthcoming, she said with a brittleness born of abashment and chagrin, "I—I thought you were going to kiss me!"

His eyes narrowed. He clucked his tongue disapprovingly. "Really, Miss Lawton. I am not such a cad as would take advantage of a defenseless young woman at a time like this." He seemed to think about that. "Or at any time, for that matter. Not that you are defenseless. In fact, though I hardly know you well I think you must surely be the least defenseless woman I have ever met. With your skilled use of teeth, feet, and walking sticks, Attila the Hun himself would not stand a chance against you."

Phoebe felt quite deflated. Highly disconcerted. Utterly mortified. And, to be quite honest, extremely disappointed.

She frowned inwardly at the way she had thrown herself at the baronet, wondering what on earth had made her behave in such a manner. Something about Sir Malcolm seemed to cause all her ideas about not troubling herself over a man to fly straight to the moon. Well, it would not happen again; that much was certain.

Sir Malcolm's attention was drawn back to where it had been before this unseemly exchange. "Move a bit to the right," he said distractedly.

Phoebe shifted. "What are you doing?"

"Just a second. I've almost got it." He frowned in deep concentration. Then a radiant smile broke over his face. *"Voila!"*

The sarcophagus door sprang open, admitting a gust of fresh air that made Phoebe realize it had been very stuffy inside the coffin. She stepped out into the room, drew a grateful breath, and pulled off her gray kidskin gloves, dropping them into her pelisse pocket. She then removed the cloak and draped it over one arm. "Thank God! I'd begun to think that someday somebody would open the sarcophagus and find us, our bodies as dessicated as real mummies's, inside."

"Not much chance of that," Sir Malcolm replied absently. He followed, cobra-headed cane in hand. "The holes in the door would have given us enough air for as long as we were trapped. And England's air is too humid for our bodies to dry out. Not to mention that if we had died, we'd have begun to smell much too badly to be overlooked for long. Our real danger was in being unable to get out, and being forced to alert the authorities to our presence."

"Do you think anyone will come back in here tonight?"

"Hard to tell. If they do, we will simply climb back into the sarcophagus and let ourselves out again when they've gone."

Untying the strings of her bonnet, which lay loosely

against the nape of her neck, Phoebe pulled the hat off. "How did you get the door open?"

"I recalled," the baronet said, "that when I leapt into the coffin and collided with you, your hair had come undressed. I merely found a pin which had not fallen to the floor, and used it to pick the lock."

Phoebe raised a hand to her tumbled tresses. "Oh, dear. I must look a wreck."

How utterly humiliating not to have realized, until he'd told her, that her curls lay in tumbled abandon over her shoulders and down her back. Still, since the baronet's opinion of her was by now most certainly shredded, this latest humiliation mattered little. She sighed.

"Actually," Sir Malcolm said tonelessly, "you look quite charming."

Phoebe's spirits lifted a trifle. She cast the baronet a furtive glance. He was not looking at her. Moving back to the sarcophagus, she reached down and began gathering her scattered hairpins, whereupon she set about securing her hair once more in a loose bun. Then she stuffed the numerous loose hundred-pound notes into her reticule, and picked up Sir Malcolm's crumpled hat and his gloves.

She turned back toward the baronet, who was standing near the eastern window, clutching his cane and peering cautiously outside. The sun had finally gone down, but it was not quite dark in the museum since moonlight glimmered in through the window and down through the stained-glass dome high above their heads.

Phoebe handed him the ruined hat and the gloves. "You forgot these."

"Oh. Thank you." He stuffed them into the voluminous pockets of his outmoded coat. "I wish we had something to eat," he remarked idly. "I am quite ravenous."

Remembering the food she'd packed before leaving her townhouse, Phoebe dropped her pelisse and bonnet on a nearby bench and opened her reticule. One of the apples she'd put in the handbag, she recalled, had rolled out of the sarcophagus during Sir Malcolm's intrusion and been subsequently eaten by the Chief Inspector. The other looked bruised and rather nasty from being trod upon while she and the baronet were trapped in the sarcophagus.

The cheese, however, while somewhat flat, had remained inside her handbag and appeared clean and edible. "Would you like a piece of this?" she asked, holding out one misshapen lump.

Sir Malcolm turned toward her. "Cheese!" His expression was like that of a young boy whose mother had just made apple pie and offered him the largest slice. "I would love it. How wise of you to bring provisions on a burglary."

Although her ego still burned from the combined effects of his scathing set-down earlier that afternoon and the more recent events in the coffin, Phoebe could not help grinning. "I told you before that I was really quite intelligent, sir. That may seem a bit difficult to credit just now, but it is nonetheless true."

"I never doubted it, Miss Lawton." Sir Malcolm returned her smile. He took the peculiar-looking mass of cheese she offered, raising one sandy brow but biting into the wad of cheddar eagerly. Phoebe followed his example.

"Pity we do not have a bottle of wine," the baronet remarked shortly.

"Yes. Or at least some water. What did you see when you looked out the window?"

"One of the guards, walking about and looking important. It appears that we are stuck here for the night, unless you are feeling brave enough to climb out the window and shimmy down the side of the wall under risk of being spotted by our keepers."

"I fear my store of bravery is all used up," Phoebe informed him with a lightness she did not truly feel. "Still, it could be worse. Without your adeptness for picking locks, we would still be inside the coffin and, later, possibly enjoying the splendors of Newgate." She took another bite of cheese. "Where did you learn such a disreputable trade?"

Sir Malcolm grinned. Despite his outmoded clothes and ruffled hair, he looked almost rakishly handsome. His next

words confirmed Phoebe's theory that he was not as innocent as he appeared.

"Partly in an Egyptian prison."

Phoebe's eyes widened. Then she laughed and looked
away. "Sir, you are bamming me!"

"I assure you, I am not. I was arrested during a demon-
stration against the European archaeological presence in
Egypt. I fear Napoleon did not make too great an impression upon the locals; he was hardly discriminating in his
art-collecting methods. At any rate, the angry mob was
coming down the street and I was trying to find a doorway
in which to hide when a merchant took issue with my
presence and called the police. He told them I had been
trying to steal a valuable artifact."

"What happened?"

"They arrested me and stuck me in their version of
gaol. I assure you, Miss Lawton, that however unpleasant
Newgate may be, it has nothing up on the dank, dark hole
in which the Egyptian police deposited me. While there,
I sent a note to my good friend, Gajib Dahl, a teacher at
the university in Cairo. He came to the prison forthwith,
and attempted to convince the police that, as an expert on
antiquities, I would never have been attempting to steal
any of the merchant's stock."

"Why not?"

"Because," Sir Malcolm said with a laugh that sounded
suspiciously like a snicker, "everything in the store was
fake. You know, the kinds of things street vendors sell to
bacon-brained tourists. Plaster 'funerary' statuary, 'solid'
gold jewelry, freshly carved 'antique' scarabs. I may not
be the most informed archaeologist, but I have never yet
mistaken a simulation for the real thing. But I suppose I'd
best not brag about that. One never knows."

"Did they believe Mr. Dahl?"

"Yes. However, after that, being cognizant of what happens to Europeans in Egyptian goal, I immediately learned
to pick locks in case I ever had need of the skill."

"And have you ever had the opportunity to use your
newfound ability in another prison?"

"No." He pinned her with an enigmatic gaze. "Why were you hiding in the sarcophagus, Miss Lawton? Were you accidentally locked in the museum? Were you frightened when you heard my footsteps? Or were you hiding in order to creep out of the coffin when everyone was gone and steal something? And do you always carry such exorbitant sums of money on your person? I could not help but notice the plethora of hundred-pound notes littered about the floor around the coffin just now, though you retrieved them with a rapidity that was most impressive."

Phoebe flushed warmly. She considered how much she should tell him, then decided it could not hurt to be honest. "Well, I told you that I collect artifacts—"

This time Sir Malcolm *did* snicker. "You mean you 'collect' artifacts from museums? How very original."

Phoebe glared. "That is not at all what I meant!"

"I'm sorry. Please continue."

"I collect antiquities when they are placed up for sale. Usually," Phoebe added quickly as the baronet stifled another chuckle. "But when I saw the Eye of Horus several days ago, I was overcome with the desire to add it to my collection. I tried to purchase it—that is where I was going when I passed you on the stairs yesterday—but the curator became absurdly furious when I inquired as to the possibility of buying it. He refused and practically threw me out onto the street."

Sir Malcolm cursed softly. "You've never touched the Eye of Horus, have you Miss Lawton?" he asked in a strained voice.

"No, and now I shall probably never have the chance," she said mournfully. Seeing his agitation, she studied him closely. "Sir Malcolm? You seem troubled."

He looked away. "Do I? Perhaps it is because I have a bit of a headache."

"Ah." Phoebe nodded. "I am not surprised. You probably got it from the stuffy heat in the sarcophagus. My companion, Matty, frequently suffers from headaches," she added superfluously.

Sir Malcolm's frown vanished. He grinned shrewdly. "Ah, yes. Your erstwhile companion. Do you speak of the one with a fondness for African exhibits? The one who leaves you sitting alone for extended periods of time and allows you to break into museums after hours? Or are you speaking of another, far more estimable lady, such as the woman who was accompanying you when we collided in front of the museum?"

Phoebe laughed. "All right, I admit I fibbed. Matty was never at the museum today."

"I did not think so. You know, Miss Lawton," Sir Malcolm said then with an abashed frown, "I must apologize for being so rude to you—both this afternoon and this evening. It was just that your appearance in the sarcophagus, when I was seeking a place of concealment, took me very much by surprise. As for my snapping at you for your opinions about men and marriage, I had no right. I spoke out of turn. Ofttimes, I fear, I am a bit too staid."

Phoebe sobered. "No, sir. It is I who must apologize. Both for biting you on the hand and for forcing my unusual views on you this afternoon. I should learn to hold my tongue. I did not mean to offend you, and I certainly did not mean to call all men apes. If you are too staid, I am much too impetuous."

His eyes sparkled behind his spectacle lenses. "I shall forgive you, if you will forgive me. What say you? Shall we start over?"

"Please." Delighted to have the opportunity to redeem herself with her idol, Phoebe felt relief wash through her like a cleansing tide. "But it is your turn, Sir Malcolm. Why were *you* trying to take the Eye?"

The baronet turned away and strode back to the window. Phoebe had noticed in the short time she'd known him that he did not often use his cane, yet he was leaning upon it now.

"I am sorry," he replied stiffly, the good humor of moments before disappearing abruptly. "I cannot tell you that."

"What? I explained my actions," Phoebe objected. "It is only fair that you explain yours as well."

"Good Lord," he said. Removing his spectacles, he rubbed his eyes. "Was I humiliated before the entire board of directors only to repeat the process before a female?"

"I do not understand, sir."

Glasses in hand, he turned. "I assure you, it is not my habit to go sneaking around burglarizing museums, any more than it is yours. Is that not explanation enough for you?"

She returned his gaze steadily. "No."

He ran his empty hand through his hair, making his sandy cowlick stand up even farther. "Well, I suppose I've ruined my professional reputation already. I might as well complete the job by filling up the prattle boxes."

Phoebe raised her chin defiantly. Her temper flared. "I beg your pardon, Sir Malcolm. I am not a gabblegrinder, and I resent the implication."

He nodded. "My apologies. I did not mean that. I am just feeling persecuted." He paused momentarily. "Very well, Miss Lawton. I shall tell you why I felt it necessary to sneak in here tonight and attempt to retrieve the Eye of Horus. It is cursed."

Phoebe gaped, openmouthed.

Turning, Sir Malcolm strode to a settee and collapsed onto it, stretching his long legs out in front of him and laying his cane on the floor by his side. His spectacles dangled from his fingers. "There," he said dispassionately. "Now you have your answer, now the cat is out of the bag, now I have put the icing on top of a very bad cake."

Phoebe stared at him, not knowing what to say. "Cursed," she repeated stupidly.

"That is correct."

When he said nothing more, she shook her head and said firmly, "You will have to do better than that, Sir Malcolm. I am not a fool just because I am a woman. I do not believe in curses."

The baronet gave her a weary glance. "Bully for you.

Neither did the members of the museum board when I tried to buy back the amulet, myself, only yesterday. And I do not think women are foolish.'' He grinned wryly. ''Unless they happen to be attempting to burglarize a national museum. You really have a chip on your shoulder about male opinions of females, don't you?''

Phoebe ignored this comment. ''You tried to purchase the Eye?''

''Yes. And, like you, I was rebuffed soundly. I ruined my entire professional reputation just to save a few lives. Rather than being grateful to me for my concern, the fools laughed and threw me out.''

Watching his broad shoulders tremble with suppressed rage, Phoebe murmured soothingly, ''Sir Malcolm, I am certain you must have a reason for thinking the Eye cursed, no matter how ridiculous or illogical others might find the idea. You do not strike me as an unreasonable man. Somewhat eccentric, yes. Unreasonable, no.''

Some of the tension seemed to go out of his body. ''Well,'' he said quietly, ''thank you for that, anyway.''

''You are welcome. But please, tell me why you believe the amulet to be cursed.''

Repositioning his glasses on his face, the baronet gazed at her earnestly. ''It is no assumption, Miss Lawton. The amulet *is* cursed. Everyone who has ever touched it, except the museum curator and myself, is dead. And now, of course,'' he added in a tone that sounded as if he were ill, ''the young guard, Mr. O'Hara, has joined the ranks of the doomed.''

''Well,'' Phoebe said. ''There you have it. If all of you are still alive, your hypothesis can have no validity.''

He laughed darkly. ''Can it not? Three men are still alive, 'tis true. But *twelve* men are dead. And one woman.''

''What! Are you certain?''

''Definitely. My friend Michael Dane, Lord Cullen, who is currently on his way home from Egypt so that we may leave for Zanizbar shortly, wrote to inform me each time another person died. At first I, too, found the idea of a 'genuine' curse ludicrous. But as the numbers of the deceased began climbing I started to wonder."

"Could not their deaths have been due to mere bad luck?" Phoebe suggested.

"Not unless you count plague, accident, and murder as bad luck."

"I would hardly call them good fortune."

"Nor would I, but thirteen deaths are far too many to be discounted to mere chance. Do you understand, therefore, why I must retrieve the amulet?"

Phoebe considered. "I can understand why you feel it necessary. But you must admit there is a possibility that all of the so-called victims died naturally—I know, I know," she said, as he began sputtering about the unnaturalness of murder, plague, and accident. "It is unfortunate they died as they did. But surely it is easier to accept natural cause as a reason, than to take stock in an ancient curse."

"I only wish it were."

"Just suppose you are correct," Phoebe said then. "What is the amulet hurting here in the museum? No one is likely to touch it when it is inside a glass box."

"That would be true except that cleaners, under command of the museum guards, come in once a week to dust things off. They are poor folk, and could easily be swayed by the Eye's beauty and value, to touch it or even attempt to steal it. The plain fact is that my conscience will not allow for the possibility that more innocent people may lose their lives just because I was stupid enough to have the amulet shipped to England."

"You could hardly have left it in Egypt," Phoebe reasoned. "You'd have had to be mad—and you'd have risked the anger of the Egyptian government. It would have seemed to them that you thought their artifacts unworthy of an English museum. Besides, the Eye of Horus is the most magnificent piece I have ever seen. And while I am sure I have not seen as many artifacts as you, I am well enough educated to recognize prime materials."

"You are right, I suppose. It was strange, though." Sir

Malcolm held up his hands and gazed at them thoughtfully. "Although I never actually held the amulet myself
until it was delivered by an Egyptian emissary at the London port, from the moment I first laid eyes on it I had to
have it. It seemed almost to have a strange power over
me."

Phoebe started. "I felt exactly the same way when I
first saw it. You may be certain, Sir Malcolm, that I am
hardly the type of woman who burglarizes museums on a
regular basis."

"My point exactly. It was as if the amulet were reaching
out, trying to make you its next victim."

"Now that is quite absurd," Phoebe said with a nervous laugh.

Sir Malcolm studied her gravely. "Absurd or not, I will
not risk any more lives. I intend to obtain the amulet."

Phoebe had a nasty feeling that she did not want to
know what he intended to do with the Eye once he retrieved it, but she could not keep from asking. "And
then?"

His jaw worked. Without looking at her, he said softly,
"And then I will destroy it."

6

"**D**estroy it!" Phoebe's heart threatened to stop. "In God's name, why? Can you not simply put it in your own collection, or somewhere else away from curious fingers? How can you destroy something so exquisite?"

"Easily." His glance returned to her face. His eyes were cold and hard. "I want the amulet destroyed, Miss Lawton, because it very nearly destroyed me."

"Again, I do not understand."

Agony flashed over his face. "One of the thirteen people it killed was my younger brother, Francis."

Phoebe felt a glimmer of comprehension. "So you are actually bent on destroying it out of an odd sense of revenge."

He made a sharp gesture of denial with one hand. "No. Well, perhaps at first. But not anymore, not since twelve others have perished as well."

She said nothing, but merely watched his face.

"I cannot help but believe that my own brother died because of my negligence."

"How so?"

"When we opened the tomb, a bony corpse was found just beyond the doorway."

"I remember reading of that."

"One of the workers, who read the inscribed curse on

the back of the necklace while it was still clamped in the dead man's fingers, begged me to destroy the amulet. I did not listen, but brushed off what sounded, to me, like a ridiculous suggestion—not to mention that I was far too busy cataloguing artifacts to pay much attention to any particular piece."

"What happened to the amulet after the tomb opening, if you did not pick it up?"

"My brother Francis removed it from the dead man's hand before the porters took the corpse away, and dropped the Eye into his pocket. He must have forgotten to put it back among the other artifacts. Two days later he died of a mysterious fever. Even then I did not realize it was due to the curse.

"The woman tending Francis went through his clothes prior to his burial. She found the Eye and took it to my partner, Lord Baxter. Lord Baxter died five weeks after taking it from her hand—and the nurse died a month after that. A fine reward for such honesty, wasn't it? That amulet could have brought enough gold to keep her and her entire family in comfort for the rest of their lives.

"Needless to say, my conviction about the curse's falsehood did a complete about-face as the death toll continued to mount. And I cannot discount the probability that, had I destroyed the amulet immediately upon its discovery, all thirteen of those people would be alive today. I am now convinced that the Eye of Horus is responsible. How can I do less than destroy the amulet so that no one else perishes for my mistake?"

Hearing this sincerely offered pronouncement, Phoebe felt ill. She turned away. Although she sympathized with Sir Malcolm's grief at the loss of his brother, and was sorry that other people had also lost their lives, every fiber of her being screamed out at the injustice of destroying the Eye of Horus for what could only have been coincidence.

Surely, she thought frantically, while Sir Malcolm must do what he felt right, she must also do what she could to stop this atrocity from happening. Turning back, she said softly, "I suppose we must all do what we feel is required in situations of this type."

"I am relieved that you understand." Sir Malcolm patted the settee cushion. "Come here. Lie down and put your head in my lap. You may use my ruined hat as a pillow. You must be exhausted. I'll keep watch."

Propriety reared its head. "No, thank you," Phoebe lied. "I am not tired."

"Don't be ridiculous, woman." Sir Malcolm smiled sardonically. "If I did not take advantage of you in the sarcophagus, I'm hardly likely to do so now."

"Oh," Phoebe said quickly, "I did not mean to imply you would." Then she laughed. "And you are right. I am very weary."

Squelching her trepidation, she lay down on the settee. Sir Malcolm pulled the crushed hat from his pocket and folded it into a makeshift pillow. Phoebe gingerly placed her head against his leg.

Her last thought before falling asleep was that, given the solidity of Sir Malcolm's leg muscles, rock hard even through the folded hat, if he ever decided to wear modern fashions he would look utterly splendid in them and would have no need of buckram wadding to pad the legs of his breeches. He was truly a magnificent specimen of manhood.

Phoebe felt a hand on her arm. Had she overslept? Was she ill? Had Matty come into her bedchamber?

"Miss Lawton?"

As she heard the baronet's voice, the night's events came flooding back in perfect clarity. She opened her eyes and mumbled, "Good morning."

Sir Malcolm grinned. His hair was mussed and his spectacles rested crookedly on the bridge of his nose. He straightened them and said, "Good morning. I trust you slept well. You looked so peaceful that I did not want to wake you until it was absolutely necessary. But dawn has come and gone, and soon the museum will open. I think we'd best get back into the sarcophagus in case someone comes into the Egyptian Room this morning to check on the crime scene.''

Phoebe sat up and watched as he tucked his hat back into his pocket, picked up his cane, and moved toward the coffin. There he turned and bowed. "Ladies first."

Yawning, Phoebe grabbed up her pelisse, bonnet, and reticule, folded them in a bundle, and followed.

They stood in the sarcophagus for thirty-five minutes. Midway through that time a guard wandered through, but noticed nothing amiss. Once the museum opened Phoebe and Sir Malcolm exited the sarcophagus, waited until fifteen or twenty other people were meandering in and out of the exhibit rooms, and then walked casually outside.

When they stood on the curb, Sir Malcolm donned the gloves he'd pulled from his pocket, hung his cane over his arm, and took the gray sarsenet pelisse from Phoebe's hands. He settled it on her shoulders, tying its ribands under her neck. Phoebe found his ministrations unsettling, but while she would ordinarily have snapped at a man who took such liberties, she found herself at a loss for words.

"Well, Miss Lawton," the baronet murmured, conspiratorially. "You said women never had adventures, yet it seems you have had quite a remarkable one."

Phoebe felt oddly bereft at the thought that they must now part. "That is true," she said absently, opening her reticule, withdrawing her own gloves, and pulling them on as she strove to understand her feelings. "But only because I went after it. As I said while we were conversing in the Egyptian Room yesterday afternoon, adventures do not commonly make themselves available to women. If we wish to have them, we must seek them out."

His good-natured expression faltered. "I hope you do not make a habit of seeking out dangerous situations, dear lady. Especially since you have no male relation to look out for your safety. Being independent is one thing; being foolhardy is quite another."

Phoebe grinned. Men never gave a woman credit for being able to look after herself. Whenever one of them found out about Phoebe's own lack of male supervision, he always seemed compelled to offer her advice on how to live her life. Sir Malcolm was no different.

Once again she was on familiar territory, and the disturbing sensation of not being in control vanished. "I shall endeavor to remember that."

"Good. I walked here yesterday, since I do not live far. But I would be happy to send my carriage back here for you. It is unmarked—I would not want your neighbors to gossip about you appearing on your doorstep in the morning in a gentleman's equipage."

Phoebe's grin deepened. "No, thank you. I will take a cab. I assure you, Sir Malcolm, that I have had extensive experience in looking after myself."

"I did not mean to imply that you had not." Sir Malcolm's hazel eyes sparkled. His sandy-brown hair still looked disheveled but somehow managed to display a perfect windswept style. "You are truly antagonistic about men intruding upon your life, aren't you, Miss Lawton?"

Phoebe's smile vanished. Remembering her father and mother, she flushed. "Perhaps. Well. You must go, and I must find a cab." Unable to help herself, she smiled again. "I enjoyed our adventure, Sir Malcolm."

"As did I. Dare I ask that you allow me to fetch your cab?" he asked with a tentative grin. "Not that you are not infinitely capable of doing so yourself, but just to salve my masculine pride?"

She laughed. "Thank you, sir. I would appreciate it."

A few moments later the hired vehicle stood at the curb, awaiting Phoebe's entry. As she turned to leave, Sir Malcolm put a hand in the pocket of his worn brown coat, then held out a closed fist. "One moment. You're forgetting something."

Phoebe looked at him quizzically, then extended her hand. The baronet dropped seven hairpins into her palm. Phoebe reached up to discover that her unstylish bun was once again tilted over one ear. "Drat," she muttered.

She would have preferred that the baronet, if he ever thought of her again, remembered her a bit more glamorously. It was bad enough that she had blithely walked out of the museum almost in a state of undress, having forgotten to put on her pelisse, but now, the additional discovery that she had also forgotten to put on her bonnet, and that her hair was nearly undone, quite overset her.

What was it about Sir Malcolm that seemed to make her common sense float away like clouds on a summer breeze? She was utterly mortified. But, she hoped fervently, perhaps since the baronet was hardly a fashion mogul, he would not have noticed her social gaffe.

"Since I seem always to be in a hurry, I frequently dress my own hair," she explained hastily, cheeks burning. She gripped her reticule tightly, as if squeezing it might lend some comfort. "As a result, since I am not quite so skilled at the task as my maid, Tribble, it is forever tumbling down about my shoulders. And here I am with no mirror to repair myself."

He chuckled. "Never fear. I have some experience in these matters." Reclaiming the hairpins, he found one more pin in his pocket and tucked all of them into her hair, deftly repositioning her bun. Then he took her bonnet from her hands and settled it expertly atop her head. As he formed a pert bow just below her left ear, he murmured teasingly, "It is nice to know there is something at which you are less than totally adept."

Phoebe felt a strange warmth pervade her body. She blushed furiously and cast her gaze around to see if any passersby had noticed his personal attentions—then realized she did not care if they had. Of what use was a reputation for being eccentric, if one did not utilize it fully?

While she realized that their present circumstances, as well as last night's adventure, had perhaps contributed to an overly simplified feeling of intimacy, she was nonetheless glad she had met Sir Malcolm, and hoped this meeting would not be their last. How strange, she thought fleetingly, that she, who had never had the slightest desire for male companionship, would be hoping to see the baronet again in order to continue their lighthearted banter.

The baronet put a hand to his head. His gloved fingers

hesitated momentarily in empty space, then he dropped his arm. "I'd forgotten I was no longer wearing my hat," he said abashedly. He gazed at her. "Well," he said at last. "It has been interesting knowing you, Miss Lawton. Perhaps we shall meet again."

"Perhaps," Phoebe agreed softly. She thought rapidly. "Do you go to the Simmons's ball tonight? I have not seen you at any tonnish functions, though I assume that is because you travel frequently. Maybe now that you are in London we will see more of you."

Sir Malcolm shook his head. "Actually, I do not get out much. I have been in London for the past year, but spend most of my time in my library, writing about my archaeological experiences. It . . ." He hesitated, then continued brusquely, "it has been difficult coming to grips with my brother's precipitate death, and I am certain that, had I gone out, I would have been less than amusing company."

"I understand," Phoebe said gently.

Sir Malcolm drew a deep breath. He smiled faintly. "And, anyway, although I would like to go to the Simmons's ball, I cannot, for I have not received an invitation. I seriously doubt anyone in town remembers me. Otherwise, I assure you I would be delighted to attend. It is high and above time I ventured out of my warren."

Phoebe felt a brilliant smile burst out upon her face. "Oh, you needn't worry about not having an invitation," she said happily. "Lady Simmons is a good friend of mine. I would be glad to speak to her."

"Thank you. Would it be acceptable for me to bring my uncle, Lord Thomas, as well?"

"Certainly." Phoebe gazed at him for several more seconds. The horses drawing the cab stamped impatiently. He looked back, his gaze warm behind the lenses of his spectacles.

"Goodbye, Sir Malcolm," she said at last. "It has been most interesting." She allowed him to hand her into the cab. As the vehicle moved away, she leaned out the window to wave, but he had already disappeared amid the milling throng.

Malcolm moved briskly down the street toward 102 Prichard Place, his London address. His walking stick dangled forgotten from his arm. To an observer it would have appeared as if a large black cobra with a golden head were climbing up his side.

He gazed at the ground before him as if it were the most fascinating thing he had ever seen. In fact, he did not see it at all. His entire world had turned topsy-turvy, and he did not know what to do about it.

He knew that, since the attempted theft of the Eye of Horus had been discovered, the museum curator would take great pains to keep the amulet under lock and key. It was also possible that the curator suspected Malcolm, himself, as the perpetrator of the crime, given Malcolm's unsuccessful attempt to purchase the amulet.

It was very sad that the young guard, O'Hara, had touched the Eye. But there was not much anyone could do about that. Instead, Malcolm knew he had to concentrate on obtaining the amulet before anyone else touched it. Since *he* had already done so, his death could come at any moment, as it had to its other unfortunate victims. Already he felt the Grim Reaper's hot breath warming the back of his neck.

He had to get the amulet back. But how?

And what was he to think of the intrepid Miss Phoebe Lawton, who had seemed as determined as he to obtain the Eye of Horus? He grinned, wondering if any other woman of his acquaintance would have sneaked into a museum at night, hidden in a coffin, and attempted a burglary.

Was the chit brave? Foolish? Or perhaps a bit of both?

Whichever, she was a taking little thing, for all her outspoken ideas about marriage and independence and men being similar to apes. And though she had disagreed on the matter of the curse, she had not laughed at him for his ideas, which most women of his acquaintance would undoubtedly have done. The *men* already had.

All in all, if one disregarded the failure of his attempted burglary, it had been an enjoyable evening. Quite possibly the most enjoyable one he'd experienced in years. And he had Miss Phoebe Lawton to thank for it.

Since Francis's death he had become used to spending his evenings at home with his books and his collection of antiquities from around the world rather than going to balls or the endless whirl of parties. What month was it, anyway? June? July? No, it was the beginning of August. That meant that this year's Season was almost over.

He was glad he'd agreed to attend the Simmons's ball. It would do him good to get out. Besides, the thought that Miss Lawton actually might want to see him again lit up the dark, inner recesses of his mind like a candle in the night.

Offhand, he wondered what his uncle Thomas, who had lived with him at his townhouse for the last three years because of a fondness for horses and a lack of funds, was doing for the evening. It would be far more comfortable to go out with a companion than alone, and he had already ascertained Lord Thomas's welcome at the ball.

Then he frowned, recollecting that his wardrobe was hopelessly out of date. He no longer had the slightest idea what gentlemen wore to social functions. Actually, he had not been the most dashing and debonair of men even before Francis's untimely demise—the dapper Francis had constantly been nattering at him to dress with more care. He regretted his lack of polish, now. What had Miss Lawton thought of his dusty, outmoded appearance?

He would have to ask Uncle Thomas to recommend a decent tailor. With this solid plan of action in mind, he lightly took the steps to his townhouse three at a time.

7

Phoebe managed to slip through the servants' entrance of her townhouse without being seen. She made her way directly to her room, where she washed and changed without calling Tribble, who had not discovered Phoebe's absence since the abigail never entered Phoebe's chambers until the service bell rang.

Phoebe then hurried to Matty's suite. Knocking softly, she turned the door handle and peeked in. The windows were swathed with heavy velvet in the grayish-lavender shade Matty preferred. The room was deep in shadow. Phoebe thought she could just make out a large lump on the mattress.

Moving on tiptoe, she crept forward. "Matty? Matty? Are you asleep? Are you still in pain? Shall I summon a doctor?"

To her relief her cousin turned over, gave a great yawn, stretched, and sat up. "Oh, heavens no. I am much better, Phoebe, just lazy. What time is it?"

"Almost eleven. How is your head?"

Matty shook herself lightly. Her gray hair stuck straight up like meringue on a lemon pie. She shook herself again, harder. Then she smiled. "Fine. It is gone."

"I am so glad."

Sitting, Matty reached out and tugged energetically on

the bellpull that hung beside the bedpost. When a maid appeared in the doorway, she said briskly, "Coffee, scones, bacon, eggs, and fresh fruit, if you please. Oh, and one of Cook's apricot tarts, if she has made any."

Phoebe laughed. "Now I know you are all right. You must be, to want a breakfast large enough for five people."

"Nothing wrong with a healthy appetite," Matty countered. "A man likes a bit of meat on a woman's bones."

Phoebe did not mention that this point was moot, since there were no men in their establishment save the butler and a few footmen. "What are you wearing to the Simmons's ball this evening?" she asked. "I trust you do wish to attend." She knew Matty would be planning to wear either purple or gray, and wished there was some way she could convince the older woman to try a brighter color.

True to form, Matty replied, "I thought I would wear my new plum satin with its matching turban, and my amethysts. I will need to go out this afternoon, however, since I have misplaced one of my lavender kid gloves. I believe I left it at Lady Tibilt's musicale last Saturday, though when I sent her a note inquiring, she said she had not seen it. I thought perhaps one of the bazaars would be the most likely place to find a new pair. And I remember you wanted a new shawl to go with your cherry-striped walking gown."

"Yes. I also wish to look for a few new ostrich feathers for my riding hat. Somehow I lost two the last time we rode through Rotten Row. Do you wish to go to the Exeter Change, or the Burlington Arcade?"

Matty shrugged. "Either. What are you wearing tonight?"

Phoebe thought for a moment. "Probably my rose silk. I have, as you know, worn it once before, but it goes so well with my new shell-pink lace fan painted with moss roses that I believe I will wear it again. And probably my emeralds, since they will bring out the color of the rose leaves."

Matty nodded approvingly. "It sounds lovely. But then you always look a veritable picture. If only you would be more encouraging to gentlemen," she grumbled. "They are inevitably charmed by you. All you would need do is crook your finger at any one of them. And, as I have said many times, you'd best do so before you run out of time."

Not wanting to hear the oft-repeated refrain again, Phoebe turned to the chamber door. "Well, I just wanted to make certain you felt better and that I did not need to send for a physician. I shall be in my room if you need me. I have developed a bit of a headache myself and think I shall lie down for a while. I feel almost as if I have not slept all night." She smiled secretly. "But of course I did. And most comfortably."

"Oh, you poor dear," Matty murmured. "Of course you must rest. We do not want you ill at tonight's ball. Would you like me to send up a maid with some rose water for your temples? Or one of Cook's headache powders? They really do work wonders." Then she frowned. "However, they also make one sleep like the dead and I could not promise you would awake in time for tonight's entertainment."

"No, thank you. All I need is complete silence for a few hours. Shall we go shopping at two?"

"Only if you are feeling better," Matty said firmly. "If you are not well by then I will insist you take a headache powder and we simply forget about the Simmons's ball. There will be others."

But not, Phoebe knew, where Sir Malcolm was certain to attend. Nothing would keep her from the Simmons's townhouse that night. "I am sure I shall be just fine."

Passing the maid carrying Matty's heavily laden breakfast tray, Phoebe escaped to her bedchamber, where she collapsed across her comforter and slept soundly until one-thirty. At that time she rose and rang for Tribble to help her dress for the afternoon's shopping expedition.

Malcolm stood in the tailor's shop on Conduit Street and eyed his reflection in a full-length looking glass. "Are you quite certain this is what gentlemen are wearing these days, Uncle?'' he inquired doubtfully. ''I confess I find it hard to credit.''

''Of a certainty, my boy,'' his uncle Thomas replied amiably. He stood not much above five feet and, with his vibrantly hued clothing, bald pate, round belly, and spindly bowed legs, resembled nothing so much as a vividly colored pot-bellied stove. He regarded his nephew's new clothing through a silver quizzing glass. ''You'll fit right in, tonight. I am so pleased you've decided to come out of hiding.''

''Do Lord and Lady Simmons give many costume balls, then?'' Malcolm asked. Though Phoebe had not mentioned that the ball was a full-costume affair, he assumed that his uncle, who got about a great deal, was fully cognizant of the particulars of each tonnish function.

Lord Thomas lowered the magnifying lens and glanced up. ''The Simmonses?'' he repeated. ''Er, yes. I believe they have been known to host one or two in the past.''

''Ah.'' Malcolm relaxed, glad to know he would not appear too ridiculous, since the other ball guests would surely be garbed similarly.

Mr. Harry Quimby, the proprietor of the shop, dusted a stray bit of fluff off of Malcolm's sleeve. The proprietor's eyelashes were extremely long and his cologne was almost overpowering. He emitted a laugh that sounded suspiciously like a giggle. Malcolm eyed him uncertainly and backed up several feet.

''Ooh, sir!'' Mr. Quimby cooed, clapping one soft-looking hand to his equally soft-looking cheek. ''I daresay once the ton gets a look at you, not only will my store be swamped with orders, but you yourself will receive more invitations than you can count. Of course, no one else could fill this costume like you do. Your figure is one in a million. Just look at those shoulders! I have never seen their match.'' He gave a heartfelt sigh and pressed his hands together expressively.

''Er . . . quite.'' Malcolm turned and frowned at himself in the mirror. ''I do not believe any of the gentlemen I've seen around town have been dressed like this, Uncle Thomas. You are *quite* sure ...''

Lord Thomas waved the question away. Removing an enameled snuff box from his embroidered coat pocket, he flipped open the container, snorted a goodly amount of the powdered tobacco, and promptly sneezed. He wiped his weepy eyes and nose with a lace-edged hanky, and gasped, "That's 'cause them's party clothes. Trust me, Nevvie."

Somehow, Malcolm did not feel totally convinced. Yet, as he had assured himself already, it was undeniable that Lord Thomas did go to numerous ton affairs, and was far more astute in fashionable matters than Malcolm. "Of course I trust you, Uncle," he replied in a voice that sounded far more sincere than he felt. He turned away from the mirror, adjusted his spectacles, and smiled half-heartedly. "Just let me change back into my old things and pay for my purchases, and we shall be on our way."

Phoebe and Matty arrived at Lord and Lady Simmons's townhouse shortly after ten o'clock that night. During the day's shopping trip, both had found the items required to complete their ensembles.

Matty's maid, Phoebe noticed favorably, had left off the purple turban and dressed the older woman's hair in a new, very feminine style, so that Matty's mouse-brown locks curled in little wisps about her angular face. She looked almost pretty—at the very least, handsome—even though she was wearing a rather drab shade of plum. The amethysts Phoebe had given her cousin for Christmas two years before glittered on Matty's hands, in her hair, and around her fingers and throat.

Phoebe, wearing her rose silk with deep flounces at the hem, lace pointelle edging around the bodice and sleeves, and matching rose-colored slippers and gloves, knew she was looking in prime fettle. She had also, as planned, worn her emeralds—a necklace, bracelet, hair clip, ring, and earrings of very large, deep green square-cut stones that sparked blue fire from their crystalline depths when-ever she moved. She was confident that the gems set off the moss rose leaves, painted on her lace fan, to perfection.

Tribble had washed Phoebe's hair in a blend of lemon juice, egg whites, and vinegar until it sparkled as if someone had combed powdered gold through its silken lengths. Then the maid had dressed it high on Phoebe's head, but had left the ends free to curl in a tempting blond swirl down her back. Hopefully the coiffure would remain in place for the entire evening. At last, with a dab of attar of roses behind her ears and on her wrists (as well as just a touch between the firm swell of her bosom), Phoebe felt herself ready to meet the harshest scrutiny.

The thought of seeing Sir Malcolm again made her stomach quiver. She took a deep breath to calm herself. When she and Matty ascended the ivory marble staircase leading up from the main hall into the Simmons's ballroom, Phoebe held her head high and smiled so radiantly that a footman nearly fell backward as she passed.

They reached the reception line at the top of the stairs just as Lord Simmons's younger brother, Lord Peter, entered the ballroom. His brilliant red hair had obviously been burnt with a curling iron in an effort to make the poker-straight locks form the fashionable windswept style. The attempt had failed dismally, only serving to make the nineteen-year-old look as if he'd thrust his head inside a fireplace and been singed by a stray spark.

When Lord Peter's gaze settled upon Phoebe he froze, striking an elaborate, awestruck pose which Phoebe supposed was meant to make him resemble a hero in an epic tale. Unable to help herself, she laughed at the absurd picture he presented.

"Good gracious, Lord Peter," she said with a chuckle. "Do I look so much like Medusa that you have been turned to stone?"

The young lordling hurried forward. "Phoebe—I mean Miss Lawton!" He colored furiously at presuming to use her Christian name. "How can you suggest such a thing? Nay, you look like Venus rising from Sandro Botticelli's shell. Your beauty quite takes my breath away."

Phoebe raised a brow, skeptically. "Truly? Unless I am mistaken, the goddess in Botticelli's *Birth of Venus* had red-brown hair rather than my own gold, was alarmingly lacking in attire, and looked as if she had eaten far too many clams in butter sauce. Should I be offended by your reference, my lord?"

Though his green eyes sparkled, Lord Peter shook his head gravely. Phoebe's nose wrinkled as the faint, acrid scent of burned hair wafted through the air.

"No indeed," he declared. "You should be honored— nay, *I* am the one who is honored. I and every other man present tonight. Honored at the opportunity to gaze upon your exquisiteness. Tell me, lovely one. Have you decided to accept my suit and make me the happiest man on earth?"

Matty, standing slightly behind Phoebe, snorted. "Piffle," she said with a deprecating glare. "Young men nowadays have no sense of the original. Venus rising from a shell, indeed."

Lord Peter glanced past Phoebe. He grinned, and looked almost handsome. Give the lad another ten years to mature, Phoebe thought fondly and, burnt hair or no, the women of the ton had better guard their hearts.

"Ah, Miss Stoat. It is a pleasure to see you here this evening, as well," Lord Peter said. "You are looking most fine. Is that a new hairstyle?"

Matty's baleful stare softened. She simpered, patting her locks with an amethyst-encrusted hand. "Why, yes. It is."

"I thought so," Lord Peter replied. "It is very becoming."

"Thank you, my lord."

Though Phoebe's quick mind had thought of several witty rejoinders she could make about Lord Peter's proffered suit, she repeated none of them. Though he always pretended to be joking when he paid her court, Lord Peter was unmistakably infatuated with her. Phoebe easily recognized the heartfelt sincerity in his pale green eyes, and did not want to hurt him by replying too flippantly.

She knew Lord Peter would outgrow his infatuation in time. She was very fond of him, and would, if it would not have abrogated her freedom from masculine authority, almost have wished he was her brother.

She ignored his renewed proposal and said, "I do hope you plan to dance with both Matty and myself this evening, Lord Peter, instead of leaving us to stand amid the chaperones and old maids. I long to see how the skirt of my new gown swirls during the waltz. You will not disappoint me, will you?"

"The waltz?" Though Lord Peter paled, he swallowed and answered steadily. "Of course, the waltz! It will be my sincere pleasure to partner both you and Miss Stoat in the waltz, dear lady."

Since more people had arrived at the receiving line during their conversation, Phoebe cast Lord Peter another smile and followed Matty on through the queue. She made certain to compliment young Lady Jane, Lord Peter's twin sister, who had been brought out last year but had not been what could be called an unqualified success by any stretch of the most colorful of imaginations.

Lady Jane was cursed with spots, and had the same unfortunately red hair as her twin. Not only that, but she had no more conversation than a fish. The poor girl was unlikely to make a match of any kind, much less a glittering one such as Lord and Lady Simmons hoped for. Still, it did Phoebe's heart good to see Lady Jane's eyes light up when Phoebe mentioned how radiant the girl's puce velvet gown made her complexion (which was in truth undeniably sallow) appear.

Phoebe sighed inwardly for the debutante, and thanked God her own excruciating youth was behind her.

Then she and Matty reached the end of the receiving line, and she let her gaze wander freely over the crowd. Lord and Lady Simmons must be pleased, she thought as she noted that the room was packed as tightly as a can of sardines and would most definitely qualify as a crush, or at the very least a terrible squeeze, and thus be considered a great success.

Men, dressed in variously colored jackets, brightly hued waistcoats, white silk stockings—many of which were intricately clocked—black knee breeches, and dancing slippers of softest leather, stood attentively beside ladies dressed in every color of the spectrum. Jewels of every type and description flashed in the candlelight cast down by two dozen huge crystal chandeliers. Satins, silks, velvets, voiles, gauzes, and lace swirled as the women, clinging to their companions' arms, perambulated about the ballroom.

As the orchestra began tuning its instruments, Phoebe felt a burst of sheer exhilaration rush through her body. She dearly loved to dance, but was the first to admit that she was not the most graceful creature in the world. The gentlemen of her acquaintance, however, bore with her ungainliness, for she not only knew how to make each of them feel as if he were the only man in the world, but she could also hold up her end—and in some cases with very shy gentlemen, both ends—of a conversation.

Thus, even though she was considered extremely odd by most of the ton because of her outrageous ideas about marriage, every gentleman in her sphere worshipped her; and, because the ladies knew she had no intention of marrying and was therefore no competition to either them or their daughters, they allowed Phoebe's peculiarities to pass without much comment.

Despite her lack of adeptness on the ballroom floor, within minutes Phoebe's dance card was nearly filled— the first dances claimed being those which did not call for such proximity as to prove calamitous to a gentleman's fine dancing slippers or his sensitive toes. Finally, the only dances remaining on her card were the waltzes, save the one Lord Peter had bravely agreed upon, as not even the most lionhearted of men could bring themselves to lead Miss Phoebe Lawton onto the floor for one of those close, intimate dances.

Nevertheless, Phoebe was satisfied, especially as her partners, after signing her own programme, made a sizable dent in Matty's as well. Then, as the orchestra glided into a minuet, she allowed herself to be led onto the gleaming parquet floor.

The first half of the evening passed splendidly. Lord Peter's slippers suffered only minimal damage, and after their dance Phoebe took a seat near the wall as the musicians began playing another waltz. She eyed Matty enviously as the older woman's partner whirled her round and round. Then, closing her eyes, Phoebe leaned her head against the back of her chair and allowed her imagination to take her onto the floor, since no brave gentleman was forthcoming.

Some ten minutes later a flurry of activity near the room's entrance made her reopen her eyes and glance in that direction. She sat bolt upright as a portly older gentleman entered the ballroom.

Matty, who had just returned to Phoebe's side, pressed one mauve-gloved hand to her lips. "Good heavens," she said sympathetically. "Have you ever seen the like? Look at that wig! And those breeches! The poor man. Who is he?"

Phoebe felt a sudden queasiness in the pit of her stomach. "I believe it is Lord Thomas Creevey," she replied. "Sir Malcolm Forbes's uncle."

Lord Thomas *did* look a sight. He was not much over five feet, and was nearly as wide as he was tall. His skinny legs did not look strong enough to support his bulk, though his feet were astonishingly large and, thus, perhaps made up for his lack of symmetry. His eyes bulged and his cheeks were scarlet, as if a great pressure were building in his head and he were about to explode.

Phoebe looked away from the man's eighteenth-century powdered wig and bell-toed slippers, embarrassed by her fellow ton members' rude stares. But when a second ripple of surprise wended its way through the crowd, she reluctantly glanced back.

A few feet behind Lord Thomas another figure, dressed with equal absurdity, entered the ballroom. Phoebe was glad she was sitting down, else she was certain she would have swooned. If it had not been for the look of utter shock in his eyes, which she had seen once before, just prior to his leaping into the Egyptian sarcophagus with her at the London Metropolitan Museum, she would never have recognized Sir Malcolm Forbes.

8

"Don't know why you wanted to come here tonight, Nevvie," Lord Thomas griped, glancing up at Malcolm. He tugged his colorful coat firmly down over his bulging stomach. Then he raised his quizzing glass and surveyed the crowd. "It'll be dull as dishwater, mark my words. Should have gone to *my* friend's party, instead."

"You said these clothes were appropriate for tonight's entertainment," Malcolm hissed.

"I never did!" Lord Thomas expostulated.

Malcolm gritted his teeth, and said harshly, "You told me the Simmonses were well known for their costume balls."

Lord Thomas flushed. "I most certainly did not. I merely answered your inquiry about whether the Simmonses had ever hosted any. But I had no idea you were speaking of this ball, tonight."

"But you said my attire would fit right in!"

"And it would have. If we'd gone to Alexander Fielding's masquerade ball, as I'd expected, we'd have fit right in," Lord Thomas countered testily. "When you said you wanted to go out tonight, I assumed you meant wherever *I* had planned to go. You never told me we was coming here. Can't blame me for this mess. Ain't as if you ever went out before."

"After this, I'll never show my face again," Malcolm replied darkly.

Lord Thomas lowered bushy brows over protruding eyes and scowled. "Here now, don't get stuffy with me. It ain't as if we has to stay here. We can always turn around and go to Zander's."

"I cannot leave. I told a certain someone I would be here this evening. I must at least let her know I kept my word."

Lord Thomas shrugged. "Suit yourself. But I'm leaving. May I take the carriage? Zander's house is a good ways away."

Malcolm nodded absently. His uncle turned and, as quickly as a spider, scurried back down the staircase. Swallowing, Malcolm began casting his gaze about the room, looking for Miss Phoebe Lawton.

Phoebe gaped at the baronet. His sandy-brown hair was covered by a powdered wig similar to Lord Thomas Creevey's. Also like the older man, Sir Malcolm wore white face powder, twin dots of scarlet rouge high on his cheekbones, and glossy red lip color.

His clothing, which fitted his wonderfully muscular frame like a second skin, would have made a court jester proud. His shoulders were graced by a jacket of pea-green velvet, every square inch of which was covered with the same color sequins. His waistcoat was lemon-yellow satin embroidered with ladybugs and nightingales. His cravat was so high he could scarcely turn his head, but had to pivot his entire body in order to look around.

His breeches were celestial blue velvet and had oval slits down the leg through which amaranthus-colored silk stockings were visible. The pant legs were so snug one could see every definition. Phoebe's gaze dropped to the inescapable swell at the juncture of the baronet's thighs, and she felt her temperature rise alarmingly. She looked lower, hastily.

On Sir Malcolm's feet, metallic-gold Arabian–knight–style slippers protruded at least five inches from his toes. The tips turned back upon themselves, secured by gold thread to their tongues, where tiny bells tinkled with every movement the baronet made. But the worst thing about Sir Malcolm's appearance was the fact that it had obviously been a grave mistake.

No doubt, Phoebe reasoned, Sir Malcolm had known his clothing was too outmoded to wear to a tonnish gathering, and had gone shopping for a suitable ensemble. That must have been when the dreadful misunderstanding occurred.

Sir Malcolm pushed his spectacles up firmly and clasped his ebony cane in one lace-gloved hand. The crowd had gathered about him in a semicircle, no one wanting to miss a moment of the spectacle. The baronet's eyes darted about frantically.

Phoebe unfurled her fan and whisked it furiously in front of her face, wondering what to do. Catching the gaze of Lord Peter, she beckoned him to her side. She whispered frantically in his ear, then sat back to see if the young man would succeed.

Lord Peter strode confidently over to the baronet. "Sir Malcolm Forbes!" he cried. "You crafty old devil, you actually did it!" He turned to one of his acquaintances, Mr. Alvarez Schwartz. "Look here, Alvy, the old fellow actually did it! Would you believe anyone would have had the nerve?"

"Eh?" Mr. Schwartz blinked and looked confused. "What?"

Clapping a hand over Sir Malcolm's arm, Lord Peter propelled him into the very center of the mass of people, like a bird flying into the eye of a hurricane. "Everyone, come meet my good friend, Sir Malcolm Forbes. Surely you've heard of him. Famous archaeologist, always donating artifacts to the Metropolitan Museum, as well as to the regent's personal collection."

Several gentlemen approached cautiously. One by one Lord Peter introduced the baronet to the group.

"So you see," Phoebe listened as the young man addressed the crowd. "It was all a lark. I was at Sir Malcolm's townhouse last night, and I bet him a pony that he wouldn't dare come to my brother's ball dressed as outrageously as a court jester. Dashed if he didn't win. Guess I'll be asking my brother for an advance on my allowance!''

When the men laughed along with Lord Peter, and shook Sir Malcolm's hand, Phoebe relaxed. Curiosity satisfied, the other ball guests began drifting away. Finally Lord Peter approached Phoebe's chair, a reluctant Sir Malcolm in tow.

''Sir Malcolm,'' Phoebe said smoothly. ''How nice to see you this evening.''

Beneath its thin coating of rice powder, Sir Malcolm's face paled even more. ''Miss Lawton,'' he muttered. ''I pray you will understand when I take my leave immediately. My mode of dress seems to have caused quite a stir.''

Phoebe cast a speaking glance at Lord Peter, who nodded and moved away. When the young man was out of earshot, she said quietly, ''You cannot leave, Sir Malcolm, or the entire ton will know Lord Peter's 'wager' was untrue. It will make him look deceitful, and make you appear cowardly. No, sir, you must brazen it out.''

Sir Malcolm scowled. ''For how long?''

''At least an hour.''

''An hour! God's precious blood. Oh, very well.'' He sat down beside her and sighed. ''I have made an utter fool of myself, haven't I?''

Phoebe shook her head. ''Not at all. By morning the ton will be abuzz with gossip about the bold Sir Malcolm Forbes, who is every bit as eccentric as his reputation has made him out to be.''

''That is good?'' he demanded cynically.

She met his gaze steadily. ''I think you will agree that it is preferable to being branded craven.''

He inclined his head. ''Point well taken.''

Suddenly he smiled his familiar crooked grin, and Phoebe caught her breath at the transformation. Immediately Sir Malcolm was metamorphosed from a ridiculous quiz into the daring rogue Lord Peter had made him out to be. Standing, the baronet held out his hand.

"Miss Lawton," he said loudly enough for those nearby to overhear. "I see you are not dancing. Are the gentlemen of the haut ton blind? How can they leave you sitting there when you are the fairest damsel in the room? I insist you allow me to partner you for this waltz."

Those guests standing nearby began twittering like nervous sparrows. Several people stared blatantly and snickered behind their hands.

Though she longed to whirl onto the dance floor, Phoebe desperately tried to rescue Sir Malcolm from his mistake. "No, thank you, sir," she said. "I am certain that after your absence from the ton, you will not wish to dance until you have refreshed your memory of the steps."

He shook his bewigged head. "Why, that is absurd. Dancing is like riding a horse, dear lady. Once one learns, one never forgets."

Phoebe glanced furtively at their eager observers. "Pray, sit down, Sir Malcolm. I do not wish to dance just now."

"What? You refuse my invitation?" He waggled his brows. Clapping a hand over his chest, he said woefully, "Miss Lawton, you wound me. Sink me, but you do. Were your words a sword they would pierce my poor, besotted heart."

Laughter mushroomed through the room.

Phoebe ground her teeth. Rising, she pinned the baronet with an ominous glare. "All right. But you deserve everything you get." As Sir Malcolm leaned his cobra-handled cane against the wall and extended a garishly clad arm, she laid the tips of her rose-hued gloves on his pea-green sleeve.

With great ceremony he led her to the exact center of the dance floor. Pushing his spectacles up firmly on his nose, he placed his fingers alongside her waist and took her hand. Phoebe took a deep breath and prayed for grace.

She quickly forgot her lack of this commodity as they began to move, however, when she noticed that Sir Malcolm was scarcely limping at all. In fact, he seemed so at home on the dance floor that he might have been dancing every night for the past ten years. She peered up at him curiously, wondering if there might not be more to this man than the bookish scholar and dusty scientist she had presumed him to be.

"Your hair looks lovely tonight, Miss Lawton," Sir Malcolm said conversationally. His blue-green eyes gleamed appreciatively behind his spectacle lenses. "I trust your maid had enough pins to secure it without having to purchase more, after your mishap in the sarcophagus."

"She did, thank you. May I inquire whether you have replaced your hat?"

"Not yet. I have an appointment to do so tomorrow, with a haberdasher whom I have known for many years. Thus, I needn't fear buying the wrong style and making another horrific spectacle of myself." He quickly explained the mistake about his evening dress.

"I thought that must have been what happened. You know, Sir Malcolm, you dance extremely well."

"You sound as if that surprises you."

"It does a bit, I confess. Your leg does not seem to trouble you at all, as one might reasonably expect. And I did not think you were the type of man who had spent a lot of time dancing, although now I see that I must have been mistaken. You are obviously an expert. But until this moment you struck me as so—" She broke off abruptly.

He quirked a brow inquiringly.

"So terribly serious," she finished. "So disinterested in the frivolities of society."

He tipped his head back and laughed. Ten years seemed to drop off his face. Phoebe gazed at his intriguingly crooked grin, spellbound. Those couples dancing nearby turned to look, and also smiled.

"Good heavens, woman," Sir Malcolm managed at last. "You make me sound like a crippled bookworm. I assure you, my leg does give me trouble at times, but it can be managed. It aches a bit after dancing, but waltzing with you is worth every minute of pain I may suffer tonight.

You think perhaps that I have spent my entire life—the part not spent climbing around in ancient tombs—in my library?''

''Actually, yes. You did tell me you seldom ventured out amid the ton.''

''That doesn't mean I cannot squire a woman about the dance floor when necessity dictates. You see, when I came to London at twenty years of age, I enjoyed at least five years amid the glitter of the beau monde before I became interested in searching for artifacts. And even while out of Britain it was often necessary to dance with the wives of pashas or other foreigners. The waltz is sweeping the rest of the world, just like it is here.''

''Really?''

''Yes. But enough about my dancing. Please explain something that has been troubling me, Miss Lawton.''

''What is that?''

''I could not help noticing that, though all the other dances on your card were filled when this waltz began, all the spaces beside the waltzes were empty—except for the one Lord Peter had claimed. Why is that? I cannot understand why the gentlemen here tonight would leave a woman as lovely as you on the sidelines during one of the most deliciously intimate pastimes in the world.''

Though pleased by his flattery, Phoebe grimaced. ''There is a very good reason, I assure you,'' she muttered. ''Though I hope you do not find out what it is.''

The words were barely out of her mouth when Sir Malcolm cried, ''Ouch!'' He looked alarmed and very surprised. ''I am so sorry,'' he apologized. ''I must have misstepped.''

Phoebe bit her lip and swallowed her rising panic.

A few seconds later, Sir Malcolm uttered a second pained oath. He blinked uncertainly. ''Miss Lawton,'' he said hesitantly, ''are you perhaps feeling faint?''

''No. I am fine.'' Phoebe wished the Simmons's ballroom floor would open up and swallow her. Naturally, it did not.

Then, Sir Malcolm cried again, ''Ouch!''

Phoebe's cheeks flamed and her mouth went dry.

"My dear girl," the baronet said uneasily. "Are you quite certain you are wholly well?"

"No. I am not." Glancing about furtively, Phoebe noticed that every eye in the place was glued upon the pair of them with conspicuous amusement. "Sir Malcolm," she said, distressed, "we should sit down. People are staring."

He peered down at her, his gaze speculative. "Miss Lawton," he murmured again. "Do you perchance have trouble with the waltz?"

Phoebe felt the sharp tang of tears prick her eyelids and make her throat tighten. "With the waltz and every other dance," she answered thickly, "though my gentleman friends always invite me to participate in those that do not bring me into close contact with their feet. I fear the only time I have the opportunity to waltz is when I ask the gentlemen myself. None of them would have the heart to put life and limb on the line, otherwise."

Behind his spectacles, Sir Malcolm's eyes blazed. "Is that so?" he asked angrily.

Phoebe nodded and blinked rapidly to keep her tears from overflowing onto her cheeks.

The baronet's jaw worked silently for a moment, and he gazed over her head as if deep in thought. Then he looked down again. There was a disconcerting glitter in his hazel eyes. "Would you mind very much if we tried something, Miss Lawton?"

Barely managing to keep hysteria at bay, Phoebe could not stifle one mournful sniff. "I would prefer to sit down, sir. I am utterly humiliated."

"I will escort you to a chair if that is what you truly want. However, you would do better to trust me. I promise what I intend will be neither painful nor unpleasant. As you said earlier, though not in so many words," he said pointedly, " 'tis better to be branded an eccentric than a pusillanimous milksop. If you sit down now, people will think you a wretched coward."

Phoebe hesitated, then gave a shaky grin. "*Touché,* Sir Malcolm. I am in your hands."

"Not yet," he answered mysteriously, "but you soon will be."

Before Phoebe knew what he was about, Sir Malcolm put both hands around her waist and swung her into the air. "Sir Malcolm," she gasped. "What do you think you are doing? Put me down at once! People are staring!"

The baronet laughed unabashedly, causing even the most polite dancers, who had avoided staring outright at the awkward pair, to turn and gape. "Of course they are. But they are seeing nothing they would not expect from such an odd couple as we. Relax, Phoebe, and enjoy our waltz."

Though the voice of reason and propriety chattered scoldingly inside Phoebe's head, she could not resist the sensuous pull of the music. Putting her arms around the back of Sir Malcolm's neck, she let him swing her around and around until she was giddy with the sheer joy of life.

All too soon, the splendid dance came to an end.

"That," Phoebe said candidly as Sir Malcolm set her gently on her feet, "was the most exhilarating experience I have ever had. I may never be able to hold my head up in polite society again, but I would not have missed it for the world. Thank you, Sir Malcolm."

The baronet's irrepressible grin made him look like a mischievous boy in a grown man's body, though at the same time he exuded a strength and masculine vitality that made Phoebe feel wonderfully feminine. She suddenly felt disturbingly warm.

Sir Malcolm laughed. "Nor would I. And as I said already, I wouldn't worry about the ton's holding your actions against you. You seem to be a favorite among them. Look there, you see? Already they are becoming involved in other things and seem to have forgotten all about us."

It was true, Phoebe saw. Wholly unexpected, insanely improbable, but gloriously true.

While moments before every eye had been pinned,

aghast, on their whirling bodies, now everyone was going on with the business of dancing and card playing and gossiping. It seemed, she thought gratefully, that her good reputation among her friends was strong enough to kill even the outrageousness of the dance.

"Is there anything to eat here?" Sir Malcolm asked then. "That made me a bit peckish."

Phoebe made a face. "Weak punch and greasy lobster patties."

"Ugh. No thank you." Tilting his head to one side, he looked her up and down, hopefully. "I don't suppose you are hiding any cheese somewhere on that lovely gown?"

Phoebe giggled. "No. I am sorry."

He sighed. "Ah, well. One cannot have everything, I suppose. Come. Let us walk outside for a breath of air. While I would never intimate that you are heavy, dear lady, it was nonetheless fatiguing carrying you held out from my body that way. T'would have been easier, and even more delightful than it was, if I'd held you closer to my chest."

Phoebe experienced a sudden flare of heat in her lower parts as she imagined being cradled against the baronet's hard body. She glanced furtively at him, wondering if he might be thinking something similar, but he was gazing purposefully toward the double French doors on the opposite side of the ballroom.

"Perhaps," he continued, "the fresh air will take the edge off my hunger."

Smiling with a wistfulness she did not quite understand, Phoebe took his arm and they moved across the crowded floor as the orchestra began playing another waltz. They stepped out onto the balcony and headed for its stone railing, below which, bathed in moonlight, lay the Simmons's formal garden. There was no one else in sight, and the sky was a clear, star-studded, midnight blue.

Phoebe lifted herself up onto the stone railing and turned slightly so that she sat facing Sir Malcolm. She studied him covertly. What was it about him that made her feel as if she could behave in any way, or do anything, such as toss herself quite shamelessly up onto this wall like a schoolgirl climbing an apple tree, without fear of reproof? She had never dreamed of feeling so . . . so *free* with any gentleman.

Then a smile tugged at her lips. "Your glasses are falling off again. You really must have your optician adjust them so they fit better. They seem to be constantly on the verge of sliding off the tip of your nose." Reaching up, she settled the spectacles more securely on his face. "That's better. Do they feel all right?"

"Perfect." He looked at her and also grinned. "Your turn."

Phoebe did not move as he put out a hand to secure her coiffure which, despite Tribble's finesse, had begun falling down her back in a wildly curling tangle. She said breathlessly, "It must have been our waltz that pulled it free."

Sir Malcolm did not reply, but went very still. His fingers clutched one stray curl. He gazed at it with a bemused expression. "My God," he murmured. "It is softer than the finest Chinese silk."

Phoebe looked up into his eyes. Instead of seeing the cosmetics plastered on his skin, it seemed as if she could see down into his very soul. What she read therein held her prisoner. She could not have moved away even if God himself had called her soul to heaven.

"You know," Sir Malcolm murmured huskily. "Your eyes really are the exact shade of a forget-me-not. And it really is my favorite color. Be still, Phoebe, for this time I truly *am* going to kiss you." Never taking his gaze from hers, he bent forward.

9

Just as Sir Malcolm's warm lips brushed against Phoebe's, a sharp voice rent the night air. "Phoebe? Phoebe, are you out here? Lord and Lady Dunstable and I need a fourth for whist. Do you wish to play?"

Sir Malcolm jerked away. His face was a mask of self-recrimination. "My God. I am sorry." He sounded choked. "I do not know what came over me. As I told you before, in the sarcophagus, I am not in the habit of taking advantage of women. This behavior is totally unlike me."

"But you didn't—"

"Please excuse me." He looked around as if dazed. "I believe I left my cane inside. I must retrieve it and be on my way. I think you will agree that I have stayed long enough to protect my reputation." He laughed harshly. "And almost long enough to ruin yours."

"But, Sir Malcolm—"

"I must go. Tomorrow I plan to visit the museum to make a final attempt to purchase the amulet. If the curator will not sell it to me, I do not know what I shall do." He gave her a final smile that did not quite reach his eyes. "Good evening, Miss Lawton."

The baronet bowed and moved away. His limp seemed, somehow, more pronounced. Phoebe jumped down off the

82

wall, put out a hand, and moved to follow him, but stopped when her cousin reached her side.

"There you are." Matty studied Phoebe somberly and shook her head. "What were you doing out here with the baronet, Phoebe? Have you no concern for your reputation? You must count yourself fortunate, my dear, that you were not ostracized by the ton for your behavior tonight during that scandalous waltz. I would not be a friend if I did not tell you that tongues are, despite everyone's fondness for you, wagging mightily. You must take care."

Phoebe barely heard her. "Do you mind if we return home, Matty? I am suddenly quite fatigued." She did not wait for a reply, but moved back into the ballroom.

Malcolm barely noticed the peculiar stares he received as he made his way out to the street in front of the Simmons's townhouse. His brain felt so addled that he stood on the curb for ten minutes before recollecting that his uncle had taken the carriage, leaving him to fend for himself. Rather than call for a cab, he began walking along the street, his ebony cane tapping the macadam with each slow step.

The sky, so clear and brilliant thirty minutes before, had clouded over as rapidly as if a giant had wiped away the stars. A fine mist filled the air, presaging the rain that began falling soon thereafter.

Malcolm plodded on, passing beneath the gaslights lining the street. He scarcely noticed the way his metallic-gold slippers sloshed through the puddles, or the chill where his amaranth-silk-stockinged legs, visible through the slits down the sides of his celestial blue velvet breeches, were exposed to the night air.

He was only vaguely aware that the rain was washing rice powder off his wig and face and onto his pea-green sequined jacket and embroidered lemon-yellow waistcoat, leaving white streaks on the velvet as if some giant bird had passed overhead. His heart was heavy, and his wounded leg throbbed, no doubt from a combination of

the damp, chilly night air and the wild, thrilling waltz he
had shared with Miss Lawton. Phoebe.

That impetuous, eccentric, thoroughly wonderful
woman.

Impetuous she might be, Malcolm admitted to himself,
but everything about her was nonetheless superb. The way
her glorious golden hair was always falling down about
her shoulders, for example. And the way she carried food
tucked away in her reticule in case of emergency. Or the
way she looked up at him with shining eyes, as if he were
the wisest man in the whole world.

He liked the way she had laughed in the face of the
entire ton tonight. And he liked the way she had *not*
laughed at him, when he had told her about the curse or
when he had appeared at the ball looking like a circus
reject. He even liked the way she seemed to be constantly
stepping on his feet.

To be perfectly honest, he liked—he forbid himself to
feel anything stronger—*her*. Yet he, who had never had
either the time or the inclination even to think of indulging
in such an illogical emotion as love, feared that after only
a few days' acquaintance he was dangerously close to
falling head over heels in love with Phoebe Lawton. And
he positively could not let that happen.

He laughed bitterly, realizing that it would not matter
even if he did succumb to the lady's charms. T'would do
him no good. Miss Lawton would never see him as anything but a ridiculous, comical, vulgar buffoon after tonight. God, he'd thought he'd embarrassed himself before
the members of the museum board. That was nothing compared to tonight's escapade.

What the devil did he think he was doing, flinging Miss
Lawton about the dance floor as if she were a marionette?
Oh, she had seemed to enjoy herself then, but by now,
having had time to consider the matter, undoubtedly she
thought him a complete and utter fool.

And then, to top matters off, he had almost kissed her
while he'd looked like one of the clowns from Astley's
amphitheater. Why, if he had succeeded she'd probably

have screamed for help and had him dragged off to gaol. For what was he but the crippled bookworm he had jokingly called himself earlier? Or a trumped-up commoner with a baronetcy he'd received from the regent like a dog rewarded with a bone for retrieving its master's socks? What did he have to offer any woman?

What indeed.

When he reached the front gates of his home, he leaned on the fencepost for a moment. He felt completely spent. Exhausted. Logical to a fault, he was aware that he was indulging in a fit of megrims which would undoubtedly pass, but at the moment he felt as if his entire world had come to an end.

Tipping his head back, he let the rain wash over his face, hoping it would wash away some of his sorrow. It did not help. Rain could not erase the image of Miss Phoebe Lawton's face, which was branded upon the backs of his eyelids so that every time he blinked he saw her lovely blue eyes and her silken hair the color of autumn sunshine.

There was only one thing he could do. He would have to avoid her completely from now on. He had no right even to think of her. Not when he had touched the Eye of Horus and would very soon join its thirteen other victims six feet underground.

He could allow himself to think of nothing but obtaining and destroying the amulet before it killed anyone else. Ruthlessly squelching the pain in his heart, he squared his shoulders and jerked his saturated wig off his head. He pushed his spectacles up firmly onto his nose, and, leaning heavily on his cane, limped up his walkway.

The following morning Phoebe rushed into Matty's room before the older woman had even risen from her bed, and shook her vigorously.

"Heaven have mercy!" Matty cried, clutching the bedclothes to her throat, her eyes wild with fright. "Has Napoleon landed? Is the French army upon us?"

"Matty, wake up," Phoebe said urgently. "We have to hurry."

As Matty's confused gaze cleared, she gawked at Phoebe, clearly astonished. "Phoebe! Are you trying to give me a fit of the heart? I was having a dreadful dream that we had been invaded by the damned Corsican—may God not rest his cursed soul."

"Then you should be grateful I woke you." Phoebe grabbed the comforter and tugged it back. "Please get up. We must hurry if we are to make it on time."

"Make what on time? I was not aware we had an appointment, especially at such an early hour. No one in her right mind gets out of bed with the chickens. Besides, I have not even had breakfast." She brightened visibly at the thought of food. "Perhaps you can ring for something, and then you may explain about our appointment as we break our fasts."

Phoebe fought for self-control, though her heart pounded fearfully at the thought of Sir Malcolm's arriving at the museum and succeeding in obtaining the Eye of Horus even before she managed to convince her cousin to rise from bed. She wished fiercely that she had been able to leave Matty in dreamland and go to the museum alone.

"We do not have an appointment, and we do not have time to eat," she said fretfully.

"Not eat? Of course we must have a little nip before venturing out into the world. A bit of bacon, some eggs, a few kippers with biscuits, sausages, and perhaps three or four of those milk-toasts Cook makes so well, and I promise that I will be more than happy to accompany you wherever you wish to go." Then Matty peered closely at Phoebe. "And you must have Tribble redress your hair. It looks dreadful."

Unbidden, Phoebe's hand rose to touch her loose chignon. When she lowered her fingers, hairpins scattered over the counterpane. "Oh, Tribble did not do my hair. I put it up myself. I did not wish to wait for Tribble to answer my bell. She is so very slow. Although she does a splendid job in both hairdressing and choosing clothing ensembles, she takes simply forever, and time is a commodity we simply do not have this morning. So please, hurry.''

"Hmph. It is not proper for you to coif your own hair, Phoebe. Also, I would be remiss if I did not inform you that your pink gown does not match that mustard-yellow mantle.''

Phoebe glanced down, unconcerned. "Does it not? I was in such a hurry I fear I did not notice. But that is neither here nor there. Truly, Matty, we must rush. We must be at the museum as soon as it opens. And that means that my hair stays messy and your stomach must remain empty for a bit longer.''

Matty balked, glaring. "Do you mean you almost gave me my death of fright merely to drag me off to that horrid museum again?'' She crossed her arms over the board-flat plane of her chest. Her thin lips tightened. "I will not go.''

"Please, Matty!'' Phoebe implored. "I would have gone without you, but it seemed important to have you along.''

Having given much thought to her previous failure to purchase the Eye of Horus, Phoebe had concluded that the curator must have given her one look, noticed the absence of a companion, and dismissed her as lacking sufficient countenance or funds to purchase a valuable artifact. If, therefore, she took Matty along and behaved with all propriety, there was a chance the curator might be convinced she was sincerely interested in purchasing the amulet and deliver it into her hands before Sir Malcolm succeeded in obtaining it himself and, subsequently, destroying it.

She added hopefully, "I realized you would be hungry, which is why I put some apples, bread, and cheese in my reticule for you to nibble on as we drive.''

"Good Lord, apples and cheese on an empty stomach? The combination would give me weeks of indigestion.''

Phoebe gazed at her pleadingly.

Finally Matty relented. "Oh very well,'' she huffed. "I will go, but first I *am* going to have my breakfast. And as for your going anywhere by yourself, I should hope and pray you have better sense than to do something so addlepated. Even your reputation, eccentric though it is and, as such, oddly smiled upon by the ton, would not survive unchaperoned capers.''

Though Phoebe sighed, she did not argue. It was obvious that Matty had given in as much as she was going to. Phoebe would simply have to hurry Matty along, somehow. Striding to the servants' bell, Phoebe gave it a hearty tug. When a maid appeared, she ordered a light breakfast of fruit and toast (earning another of Matty's fiery glares) and then moved to the older woman's armoire, from which she pulled a plain gray cambric walking dress. By the time her cousin's abigail entered the room, Phoebe had an entire ensemble laid out.

Thirty minutes later the Lawton carriage sped toward the London Metropolitan Museum. The carriage tipped and swayed, jouncing and bouncing through potholes large enough to swallow small cows. Once, they hit one of the gargantuan caverns with enough force that both women were hurled into the air.

''Dear God!'' Matty cried as she thumped back on the seat. Her face was as white as flour. ''We are going to be killed. I just know it. We are going to die.'' Putting her hands together, she bellowed a prayer.

Ignoring the apocalyptic declaration as well as the ear-splitting cries for heavenly intervention, Phoebe chewed her lip, worried that they would not arrive at the museum in time. It had already been open for fifteen minutes, plenty of time for Sir Malcolm to have succeeded in his dastardly errand.

She clung to a hanging carriage loop and tried not to dwell on what Sir Malcolm would think if he arrived during her attempt to buy the amulet out from under him. She could not avoid the niggling worry that he would very probably consider her act blatant disregard for his tale of the Eye's curse. She felt profoundly sick at the thought of earning his distrust and ill regard.

Nonetheless, although she knew she risked the baronet's ire, she *had* to attempt to save the Eye of Horus from his unreasonable plan of destruction, else she would be foregoing every drop of archaeological blood in her veins. She could not live with herself if she did not at least try to stop him from committing such an atrocious act.

Thrusting her head out the carriage window, she cried, "Faster, John! Faster!"

The driver, who sounded as if he were having the time of his life, shouted a command that made the swiftly galloping horses throw themselves even more heartily into the task. The carriage hurtled along the pavement toward its destination, one passenger hanging on and praying for dear life—or if that was lost, eternal salvation—and the other loudly urging more haste. Then, without warning, the vehicle slid to a stop, bumping hard against the stone curb. They had arrived.

Matty slumped against the wall. "Praise be," she managed brokenly.

Without waiting for the postillion's assistance, Phoebe wrenched the carriage door open and leaped down to the road without bothering to lower the steps. Her head wagged from side to side as she searched the street for a carriage that might belong to Sir Malcolm. No other vehicles were in view.

Though she remembered the baronet's indicating that his townhouse was not far from the museum, and thus he might have walked from thence and might already have destroyed the Eye, a glimmer of hope flickered in Phoebe's breast. She had a fleeting glimpse of Matty's pasty complexion as the postillion lowered the carriage steps and the older woman lurched unsteadily out of the vehicle.

Phoebe did not wait for her cousin to recover. Instead she ran as fast as her legs would carry her up the museum's marble steps. The guard standing at the museum entrance turned in surprise at her precipitous arrival, but managed to wrench open the door just before she ran headlong into solid mahogany.

"Thank you," she called, scurrying through the foyer, faintly aware that several other museum patrons were staring after her with open stupefaction.

As she reached the foot of the staircase leading to the curator's office she passed a tall, handsome young man with hair so blond it was nearly white. He appeared to be headed for the exit. Phoebe recognized him, from her earlier attempt to purchase the Eye of Horus, as one of the museum board members.

In the center of the stairs, a second board member, older and distinguished and whose ears stood out from his head like teacup saucers, flashed by.

At the head of the stairs, a third member of the museum board, dark and with a menacing aspect possibly due to his thick, bushy black eyebrows, moved down the stairs as Phoebe rushed up them.

Without giving any of the men a backward glance Phoebe sprinted down the corridor toward the curator's office. There, skirts flying, she slid to a stop. She was glad she'd worn walking boots with a rough sole, else she'd probably have slid right on past the door and hurtled through the large plate glass window at the end of the hall.

Mr. Grundle's office door was closed. Phoebe rapped sharply on its frosted glass panel three times in quick succession. There was no reply.

"Mr. Grundle?" she called softly. "Are you in?"

Her inquiry was answered by total silence. She glanced at the door handle, but managed to resist turning it and entering without being invited.

"Sir!" Phoebe knocked again, harder. "Are you present? I must talk with you."

When there was still no reply, she bit her lip, tamped down her scruples, reached for the door handle, and turned it firmly. She heard Matty, breathing hard as if she had also run up the stairs, behind her.

"Phoebe?" *Gasp.* "You cannot go in there"—*pant*— "without the curators"—*puff*—"permission! You could be arrested!" *Wheeze*. "Think of the scandal!"

Phoebe pushed the office door open, but did not reply. She could not. Words could not get past her throat, which had abruptly closed off so that she could barely breathe, much less utter words to describe her horror.

In the back of her mind she realized then that she did not have to speak of what she saw, for Matty, despite her remonstrations, had peered into the room over Phoebe's shoulder and promptly crashed to the floor in a dead faint.

10

In the next few seconds the scene in the museum curator's office seemed to shimmer with crystal clarity. Phoebe saw the long, gleaming oak desk and smelled lemon and beeswax polish. She saw several old paintings along the walls. She saw a vibrantly colored Oriental rug. She saw a large safe on one wall, its door hanging slightly ajar.

And, sprawled beneath an open window, she saw Jacob Grundle, the museum curator, crumpled in a motionless—and very dead—heap.

Sir Malcolm appeared quite suddenly, as if he had arrived just minutes after Phoebe and Matty. He wore another of his outmoded coats, this time in pine-green wool, as well as a pair of worn, unpolished Hessians. However, a new hat of softest beaver sat atop his sandy-brown hair, and his hands were encased in an obviously new pair of leather gloves.

Standing behind Phoebe, he bent to ascertain Matty's well-being, then rose and moved past Phoebe into Mr. Grundle's office. A startled oath burst from his lips when he saw the curator's corpse. Leaning his cobra-handled cane beside the door, he hurried to kneel at the dead man's side. He removed and stuffed his gloves in his pocket, felt for Mr. Grundle's pulse, shook his head, and then looked up.

"You know what this means, do you not?" he asked Phoebe. "The Eye of Horus has been at its deadly work once again. Poor Grundle. Of course, it was just a matter of time."

Matty stirred and sat up. "What happened?"

Phoebe turned to her cousin and, helping her to her feet, straightened Matty's gray bonnet. Then she ushered the older woman to a low bench about twenty feet down the hall. "You fainted after seeing Mr. Grundle's body."

"Oh, sweet Lord!" Matty moaned and clasped Phoebe's gloved fingers in hers. "That poor man. He is dead, then?"

"Yes. Sir Malcolm Forbes is here, with the body. He came up the stairs just after us."

"But how did the curator die?"

"I do not know, but it looked to me as if he had suffered a heart attack or a stroke."

Releasing Phoebe's hands, Matty slumped on the bench as if exhausted by the ordeal. "I am glad Sir Malcolm is here. He will know how to deal with this calamity."

For once in her life Phoebe, too, was relieved to have a man present to deal with the situation. Though she knew she could have handled things had she been forced, it was still a comfort, for a change, to let Sir Malcolm's competent shoulders carry the weight of responsibility. And, oddly, she felt not even a little put out by the way he had taken control of the matter and relegated her and Matty to the background.

"Yes," she agreed readily. "I am also." She turned to go back into the office to offer the baronet her assistance.

"Phoebe!" Matty cried after her. "Surely you do not intend to go in the room with the body!"

"I will be fine."

Ducking her head to avoid her cousin's horrified gaze, Phoebe moved swiftly back down the hall and entered the office just as Sir Malcolm strode to the open safe. He stood there for several moments, rifling through the vault's contents. Then he walked quickly back toward the body. He bent down and flipped the curator's obese corpse over, so that Mr. Grundle lay faceup, staring blindly at the ceiling like a bloated, beached fish.

Looking into the curator's sightless eyes, Phoebe suddenly felt nauseated. She shuddered as Sir Malcolm's hands searched through Mr. Grundle's pockets. "Should we not alert the authorities?" she asked shakily.

He gave a terse nod. "In a moment. I'm looking for the Eye of Horus. You remember, on the night we were in the sarcophagus, that Mr. Grundle mentioned he'd put it in his safe?"

"Yes." Phoebe's heart lurched as she understood his implication. "It is not there? Nor on his person?"

"No. I wondered if he'd been holding it when he died, or if he might not have put it in his pocket. But he doesn't seem to have it on him, and it is nowhere nearby on the floor." A sigh dredged its way out of his chest. "It appears to be missing."

"How can a rare, priceless artifact just 'be missing'? It couldn't have walked away on its own. Someone must have taken it. Before"—Phoebe paled—"or after Mr. Grundle's unfortunate demise."

"Perhaps, but no one else was here when we arrived."

Phoebe spun around to face him. "But there *was* someone else going down the stairs when I came up them. Some*ones,* actually. Three of the museum board members. I remembered their faces from my own unsuccessful attempt to purchase the amulet."

Sir Malcolm's expression sharpened. "Do you know their identities?"

"No."

"Describe them."

Phoebe closed her eyes and concentrated. "One was quite young, and had hair so blond it was almost white; one was fortyish, balding, and had very prominent ears; and the last was about the same age as the second man, but was dark and had thick black eyebrows."

"Ah," the baronet murmured, still kneeling beside the

body. "Most interesting. Mr. Montgomery Milhouse, the earl of Bumstead, and Lord Deauville, I assume. As fate would have it, it just so happens that Mr. Grundle informed me that each of those three men had previously attempted to purchase the amulet for very large sums of money. Interesting, indeed."

"You think one of them stole the Eye?" Phoebe asked breathlessly. "And possibly murdered Mr. Grundle?"

"One of them may have taken the amulet, but I do not think anyone murdered the curator." Sir Malcolm adjusted his spectacles. His hazel eyes scanned the room again. "It doesn't look like foul play was involved. Grundle appears to have suffered a heart attack or stroke, undoubtedly as a result of the curse.

"However, the lack of foul play does not rule out the possibility that one of the three men could have come in here, seen Grundle's body, and seized the opportunity to take the amulet." Sir Malcolm's expression turned even more grim. "If that is so, more deaths will follow the curator's because of the curse. Besides mine and the young guard's who picked up the Eye the night of our attempted burglaries, that is."

Phoebe didn't know how to respond. What could she say that would not expose her total incredulity toward Sir Malcolm's conviction? Though she wondered how anyone could believe in such a ridiculous thing as a curse, she still had no wish to offend him.

Sir Malcolm stood. "I must send one of the museum guards for the Chief Inspector. You and Miss . . . What was your companion's name again?"

"Stoat."

"You and Miss Stoat had better stay here. The inspector will undoubtedly wish to speak to you."

Phoebe's eyes flew open wide. "Good gracious! Surely he will not think we had anything to do with the curator's death!"

"Assuredly not. But he will want to know if you saw anything suspicious, or if you touched anything."

"Oh, we didn't," she assured him. "But *you* touched

something. You searched the room for the missing amulet, and then you turned Mr. Grundle over.''

He looked pensive. "So I did. But I hope you will leave that bit of information out of your statement."

"Why?"

"It would be most unfortunate if the *Times* got wind that a rare and valuable artifact had been stolen from the museum. Everyone would be on the lookout for it, and if innocent people happened upon the amulet they might be stricken with the curse. I do not think that is likely since, if one of those three board members you mentioned did steal the amulet, he will quickly hide it away. But it is still best not to risk more lives.

"Also, given the excitement of Mr. Grundle's death and his body's subsequent discovery, the Eye's disappearance will probably not be noted for several days. That will give me more time to search for it and hopefully destroy it before it can do any more harm."

Phoebe thought for a moment. He had a point. Though she was not worried about innocent people suffering from the mythical curse, she still did not want anyone to get to the amulet before *she* did. Sir Malcolm was only one man, and surely stood no better chance of finding the Eye before Phoebe herself. Nevertheless, the fewer people searching, the better.

"I will not tell anyone that you touched anything," she promised.

Sir Malcolm's expression seemed to soften. "Thank you, Miss Lawton." He stood and went to find a museum guard. As the guard, after surveying the scene, turned to go down the stairs to alert his superiors, the baronet asked quickly, "Excuse me, but do you happen to know where Officer O'Hara is today?"

The young man nodded. "Aye. He stayed home. Sick as a dog. Poor bloke hasn't been able to get out of bed for days. The illness just came upon him, sudden-like." Then the guard turned and hurried down the stairs.

Phoebe, meeting Sir Malcolm's grave gaze, felt an icy chill ripple down her spine. She did not need to ask what the baronet was thinking—and found herself wondering for the first time if he might not be right. She was relieved when more policemen hurried into the hall and things became too frantic for her to dwell on the possible cause of O'Hara's illness.

She and Matty spent the remainder of the day repeating, endlessly, the story of how they had happened upon Mr. Grundle's body. By evening the cause of death had, as Phoebe had expected all along, been ruled due to "natural causes."

As the officers carried the body away, Sir Malcolm looked at Phoebe and muttered, "They do not know how wrong they are about what killed Mr. Grundle. And now poor O'Hara is ill." He cursed viciously. "I *must* find the amulet. How much more evidence is needed? When will the fools realize that touching the Eye is more deadly than drinking a tankard of arsenic-laced wine?"

"So you still mean to destroy the amulet?" Phoebe asked softly, already knowing the answer to her question.

The baronet looked surprised. "Of course." He withdrew his gloves from his pocket and pulled them on. Then he reached out absently as if to secure Phoebe's chignon, which she vaguely realized had slid out from beneath the back brim of her chip-straw bonnet and was once again close to cascading about her shoulders.

Suddenly, without touching her hair, Sir Malcolm flushed deep red and jerked his hand away. He cleared his throat and backed up a few steps. "What other choice do I have?" he asked gruffly, not explaining his hasty withdrawal. "I am the one who brought the execrable thing into the country. I have an obligation to see that it does no more harm."

Phoebe did not offer a solution. She could say nothing comforting since, despite feeling a certain amount of discomfort and uncertainty about Officer O'Hara's indisposition, she still felt every bit as obliged to stop Sir Malcolm from bringing his dastardly plan to fruition. If only there were some way she could find out where he meant to search first, and thus search the place before he did.

As she was thinking, an odd expression spread over Sir Malcolm's face. "Miss Lawton, it just now occurs to me to wonder what brings you to Mr. Grundle's office this morning."

Phoebe's mouth opened and closed. Finally she shrugged. "I intended to try to purchase the amulet once more, myself."

Sir Malcolm's eyes darkened behind his spectacles. "In God's name, why?"

Viewing his rapidly deteriorating temper, Phoebe rushed on. "I know you believe the Eye is cursed, but I thought maybe I could buy it and have Mr. Grundle deliver it to my collection room. I thought he could place it in a specially made viewing box, and I'd never have had to touch it. I am sorry, Sir Malcolm," she finished sorrowfully. "I know you must feel betrayed. Please try to understand that I only wanted to preserve an historical artifact."

The baronet seemed to weigh her words. At last he nodded. "I do not blame you, Miss Lawton. In your position, I'd have done the same thing. But you must promise me you will not do such a foolish thing again."

"I do," she answered fervently.

And she would keep her promise, she added silently. She would not try to buy the amulet again. She would try to retrieve it from the thief. Then she would, without physically touching it, take it to her collection room. Once there, in the wildly improbable chance that Sir Malcolm was correct about the curse's validity, she would position it in the viewing box with a stick.

"I am relieved to hear it. Well, I must be going." Sir Malcolm retrieved his walking stick from where it leaned against the wall in Mr. Grundle's office, and then raised his new hat. "Good day, Miss Lawton." He turned toward Matty, still seated twenty feet away. "Miss Stoat."

Phoebe gazed after him until, leaning on his ebony walking stick, he disappeared down the staircase.

That night, after Tribble had brushed out Phoebe's long golden hair, woven it into a thick braid, and helped her into a sapphire-blue silk bedgown edged with black Spanish lace, Phoebe began pacing the bedchamber.

She stared, unseeing, at her bare toes as they flashed from beneath the hem of her nightrail. Who had stolen the Eye of Horus? And why? How could she get it back?

More importantly, how could she obtain it before Sir Malcolm found and destroyed it?

After what seemed only a few seconds the porcelain clock atop the fireplace mantel chimed three times. Realizing she'd been circling her room for hours, Phoebe ran a hand over her tired eyes. Somewhere there was an answer to this dilemma, and she would keep walking until she reached it, even if it took all night.

Feeling peckish, but not wanting to disturb the household, she consumed the cheese, bread and apples she had placed in her reticule earlier that morning but had forgotten to remove and send back to the kitchens. Then she resumed her pacing.

By morning she knew precisely what she had to do.

Since he was, by nature, an early riser, Malcolm was awake, dressed, and seated at the polished maple dining table in his breakfast room by eight o'clock the next morning.

He was preparing to taste a delectable concoction of crushed grains grown in his own fields in Sussex, diced pineapple from his orangery in Yorkshire, milk from his herd of velvet-eyed Jersey cows, and one raw egg. He had just spooned up a large portion of the mixture and was directing it toward his parted lips when he looked out of the picture window leading toward the street. Seconds later he uttered a startled oath, dropped his spoon, and leapt to his feet.

Removing his spectacles, he cleaned them swiftly with a handkerchief and plunked them back down on his nose. He gaped out the window toward the road, where a rickety cab had drawn to a halt and a woman—whose broad-brimmed, violet-laden straw bonnet was askew and whose coiffure looked heartbreakingly near to cascading down her back in a glorious honey-gold waterfall—climbed out of the dilapidated vehicle, handed its driver a coin, and turned purposefully toward 102 Prichard Place.

Malcolm felt his heart leap in his chest like a wild hare trapped in a wire cage. Good God. This could not be happening.

Surely the woman had more sense than to appear on a bachelor's doorstep early enough in the morning to raise even the most open-minded person's eyebrows. And—here he searched the area behind Phoebe futilely, then cursed with the graphic competence of a sailor—without a companion! Though delighted to see her, he felt as irritated by her unwise actions as if he sat naked on a horsehair sofa.

Damn the woman! She seemed to make a habit of leaping into scandalous situations with a single-minded lack of forethought. Of course, he thought savagely, the cause of Phoebe's hoydenish behavior was obvious. Without male supervision she had plainly run wild.

Truly, someone ought to take the chit in hand before she ruined herself utterly. Being considered eccentric only carried one so far. Judging by her behavior, it was astonishing that her reputation had not self-destructed eons ago.

Malcolm sprinted for the door in an attempt to reach it before Phoebe rang the bell and alerted his starchy butler, Fobbs, who had been with the Forbes family for nigh on fifty years.

A frightful stickler for propriety, Fobbs looked like nothing quite so much as a beanpole that had sprouted the head of a bulldog. He terrified Malcolm's friends and acquaintances. He even, truth be known, rather terrified Malcolm. (It was dashed difficult ruling over someone who had known one when one had been in short pants, and had even paddled one's backside when one had carved one's initials into the staircase banister at one's ancestral estate.)

Through the long window in the foyer Malcolm saw a slender, lavender-clad female arm and a hand encased in purple kidskin reach up and rap the gold pharaoh's-head knocker sharply against its metal rest. He came to a skidding halt just in time to see Fobbs step out of the shadows and open the door.

For an eternity the butler said nothing. He glared down at the visitor forbiddingly. To Malcolm's eye Fobbs looked like a misshapen giant beside Phoebe's petite, curvaceous femininity.

Phoebe's face mirrored her amazement but, surprisingly, no trepidation, at Fobbs's hideous countenance. She held out a card with one corner bent over, indicating her presence in the townhouse. "Please inform Sir Malcolm that Miss Phoebe Lawton is here."

"His lordship is not at home," the butler rumbled balefully. "Perhaps you might try later. But I do not know that he will be at home then, either. If I am the one unfortunate enough to open the door to you, missy, the baronet will *never* be at home. Sir Malcolm does not cavort with lightskirts, which is what you must be since no decent woman would dare pop up on a gentleman's doorstep practically in the middle of the night."

Phoebe raised one golden brow. "Sir," she said haughtily, "do you perchance have difficulty seeing? You'd best have your vision examined. It is well after eight o'clock, and the sun is shining. Now, fetch Sir Malcolm. At once."

The butler's face turned a vibrant vermilion. He opened his mouth to deliver what would undoubtedly be a scathing set-down.

"Fobbs!" Malcolm said sharply. "That will be quite enough! How dare you speak to one of my guests like that?"

Fobbs turned to gape at the baronet. He blinked, clearly taken aback at being spoken to in such a manner. His mouth hung open and his eyelids fluttered rapidly. Then, turning back to Phoebe, he said quietly, "My apologies, madam. It appears I have committed a grave error. I pray your forgiveness."

The tiny silk violets on Phoebe's straw bonnet swayed as if blown by a gentle breeze as she inclined her head graciously. "Given."

"I will see Miss Lawton in the library, Fobbs," Malcolm said. "Be so good as to bring us some tea."

The butler's heavily lidded eyes widened a fraction. "The library, sir?" he asked, a note of bewilderment in his gravelly voice.

"That is what I said, Fobbs."

Though he looked as if he had swallowed a toad, the butler nodded stiffly and moved away.

Malcolm turned back to Phoebe and waved a hand in the direction he wished her to proceed. "If you will be so good as to come with me, Miss Lawton."

11

As they walked toward the back of the house, Malcolm fought to retrieve his sense of equanimity and tried to think of something to say that would not betray his shock at finding Phoebe on his doorstep at 8 a.m. But he had no idea what one said in such a situation. Not only was he unused to the privacy of his townhouse being violated, but Phoebe's unexpected appearance had filled him with an astonishment so great he seemed to have swallowed his tongue.

The hallway was very narrow and, despite his frustration with Phoebe, Malcolm was deliciously aware of her warmth each time she bumped into him as they moved through the corridor. She felt soft and warm, when her arm touched his, and smelled as heavenly as a meadow full of summer flowers.

It occurred to him that everything about Phoebe reminded him of summer—late summer or early autumn, to be precise.

Her huge eyes of forget-me-not blue. Her curly golden hair that always looked a mere breath away from tumbling down her back in wild abandon. Her delectable perfume, with its spicy topnotes smelling of late-summer leaves just before they turned color, and its bottom notes exquisitely resembling the scent of rain following a thunderstorm.

She reminded him of sunshine. Of lush green grass. Of bumblebees thrumming along atop a gentle breeze as they searched for pollen to make enough honey to see them through the winter and into another spring. Having Phoebe live with one would be enough to get any man through a hundred winters, back to back.

But it was not just Phoebe's appearance or scent that reminded Malcolm of warm late-summer afternoons. There was a freshness about her. Its origin was a mystery. It was just a part of *her*.

They paused at the library door. Still without speaking, Malcolm turned its brass handle and stepped aside to allow her to precede him.

As he ushered her into the library, he again noticed that her chignon, visible beneath the rim of her bonnet, was precariously loose and lay low against the back of her neck. He raised a hand to press home a nearly liberated hairpin, then jerked his fingers away, as certain as he'd been the previous day outside the curator's office that if he touched Phoebe's silken curls he would grab her, pull her into his arms, and kiss her until she was breathless.

He swallowed past an extreme tightness in his throat. "Sweet heaven," he muttered, "help me."

Turning, Phoebe peeped up at him from beneath the broad brim of her straw bonnet. Her luscious blue eyes were wide, her pupils dilated. Probably, Malcolm realized, from finding herself alone with him in an undeniably compromising position. They also reflected a good deal of what could only be excitement.

Her reckless nature, he thought savagely, *would* find this outrageous situation thrilling.

"Did you say something?" she asked breathlessly. Her lips looked full and moist—delightfully kissable.

Malcolm was nearly overcome with the desire to do just that. He managed to say sternly, "Nothing important."

The loose hairpin fell silently to the carpet as she swished past him into the library with a whisper of full silk skirts and a cloud of that marvelously scented perfume. Malcolm's gaze dropped and was trapped by the small golden pin as it glittered up at him from the floor. He stared at it dumbly.

At length, realizing he was making a cake of himself, he managed to drag his gaze back to his companion. Phoebe had made her way to an emerald-green velvet armchair. There, she gracefully sat down amid pillows Malcolm's late mother had embroidered, long ago, with fox-hunting scenes.

Settling her skirts about the legs of her chair, Phoebe brushed her purple kid gloves over her lap, smoothing invisible creases. Her lavender gown was made of a fabric so delicate and transparent that Malcolm thought he could almost see her frilly underthings (God help him!) through its shimmering surface.

Soft leather slippers of a slightly darker purple than her gloves peeped side by side from beneath her lacy hem. Her feet looked small and dainty and infinitely appealing. Malcolm swallowed again. Strange, that, he thought dizzily. How could *feet* be appealing?

His head seemed thick; his brain, fogged. His ears buzzed. He told himself firmly that he should grab Phoebe's arm, march her right back to the front door, and send her straight home. He should escort her, bodily if necessary, out to another cab or to his own unmarked carriage and see her safely on her way back to wherever she had come from—which almost seemed, from the way she constantly tempted him to do things totally at odds with his prudent personality, from the Serpent himself.

Malcolm knew that Phoebe's coming to his townhouse was utterly improper. He had no doubt that, had he been any other man, it would have been tremendously unwise. And he knew he should be mortified by her forwardness, no matter what reason she had for her action.

But he merely stood there, gazing at her as if she were the most beautiful thing he'd ever seen in his life. Which she was.

He was aware of an odd tugging sensation in his chest, a feeling somewhere between pleasure and pain. All he seemed capable of comprehending was how splendid, how supremely magnificent she felt here, in his library, his private sanctuary, where he never allowed another soul— not Fobbs, not maids, not even his mother, who had once visited from Upper Cumberland before her passing (that was when she'd brought him the embroidered pillows.) Though the servants had never questioned his authority, he recalled, his mother had been quite put out at being refused admittance.

The library was the one place Malcolm had always kept completely to himself. A man needed a space all his own, and the library was his. He did all his serious thinking here, and he liked to be alone when he did it. The library was the place he always came to sort things out—such as why Phoebe Lawton disturbed him so deeply that he never quite seemed to lose consciousness of her.

He had spent a good deal of time here lately, trying to comprehend that sticky matter. He had not yet succeeded. And, he realized then, the library was not the only place he thought about Phoebe. She was always there, always at the forefront of his mind, whether he was studying some ancient tome, taking tea and biscuits, or working in his perennial flower garden.

He'd had to abandon the flower patch. One afternoon, when Fobbs had gone out to inquire if Malcolm wished to take tea in the garden, the baronet had realized he'd spent nearly four hours staring mindlessly at the clump of forget-me-nots he'd planted just after his failed attempt to purchase the Eye of Horus, but seeing only a pair of very fine eyes in precisely the same entrancing shade of blue as the tiny flowers.

Now, more than ever, it was his favorite color.

Abruptly he noticed that Phoebe was staring at him as if she were certain he'd lost his senses. He flushed as he realized he'd been goggling at her as if she were the last woman on earth, and he the last man.

In order to forget his aching longings, he narrowed his eyes and asked gruffly, "What are you doing here, Miss Lawton? You should know better. Your actions are rash and extremely unwise."

Phoebe dropped her gaze and looked down at her gloved hands, now clasped neatly in her lap. "I . . . I know. But I had to come. I had to offer my services. There must be something I can do."

Something she could do? Good God, there certainly was. Lurid images wrapped themselves lewdly around Malcolm's brain, but he cleared his throat and concentrated on the words that followed this unwittingly inviting statement.

"I feel responsible, somehow," she continued, raising her hands only to drop them again, helplessly. "As if I should have been able to keep Mr. Grundle from dying. I cannot seem to get that poor man out of my mind. I feel somehow responsible for his death."

"You had nothing to do with it. It was the amulet. The curse."

Phoebe nodded. She tilted her head to one side. Visible at the edges of her bonnet, her hair gleamed in the sunlight shining through the leaded panes in the library window. "That is what you told me before. Nevertheless, I feel so awful about it. And I keep thinking about that poor young guard, Officer O'Hara. Do you truly believe he will die, as well?"

"I wish I could believe otherwise. But if the past is any indication of the future, I fear so. Now, with his illness . . ."

"What of you, Sir Malcolm? Is there no way to save you?" An emotion that looked remarkably like sorrow flickered in the depths of her eyes.

Malcolm studied her face. His heart leapt wildly. Was it possible? Could Phoebe be feeling something more than friendship for him? Or did she merely see his interest in her—which she had to have noticed unless she was blind—and feel sorry for him?

Dear God, what a tangle.

Were the Fates so twisted that they offered him love only to snatch it out of his grasp forever? Had the Dames of Fortune been leading both he and Phoebe toward this moment all their lives, out of some twisted sense of humor? Or was he merely being fanciful—something he knew he had never been a day in his life before meeting Phoebe?

He could deny it no longer. He *was* in love with her. So madly in love with her that he feared he would explode with happiness if she merely smiled at him again.

Even yesterday, while in the midst of the police investigation, he had been more aware of Phoebe than of the corpse in the museum office. Of her softness. Her scent. The way it felt to watch her mouth as she answered the chief inspector's questions. The way her soul seemed to reach out through time and space and touch his with compelling sweetness.

Before meeting her, his every waking thought had been about when, where, and how the curse would strike him down. Now that thought hardly ever crossed his mind. When it did, it incited not fear, but only a deep regret at never again being able to gaze into Phoebe's vivid blue eyes.

Why had he finally found the woman of his dreams only to lose her forever? It was so damned unfair!

He clenched his hands into fists to keep from going to her and taking her in his arms and telling her everything in his heart. Although he knew she might very well laugh in his face, since he was nothing but a crippled bookworm and she was a veritable goddess, he longed to speak of his feelings. Yet even if the gods smiled upon him and she returned his love, he knew he could still say nothing. Not when, without a shadow of a doubt, he was doomed. It would be the height of dishonor.

Better that only one heart should break—his.

He rounded his desk, deliberately putting its wide expanse between them. At that moment a quiet knock sounded on the library door. "Come," Malcolm called.

Fobbs entered the room, looking neither right nor left as if out of respect for his master's haven. He set the silver tea tray on the desk. Then he raised his gaze inquiringly.

"Thank you, Fobbs. Please have my unmarked carriage brought 'round."

The butler bowed stiffly and left the room.

"Would you pour, Miss Lawton?"

Phoebe completed the task with such grace it seemed as if she'd been pouring Malcolm's tea all her life. They each drank a cup of tea and ate a scone. When they finished, Malcolm set his delicate Limoges cup down in its saucer. Phoebe did likewise.

Opening his hands, Malcolm tapped his fingers lightly on the desktop. "You spoke of 'offering your services.' Would you care to be more precise? Please hasten. We must get you home as quickly as possible so that no one sees you leave here." He wished more than anything that he did not have to be sharp with her, but, since she seemed totally unconcerned about her welfare and reputation, he felt honor-bound to be concerned on her behalf.

Phoebe straightened. Her gaze hardened at his curtness. "As you wish. I came here to offer my services in retrieving the Eye of Horus."

"Your services?" Malcolm frowned. "Miss Lawton, the very idea of you attempting to nab a thief is—"

She interrupted. "You cannot refuse my aid, Sir Malcolm. More people will die if they touch the amulet."

He nodded tersely. "True, but—"

"We cannot risk more deaths."

"I have no intention of risking them. I have every intention of obtaining and destroying the amulet before anyone else touches it."

She seemed to wince. "Yes, I realize that." She fiddled with the lacy grape-colored reticule she held in her lap. "Have you decided where to begin searching?"

"I have. One of the three gentlemen you mentioned seeing on the museum stairs yesterday, Lord Deauville, is giving a bachelor fete for his younger brother this evening. I thought I would begin my search by examining his townhouse. Inquiries have led me to believe that he has not left town since Mr. Grundle's death, which means if he has the amulet it is most likely somewhere in his London home."

"Oh," she said interestedly. "Do you think so?"

"Yes. And, thanks to your kindness at having Lord Peter explain my outrageous garb the other evening, I have been accepted by the ton and therefore received an invitation to Lord Deauville's bachelor fete only this morning."

Phoebe beamed. "Wonderful! I shall go with you."

A wry smile quirked Malcolm's lips. "Women are not invited to bachelor parties, Miss Lawton. At least, not gentlewomen."

Phoebe shifted restively. "Sir Malcolm, you cannot deny that the quest would be easier with two searchers instead of only one."

His smile vanished. "Perhaps that is so, but what kind of villain would I be to risk a woman's life?"

"The risk is my own to take," she retorted heatedly. "While I appreciate your concern, sir, it is out of place. You are not a member of my family. My actions are completely under my own jurisdiction, and I would thank you to remember that." Closing her eyes, she waged an obvious battle with her rampant emotions. Then she took a deep breath, and her voice softened. "Please, Sir Malcolm. Let me aid in the search. You would be a fool to refuse my help."

"I would be more foolish to accept it. It is out of the question."

"But why?" Phoebe argued, again looking perilously close to losing her temper. Her eyes flashed blue fire, and her cheeks flushed beautifully. "You are being unreasonable. I do not have to touch the amulet, you know, and you told me that only those who touch it die."

"That is so. But *you* are not going to be given the opportunity to forget your good intentions, dear lady. Given your impulsive nature, that would be a definite possibility if the amulet were within your reach."

"But I wouldn't—"

He held up a hand. "Accidents happen. And you must also remember that whomever stole the amulet poses a potentially lethal danger."

Phoebe turned away, her face stiff with disappointment and fury. Several strands of her hair had slipped from beneath the back rim of her bonnet and rippled down her slender back. Malcolm's fingertips tingled with the urge to touch her golden tresses.

He drew an unsteady breath. He wished he could let her help. It would be wonderful having her by his side. But she would undoubtedly place herself in danger. Recklessness was part of her nature. It would be too risky.

Though he was loathe to see her go, he stood abruptly. "If that is all you wished to speak to me about, you may consider the matter closed. Now, you must leave."

Phoebe whirled back to face him. "But—"

"No buts."

"If you will not let me help, Sir Malcolm," she said stormily, "I will launch my own investigation."

An icy chill threatened to freeze the marrow of Malcolm's bones. "No. You will not. You will not look for it, and, if you do by some odd quirk of fate stumble upon it, you will definitely not touch it. Do you hear me, Phoebe?"

Without answering, she jumped up and flounced out of the library.

Malcolm followed her back down the hall. He stood in the open doorway as Fobbs handed her up into the unmarked carriage. Phoebe did not even glance out of the window as the vehicle pulled away.

Malcolm walked back to his library. There he glanced down at the Persian carpet, where a solitary golden hairpin winked up at him. He bent down and picked it up between thumb and forefinger, then wandered over to sit behind his desk and gaze pensively at the emerald-green velvet chair Phoebe had recently vacated.

When another knock came on the door, he started. "What is it?"

Fobbs opened the door slowly. "Do you wish me to take the tea tray, sir?"

Malcolm lowered his brows. "Of course not, man. You know no one is allowed in my library."

Silently, the butler withdrew.

Taking his pocketbook from his coat, Malcolm tucked the hairpin inside. He should be angry with Phoebe for coming here. He ought to report her careless actions to her closest male relative. But she had none. As she had often declared, no man held any control over her life. It was a pity, since the woman desperately needed controlling before she made some foolish, possibly fatal error in judgment.

But though he tried very hard, he was unable to raise any genuine displeasure at her unexpected appearance. Finally he removed his spectacles, laid them on his desktop, and leaned his head against the back of his chair. He closed his eyes and indulged in a scrumptious daydream in which Phoebe's sunlit locks tumbled freely down her back and his fingers swept them aside, facilitating the tender kiss he laid on the satiny, delicately perfumed skin at the nape of her neck.

He almost wished he were not a gentleman. He almost wished he had given in to his primary impulse upon seeing Phoebe on his doorstep, that he had taken her in his arms and kissed her wildly—just to teach the foolish, headstrong girl a lesson about the witlessness of injudicious behavior.

God, but she needed to be brought under control.

The next time she surprised him with one of her shenanigans, he vowed, he would consider himself honor-bound to step in and administer the discipline the chit so desperately needed, before she got herself so deeply into trouble that no amount of dexterity could extract her. Loving her, how could he do less?

Opening his eyes and sitting up, he smiled, slowly. As he replaced his spectacles on the bridge of his nose, he realized he was looking forward to Phoebe's next indiscretion with great pleasure.

12

As Malcolm had mentioned to Phoebe, thanks to Lord Peter's intervention at the Simmons's ball, the foyer table at 102 Prichard Place was nearly bowing beneath the weight of invitations piled thereon, including the one to Lord Deauville's bachelor fete. Still requiring suitable London attire, Malcolm spent the afternoon visiting various shops suggested by his newfound friends, and in a matter of hours he thought he looked as fine as any English man-about-town.

When his newly hired gentleman's gentleman, Gibbet, had deftly tied Malcolm's cravat into a perfect mathematical and announced his lordship ready to take the ton by storm, Malcolm sent for his carriage. Ten minutes later that vehicle stopped before Lord Deauville's large townhouse, from which raucous shouting could be heard even on the street.

Malcolm stepped out onto the curb and gazed up at the house. Standing out here, he thought dimly, the music and laughter were so loud he could scarcely hear himself think. He hated the thought of entering the building and submitting his ears to further torture, but, since he would be dead soon he decided it really didn't matter much if he were nearly deaf by the time he returned home.

It occurred to him that he would far prefer spending his

remaining earthly time with Phoebe, perhaps exploring some remote, exotic port of call, than going to a bachelor party where crude lightskirts and lecherous men would undoubtedly be indulging in orgies before the party was over. He would even prefer just sitting before a fire, talking to Phoebe. Or reading aloud from one of his ancient texts. She would probably like that.

Doing anything with Phoebe would surely be more enjoyable than going to Lord Deauville's crowded, deafening bacchanal. However, Malcolm knew he had no choice but to attend, so he resignedly instructed his coachman to go home and return in two hours. He watched the carriage drive away, then started up the townhouse steps, clutching his cobra-headed cane in his hand.

The front door swung open the moment he dropped the brass gorgon-headed knocker against its metal rest, and he found himself swept into a fast-moving current of human bodies.

Lord Deauville's butler appeared and took Malcolm's hat and gloves and disappeared without speaking; then a squat crystal glass, filled to overflowing with a mixture of Russian vodka and a sweet, potent liqueur was thrust into Malcolm's hand. Though he had never been overly fond of alcohol, Malcolm took a large, bracing swallow, shuddered as his throat closed against the fiery liquid, and began to survey his surroundings.

As expected, many of the guests were already partially naked. This observation made Malcolm gulp more of his beverage. Glancing down, he observed with surprise that this second swallow had emptied his glass. A passing servant, perspicaciously noting this fact, immediately replaced the baronet's empty glass with a full one, which Malcolm set, untouched, on a round marble table. He then resumed his study of the crowd.

The women, all supremely beautiful and with bodies Eve herself would have envied, had obviously been handpicked for the evening's entertainments from the ranks of London's finest courtesans. Yet as physically perfect as they were, none could compete with Phoebe's summer loveliness. Malcolm was glad his spontaneous little darling was at her own home, safe and sound and probably already abed.

Phoebe studied her reflection in her bedchamber looking glass. Despite her nervousness, a little smile teased her lips. How fortunate, she mused smugly, that she had gone visiting Lady Jane Simmons that afternoon.

She had felt sorry for the homely debutante and had gone to the Simmons home to befriend Lady Jane, as well as to try to forget that Sir Malcolm would be beginning his search for the Eye of Horus that very night.

To her delight Phoebe had found Lady Jane, though of a serious nature, far more interesting to talk to when not surrounded by people expecting her to be pert and vivacious—character traits Phoebe now realized the girl exhibited only with people she knew well. With unfamiliar people, as Phoebe had already observed on numerous occasions, the girl exhibited no more animation than a tree stump.

When Phoebe innocently inquired if Lord Peter planned to attend Lord Deauville's bachelor fete, Lady Jane had proven a veritable treasure trove of information. It happened, the redheaded girl had told Phoebe, that Lord Peter, who was good friends with Lord Deauville's younger brother for whom the bachelor fete was being thrown, had actually helped plan the evening's entertainments.

Lord Peter, like many brothers, had taken immense pleasure in shocking his twin by telling her about some of the planned divertissements. And Lady Jane, like many shy young debutantes thrust right out of school and into the harsh whirl of society, yearned for friends and was more than willing to indulge Phoebe's curiosity by passing the scandalous information along.

The things, Lady Jane had declared in an appalled but fascinated tone, that young men found enjoyable!

Phoebe's devious mind had immediately recognized a plan for gaining admittance to the Deauville townhouse— a plan she had instantly set into effect. It had taken only a few coins to one of Lord Deauville's maids, and Phoebe was supplied with information and a costume that would enable her to slip among the fete guests without being observed. Or at least, she amended, without being recognized, for no one who knew the proper Miss Phoebe Lawton would ever recognize her in her present attire.

Now she smiled at her reflection even more broadly. If all went well this evening, she would locate and seize the missing amulet without anyone being the wiser—and the Eye of Horus, safe and sound away from Sir Malcolm's plan of destruction, would be hers.

Tucking an errant strand of blond hair under the white, lace-edged mobcap nestled pertly on her head, she then tugged futilely at her miniscule black frock in an effort to make it cover more of her body. She wondered whether Lord Peter had been the one responsible for deciding the maids serving at Lord Deauville's bachelor fete would wear such outrageously revealing attire. If so, apparently she had not known the young man quite so well as she'd assumed.

She scrutinized herself carefully. A black lace riband circled her throat, making her neck look very white. Her low bodice barely hid her nipples. She tugged the neckline up a fraction only to have it slide right back to its former position. Though secretly proud of her lush cleavage, Phoebe now fervently wished that her breasts did not look quite so much like melons ready to pop out of a farmer's heavily laden basket.

The sleeves of her little black dress were made of poufed white gauze, framing the gentle slopes of her upper arms. Long black lace mittens, cut so her fingers were bare, ended just above her elbows. A pert white apron edged with fluted black piping, black lace stockings gartered at the tops of her thighs, and little black kidskin slippers completed the ensemble.

She gave the short skirt another yank, but when she pulled the skirt down in front, it displayed a distressing tendency to ride up in the rear. Muttering with annoyance, she jerked it back down over her exposed derriere, where she wore the skimpiest pair of black lace drawers she had ever seen.

She bit her lip and wondered if she had the nerve to go through with her plan. But, truly, she had no choice but to try. She would just have to hope she saw no one she knew. After all, she could not very well wear a modest gown when all the other serving wenches would be dressed as scandalously as she was now.

She had painted spots of rouge on each of her cheek-bones, making her look, she thought disgustedly, like a child's doll. (Or perhaps more appropriately, she thought with a heated blush, a man's toy?) Her lashes had been darkened, and her full lips, gleaming with rose-tinted oil, definitely seemed to be pouting for a kiss.

It was a good thing, she thought, that she and Matty had gone to Hatchard's bookshop that afternoon. Matty, no doubt, was tucked up in bed with one of her new novels. And, since Matty usually read until well after three or four in the morning, provided the book was a good one (and Phoebe had seen to it the older woman had purchased four novels, to be absolutely certain one would prove satisfactory), Matty would undoubtedly not rise until well after noon the following day.

Once again Phoebe sneaked out of her townhouse and, several streets away, flagged down a cab. The driver's eyes nearly popped out of his head when he saw her costume, but he laughed and nodded when she informed him that she had been hired to act as a maid at Lord Deauville's bachelor fete.

"Yis, oi knows where that plaice is," he cackled. "Oi 'ear they's 'aving a grand time there tonight. Git in, me foine one, and oi'll 'ave ye there in a trice. Wouldna want ye to miss any chances to make a bit o' blunt on t'side, an' if we don't git ye there quick-like, all the rich blokes will be taiken. Ever done this afore?"

Phoebe's response was slow, since it took several moments before her brain comprehended the meaning behind the man's garbled accent. "Er . . . no."

"Well, taike a bit o' advice from me. Don' go for the

young 'uns. T'older t'better. They's the ones wi' plenty o' the ready.''

"Thank you." Phoebe climbed into the vehicle, unavoidably exposing her long, lace-stockinged legs.

The driver cracked his whip over the horse's head, and the cab rattled along the street in a southerly direction. Nervous, Phoebe rubbed her lips together to distribute her lipcolor evenly. Since she did not know the layout of Lord Deauville's townhouse, the best she could hope to do was to slip away and search without being observed. She crossed her fingers. Though she did not feel completely prepared for this endeavor, with luck all would go smoothly.

The cab stopped in front of a large, brilliantly illuminated house. Phoebe climbed out and offered the driver a silver coin.

He exposed blackened teeth in a friendly smile, but shook his head. "Oi, ye keep it, lass. An' I 'ope ye make lots more t'night." Cracking his whip, he drove away.

Loud music seemed to shake Lord Deauville's townhouse windows. Phoebe thought she could feel it vibrating the road. Her scantily clad legs trembled, but she made them move one in front of the other until she had circled the house and discovered the servants' entrance around the side, which the maid who had sold Phoebe her costume had informed her was there.

She watched and waited until she saw no movement through the little window to the right of the door. Moving as if she had every right to be there, she opened the door and stepped into the house. She had no time to examine her surroundings, for at that moment a harried-looking man in a stained cook's uniform and white doughboy hat popped out from behind a corner, saw her, screamed something in French, and thrust a tray laden with tiny canapes formed in obscene shapes into her hands.

"Allez! Allez!" he screeched, gesturing in the opposite direction.

Phoebe swallowed hard and began walking down the long hall. Several other women, dressed exactly as she was but carrying empty trays, rushed past in the other direction. A set of swinging doors swayed to and fro at the end of the hall. Phoebe hesitated, then drew a deep breath, pinned a flirtatious smile to her face, and pushed through.

Though many of the gentlemen looked familiar, parts of them did not. Quite a few men had discarded their expensive jackets, waistcoats, and intricately tied cravats, and their lawn shirts hung open, exposing hairy and hairless, muscular and flabby, white and tanned chests in a profusion the likes of which Phoebe knew she would never see again if she lived for a hundred years. Or, she thought with a shocked giggle, unless she took up a new profession.

A number of gentlemen with heavily painted females in tow were ascending and descending the grand staircase. The women were in a similar state of undress as the men. Their gowns were either unbuttoned or unlaced or just plain missing. Some of them pranced about in their lacy underthings, buttons and tapes showing, or with bare private parts exposed to the eyes of all and sunder. It occurred to Phoebe that she did *not* know any of these women.

One of the gentlemen without a companion on his arm sidled up to her, a leer on his face. Though she did not know him well, Phoebe recognized him as Lord Jeremiah Finch, an earl's second son with a wife and eleven children. She felt a surge of sympathy for the man's poor spouse.

Lord Jeremiah seemed at least three sails to the wind. He swayed unsteadily. "Ain't you a pretty one! Come here, darling, and give me a kiss. Then maybe I'll take one of your little treats there and give you a coin for your trouble. Or perhaps buy something else you're selling. Something much more expensive. Would you like that, eh?"

Phoebe easily slipped out from under the perspiration-stained shirtsleeve that tried to drape itself over her shoulder. The man's white fingers closed spasmodically on nothing but air, and he cursed, plainly disappointed at missing the plump breast he'd been seeking.

"Here now," he snapped. A lock of greasy black hair fell over his brow, but he made no effort to push it out of his eyes. "That's no way to act. Don't expect me to be nice to you if you aren't willing to be nice to me."

Turning away, Phoebe pointedly ignored him.

"Fine," he snarled. "I don't need your company. Plenty of quail in this covey, you know. Bitch." Spinning about, he walked away.

Just then, a bustle in the doorway behind Phoebe made her dash to one side.

The wide double doors swung open, revealing four more half-naked maids leaning over and pushing a huge, whipped-cream-covered cake, on a rolling platform, before them. The women proceeded to the center of the room, their wiggling, lace-clad fannies being pinched or patted by every male they passed. None of the maids seemed displeased by the intimate attention.

Phoebe set her tray down on a marble table beside someone's forgotten drink, and backed into a corner behind a potted rubber tree. The crowd seemed unusually excited by the thought of eating cake, she mused, watching their eager faces. Perhaps Lord Deauville's cook had a special recipe.

She decided to give the group a chance to become engrossed in their dessert before she slipped up the grand staircase and began searching for the amulet. The traffic going up and down the stairs had thinned out considerably. If she passed anyone, she would try to appear as if she, too, were on her way to an illicit assignation.

When the crowd closed around the enormous cake, Phoebe wasted no time. Leaving the cover of the rubber tree, she crept around the low marble table and gripped the carved mahogany banister.

She moved swiftly, gliding up the maroon-carpeted steps. At the top she decided to go left, turned, and walked purposefully down the hall, hoping no one would look up and see her through the wooden railing that ran the length of the second-floor corridor. Below, a drumroll sounded.

Phoebe grinned, shaking her head at all the fuss over a mere cake. But, as Lady Jane had said, men did do the strangest things for entertainment. And common knowledge had always insisted that the way to a man's heart was through his stomach.

Suddenly a huge cry erupted from the lower level. Phoebe glanced back down at the crowd. She almost toppled over the banister when she gaped down at the scene below. Lady Jane had made no mention of this! Apparently Lord Peter had rightfully considered this bit of "entertainment" far too bawdy for his twin's ears.

The top half of the cake had flipped to one side, exposing an inner compartment. Standing inside this narrow hold was a woman. A totally, stark, raving, bucknaked woman with the most enormous breasts Phoebe had ever seen.

The woman turned in a full circle. Phoebe gaped at the barest hint of what appeared to be whipped cream covering the most intimate of feminine body parts. Long curly hair the color of French brandy swirled down the woman's shoulders past an astonishingly narrow waist, and settled around gently rounded hips. There was whipped cream on the tips of her red hair.

The woman turned away from the staircase, facing the largest number of people. She had flung her arms high in the air and, as the orchestra began playing a tune mindful of far-off desert sands, began twisting and swaying in an erotic dance. Phoebe could now see only the woman's outline.

Phoebe clapped her mouth shut and willed her feet to move.

What had she gotten herself into? Good lord. If this was the kind of thing that went on at men's parties, she had no business here at all! Sir Malcolm had been absolutely right! Truly, she must stop leaping into situations she did not adequately understand!

Momentarily she became aware that the rebuffed Lord

Jeremiah Finch was gazing up at her. His face was con-
torted in a frenzy of rage and desire. She could tell from
his red cheeks and angry expression that he was still thinking about her rejection.

Lord Jeremiah cast a last glance at Lord Deauville and
the dancer, now locked together on the ballroom floor, and
began weaving through the entranced crowd in the direction of the staircase. Fear clutched at Phoebe's heart with
ice-cold fingers. Pivoting, she ran along the passage until
she had left the crowded ballroom far behind.

She passed several amorous couples, but none of them
paid her any mind. Ahead was darkness, terrifying darkness, but behind lay a threat even more alarming. She
knew that if Lord Jeremiah caught her, he would not release her until he had satisfied his lust.

Footsteps, strangely faltering as if her pursuer weaved
unsteadily to and fro, pounded after her. Drawing ever
nearer, they seemed to echo off the walls until Phoebe
was uncertain if they were behind or just up ahead. She
swung to the left, gripped a door handle, wrenched it open,
and stepped into the darkness, praying that there was no
amatory couple within the room.

Closing the door she leaned back upon it, trembling. As
she heard Lord Jeremiah's unsteady footsteps continue
down the hall, she opened the door a crack and peeped
out. Her pursuer's swaying form disappeared around the
far corner.

Deciding to give him a chance to tire of searching for
her, Phoebe reclosed the door, took a deep breath, and
examined her surroundings.

She was in an empty bedchamber. A large, circular bed
rested at the far end of the room, while tables, chairs, an
armoire, and a bureau sat nearby. A fireplace loomed off
to the left, where, to her surprise, a fire flickered and
danced. On the mantel, a clock ticked steadily. After fifteen minutes, when she had not heard Lord Jeremiah pass
by on his way back to the party, Phoebe decided he must
have known another way downstairs.

Unwilling to put off her search for the amulet any

longer, she turned and opened the door—and found herself face to face with Sir Malcolm Forbes.

The baronet was not smiling. His lips were so compressed they were barely visible. He loomed over her, his hot gaze scorching her skimpily clad body. Behind his spectacles his eyes glittered strangely as if he had had too much champagne, yet they shone with a clarity that defied this suspicion.

His tall, muscular frame looked almost as if he were trembling, but he did not appear afraid. Rather, undistilled rage emanated out from him in invisible yet tangible waves. He looked, Phoebe realized with a quiver, even more bent upon her destruction than Lord Jeremiah.

Sir Malcolm took a step forward while Phoebe retreated into the room. His expression changed. Reaching back, he set his cane against the wall, closed the door, and latched it securely. His lips curved up in a devastatingly sensual smile.

"Enjoying the party, Miss Lawton?" he asked silkily.

13

Phoebe looked as if she could not have spoken even if her life had depended upon it. Except for the two round spots of rouge over her cheekbones, she was as pale as death. With difficulty Malcolm kept from wrapping his hands around her neck and finishing the job.

"I myself particularly liked the bit with the cake," he said conversationally.

Phoebe didn't say anything.

Malcolm smiled with a conspicuous lack of joviality. "It is quite the norm at bachelor fetes to have naked women doing all sorts of intriguing things. But I suppose you were not aware of that fact when you decided to come here tonight. Or perhaps," he revised, gazing at her interestedly, "you *were,* and there is a side of you with which I am not familiar."

She still did not speak.

"I do hope I did not disturb you and the man who followed you up here," he said apologetically. "I saw you go up the stairs, and then I watched your gentleman friend follow, and assumed you and he had something very important to discuss. But do you know what?"

Phoebe shook her head.

"I was simply unable to suppress my curiosity about your presence at Lord Deauville's this evening, and had to come directly up to inquire." His voice betrayed a glimmer of the excitement that consumed him now that Phoebe had, as he'd expected, committed another foolhardy act. He well remembered the vow he'd made to himself in his library that same afternoon: the next time the chit put herself in jeopardy he would be honor-bound to step in and administer a modicum of the control she so desperately required.

His entire body tingled with anticipation. He was thrilled with the opportunity to discipline this wayward, foolish woman. By the time he finished with her, she would know better than to hurl herself thoughtlessly into unwise, possibly dangerous, situations.

"And to be perfectly honest," he finished contritely, "I simply could not bear not knowing what you and such a low-life reprobate as that man could possibly find of importance enough to discuss that it was necessary to search out one of Lord Deauville's bedchambers in which to conduct your conversation."

Phoebe finally opened her mouth but only managed to stammer, "I—I—"

"Be silent. Someone is coming." The words flashed out of his mouth like lightning bolts. He tipped his head to one side as he listened to a set of unsteady footsteps go past the door and continue in the direction of the party.

He clucked commiseratingly. "Oh dear. I fear your friend tired of your game of hide-and-seek, and went back to the main group to find other sport. That should not be hard, given the plethora of intriguing things Deauville has planned for this evening."

Phoebe blushed furiously. Malcolm could see the color flood her cheeks even in the shadowy bedchamber. He smiled to himself. She would be blushing further before long.

At last managing to free her voice, Phoebe said sharply, "Sir Malcolm, you are deliberately trying to make me uncomfortable. I realize my coming to Lord Deauville's bachelor fete was unwise, but there is no need for you to speak so outrageously. No harm has been done. You need not concern yourself any longer. I will take myself home at once.''

Malcolm curled his lips in a parody of a smile. ''Oh, no,'' he whispered. ''I'm not letting you out of my sight until you are safely back on your own doorstep, my dear.''

When he'd seen Phoebe ascending the stairs, her little black skirt bobbing invitingly about her shapely thighs, his eyes had practically bugged out of his head. And when he'd noticed her pursuer, his heart had leapt into his throat. He had followed immediately, and had observed Phoebe peeking out into the hall after her admirer had wobbled past the bedchamber. Then, certain she would not open the door if he merely knocked, he'd waited in the shadows until she'd attempted to exit the chamber.

Now he stood gazing down at her, feeling the glass of liqueur-laced vodka he'd drunk fizz through his veins and make certain parts of his anatomy exquisitely sensitive. He shook his head in order to clear his thoughts.

Although he'd always been attracted to Phoebe, now, seeing her garbed in no more than a shred of black satin nearly made him lose his much-prized self-control. Her legs, long and slender in lacy black hose, seemed to beg his touch, and her magnificent bosom, full and lush and nearly pouring out of her low-cut bodice, appeared to yearn for his caress. He took a step forward. His manhood, hot and hard and heavy against his thigh, throbbed with anticipation.

Alas, however, he was fully aware that he had not drunk so much that he could feel justified in giving in to his desires, no matter how badly he wanted to. At that moment he sincerely wished he had drunk his second beverage, instead of leaving it, untouched, on the marble table. As he contemplated Phoebe's shapely form, though, he decided that although he was not so far gone as to allow himself to take the ultimate liberty, it couldn't hurt to give the chit a damn good scare.

His smile widened. ''Are you perhaps curious why that man was following you, Miss Lawton? Or why so many other couples have been traipsing up and down the main staircase all evening?''

"Yes," Phoebe admitted, then eyed his evil grin suspiciously. "Not really," she amended hurriedly.

"Too bad. Because I am going to educate you as to that reason."

Her eyes were wide and luminous. "I beg your pardon?"

Malcolm moved closer, his advancing steps matching her retreating ones. He cast a purposeful glance behind her, then shifted slightly so that she was also forced to adjust her movements. By the time she had backed up as far as she could, the backs of her thighs rested against the edge of the huge circular bed.

Phoebe put one black-lace-mittened hand behind her, apparently in an effort to find her way around the obstructing object. Her long, bare fingers edged right, then left, pressing cautiously into the plush fabric. Her eyes widened still farther as she realized what the obstruction was.

"Sir Malcolm," she squeaked, "do you think you might not stand so close? I find myself feeling quite cornered, and cannot like it. I feel rather like a fox pursued by a hound. I vow," she added with a semihysterical giggle, "I shall never hunt again."

"I do not think I can do that," Malcolm replied in a dulcet tone. Then he quirked a brow contemplatively. He glanced at the fireplace. "Did it not strike you as odd when you came in here, that Lord Deauville's servants would have fires burning in unoccupied rooms?"

Phoebe swallowed. "I did think it a bit strange," she allowed, clearly attempting to appear nonchalant, but succeeding only in looking and sounding delightfully innocent.

"Oh, it is not strange at all. Lord Deauville is a very considerate host. He did not wish his guests to get cold. Knowing that most of these rooms would be filled all evening, he took great care to ensure their warmth when his guests came up here to utilize that very comfortable-looking piece of furniture just behind you."

Phoebe's fingers once again traced the bed's velvet spread. "Good heavens, Sir Malcolm. What a thing to say. I am shocked."

"You will be more so," he promised with another devilishly crooked smile. He took another step forward, closing the narrow gap between their bodies until her rapidly rising and falling cleavage brushed his chest with each of her tremulous breaths. His manhood throbbed, almost painfully, in response.

Knowing he needed every ounce of his self-restraint, if this lesson in controlling one's impetuosity were to be a success rather than a catastrophe, he viciously tamped down the lust clamoring in his brain. Then he stepped even closer.

Phoebe, already leaning backward, lost her balance and fell, arms flailing, onto the bed. "Good heavens, Sir Malcolm," she squealed again, propping herself up on her elbows, her mittened hands pressed against the counterpane. Her little mobcap fell lopsidedly to one side of her head, obscuring one exquisite blue eye. "What are you doing?"

A deep-throated chuckle escaped Malcolm's lips. "This, Miss Lawton," he replied softly, pushing against her shoulders until she collapsed fully onto the mattress. He brushed the mobcap off her head, exposing her glorious autumn-gold curls, and touched his lips to hers. "This."

Sir Malcolm's fingers gripped Phoebe's bare shoulders firmly, causing a strange heat in her lower parts. His eyes were wild, and seemed to be shooting blue-green sparks from behind his spectacle lenses.

Phoebe could feel the velvet bedspread beneath her shoulders, but the delicious sensations it caused, rubbing against her flesh, were as nothing compared to the nearly unbearable pleasure she felt when Sir Malcolm lowered himself to lean on one elbow beside her. Her heart pummeled the inside of her chest, and she felt his also, pounding like an African drum, where his side pressed against hers.

A tiny sob escaped her lips, but whether of fear or excitement she did not know. She only knew that Sir Malcolm's wild behavior had awakened something equally feral deep within her. Something she had not, until this night, known existed—but which, newly awakened, demanded to be set free.

When she felt his leg press between her knees, it seemed as natural as breathing to spread herself for his touch. He groaned and she arched against him. "Please, Malcolm," she whispered brokenly. "Please."

Sir Malcolm's eyes blazed down at her, his expression blindingly fierce, but Phoebe felt none of the fear she'd experienced when she'd seen the same desire on Lord Jeremiah's face. The baronet brushed his spectacles off his face with one impatient stroke. They fell off the bed and landed, with a muffled thump, on the thick bedchamber carpet.

"Please," Phoebe whispered again.

Sir Malcolm cursed. Closing his eyes, he bared his teeth in a grimace that looked as if he were in pain. "Easy," he muttered softly. "Slow down, Malcolm."

"Malcolm," Phoebe pleaded yet again, asking for something she did not understand, but knew only he could give her.

Hearing his name seemed to inflame Sir Malcolm to the point of immolation. His mouth descended upon hers like a ravenous hawk upon a delectable partridge. "Yes, my darling," he answered huskily. "Yes."

The flames of desire roaring around their bodies threatened to consume Phoebe entirely. Sir Malcolm's tongue traced her lips, dipping in and pulling out like a hummingbird sipping the sweetest nectar. One of his hands again gripped her shoulder. The other, with devastating slowness, released her hair from its chignon and raked through her long curls.

Following one long tress with his fingertips, he traced it to where it ended just above Phoebe's indecently low bodice. His hand hovered momentarily, then brushed the lock of hair aside and skimmed her rounded curves, dipping lower to explore the humid valley between her breasts. He gave a slow, pleasured sigh.

Phoebe's eyes followed his every move, irresistibly drawn to the contrast between his tanned fingers and her own white skin. His hand slipped lower and cupped her entire left breast in his palm.

Phoebe trembled. Her body, with a will of its own, arched sharply against the knee still pressed between her thighs.

Sir Malcolm sucked in his breath. Then he spoke. Phoebe tried to listen, tried to comprehend, but was consumed by her maiden's passion, the desire evoked only once in a lifetime when a woman is first touched by a virile, experienced man.

"You silly, foolish girl," the baronet murmured, running his lips over the curve of her breasts. "Have you no comprehension of what that man—that bastard—could have done to you if he had found you in here? How do you think I could have lived with myself if you had been ravished, when it was I who ignorantly told you where I would be searching for the amulet tonight? I should have known you would follow."

Phoebe, lost in his touch, heard barely a word.

"You fling yourself into every situation, wise or unwise. You think you are so fortunate to have no male relatives to oversee your actions." He laughed drily, his breath hot against her flesh. "You are wrong, you know. I have met many women in my lifetime, but I can honestly say I have never known one who needed the guidance of a man more than you do."

Phoebe gazed up at him. Distantly, she comprehended his words and knew them to be true. But she also knew that he needed her as badly as she needed him.

This realization brought no self-recrimination, only a longing to have Sir Malcolm by her side forever. He was the only man she had ever wanted, and she knew he was the only man she would ever want.

Sir Malcolm's hands caressed her continually, brushing up and down the length of her body. As his fingernail grazed one of her nipples, her entire body tensed. "Please, Malcolm," she begged again. "Love me."

She could feel that part of him that made him male, that part she had always wondered about but had expected never to know since she had never planned to marry, pressing hot against her thigh. She slid her free leg up and down his, innocently seductive.

He shuddered and kissed her again, roughly. His hair was thick beneath her hands. She entwined her fingers into it and pulled him closer. He ground his lips against hers.

"Phoebe," he murmured. "My God, Phoebe."

His mouth glided down her neck and came to rest at the base of her throat. His tongue flicked there, inflaming her further. His fingers continued working their magic atop the peak of her breast. She pressed herself into his hand.

The pleasure was too much to be borne, and far, far too wonderful to resist.

14

Phoebe felt ravenous, starved for Sir Malcolm's touch. It was as if she'd been searching for him all her life and had rejected every offer of marriage, no matter how grand, because her soul had known he was coming soon, soon.

"Phoebe," he whispered urgently. His words came on a groan. "I must know. Do you want this? Do you want me? Tell me you want me, Phoebe. God, I want you. Tell me now, if you want me to stop, for I will be unable to stop in another moment."

"Yes, Malcolm, yes," she answered. "I do. I do want you."

Eagerly questing, Sir Malcolm's fingers slipped lower to touch the bare, silken flesh just above Phoebe's stockings. As they did so, Phoebe cried out, startled and carried away by the unfamiliarity of the caress.

Her cry seemed to awaken Sir Malcolm from his dazed stupor. He jerked his hand back, away from the juncture of Phoebe's thighs, then rolled to lie beside her, staring up at the ceiling. His breath came in heaving gasps. He ground his teeth together in an audible grimace.

"What in God's name am I doing?" he rasped. "My God, I nearly ruined you. I thought I was in control, but with you I seem to lose every shred of control I possess.

I call you impulsive, but it is I who am uncontrolled when you are involved."

Phoebe lay trembling, uncertain what she had done to make him retreat both physically and mentally.

When it became clear that Malcolm had no intention of returning to her, she raised shaking hands to adjust her dishevelled bodice. She pushed her skirt back down so it covered her thighs, then sat up and ran her fingers through her hair, trying to restore some semblance of the order his hands had demolished. She tried to regain her composure, tried to make pinning her hair back into a chignon a long enough act to grant enough time for her to understand what had happened.

After several minutes Malcolm's breathing slowed. Leaning over the side of the bed, he picked up his spectacles, set them on his nose, stood, and moved to face the chamber door. Without turning he said woodenly, "I will wait for you in the hall. Then I will escort you directly home."

Now that her mind was clearing, Phoebe remembered why she had come upstairs originally. "The amulet," she said. Her voice, still thick with passion, sounded like the croak of a consumptive frog. "What about the amulet? What about our search?"

He gave a terse shake of his head. "I will return to Lord Deauville's bachelor fete after I have seen you safely inside your own townhouse. *I* will resume *my* search, then." Opening the door, he picked up his cane from where it leaned against the wall, and left the room.

Phoebe felt confused, befuddled, disoriented. She adjusted her mobcap over her chignon and tidied herself as best she could. Then she went out into the hall. Without a word, Sir Malcolm took her by the elbow and led her swiftly downstairs.

When the butler had brought the baronet's hat and gloves, Phoebe and Sir Malcolm left the townhouse. They walked to where his carriage waited. He opened the door and thrust her inside. As she stepped up into the vehicle she noticed the coachman's poorly concealed grin.

Sir Malcolm spoke to the driver and then climbed in and sat opposite Phoebe. He did not look at her, but instead gazed out of the window. "I have instructed my coachman to take us to my townhouse, since it is not far from your own. We will walk to your home from there," he continued tonelessly. "Your reputation will be safer if my servants believe I am conducting an illicit liaison with a trollop than if I asked my coachman to drop you off on your own doorstep."

"Your butler will not believe it," Phoebe retorted, remembering Fobbs's stinging remarks.

"He will believe what I tell him to believe," Sir Malcolm returned brutally. "It is the only answer. All servants, no matter how loyal, gossip amongst themselves. Though I trust my own staff more than most, I still have no wish to risk your reputation any more than you have already done tonight."

Phoebe did not reply. Her stomach roiled queasily. She felt sick at heart, believing she had earned the baronet's disgust by her brazen behavior.

Sir Malcolm must surely believe her as bad as one of the courtesans at Lord Deauville's, given the heated way she had responded to his caresses. She had always heard that gentlewomen were supposed to be uninterested in sexual matters. Sir Malcolm's response to her passion proved it.

They arrived at Sir Malcolm's townhouse. The carriage slowed to a stop at the front of the building, and Phoebe and the baronet climbed out. As the carriage drove around the side of his townhouse, the baronet instructed Phoebe to wait on the steps while he went inside for a moment. He returned thirty seconds later with a long, black, woolen cape. He wrapped it securely about her shoulders. Then, gripping her right arm he propelled her along the street.

Stopping half a block from her residence, he muttered, "Go the rest of the way by yourself. I shall watch to make certain you get inside. Tomorrow I will call upon you and we will discuss this matter."

*   *   *

Malcolm lay awake long into the night. By morning he had decided upon the solution which he believed to be the only logical answer to his dilemma. Thus, he arrived at Phoebe's townhouse before the clock chimed ten times.

A solemn-looking butler who looked like a retired prize fighter opened the door, his expression showing grave disapproval at Malcolm's temerity in visiting before the sun was fully in the sky.

"Yes?" Mames inquired stiffly. "How may I serve you on this early morning, sir?"

Malcolm was momentarily taken aback as he realized that Phoebe's butler was every bit as disturbed by his early visit as Fobbs had been by Phoebe's. "I am Sir Malcolm Forbes." The baronet placed his card in the butler's white-gloved hand. "I wish to speak to Miss Lawton."

The butler sniffed, but led Malcolm to a bright yellow salon. There he turned. "May I take your hat and gloves, sir?"

"No, thank you," Malcolm replied. "I will not be here long."

The butler bowed and withdrew. Despite his still-simmering fury at Phoebe, Malcolm had to smile upon seeing this sunshiny room that reminded him so vividly of that impolitic lady.

Gripping his cane tightly, he moved to stand near a long glass window. Brushing aside its white ceiling-to-floor cutwork draperies, he gazed out into a small, colorful flower garden. In his mind's eye he imagined Phoebe kneeling beside a particularly vibrant clump of yellow asters, her glorious golden locks covered by a wide-brimmed straw hat encircled with a broad, cocoa-brown ribbon, and her hands covered by tanned-leather gardening gloves. She wore a dress the color of an autumn sunflower, and when she looked up with her glorious eyes of forget-me-not blue, she was laughing.

When she entered the salon, however, though she *was* wearing a yellow morning gown, and her eyes *were* lustrously blue, she was not smiling. She also wore no gloves, nor a bonnet over her beautiful hair. Malcolm turned as she opened the drawing room door and then closed it softly behind her. She was alone.

"Miss Lawton," he said with a resigned sigh, "I know it seems I am forever asking you this question, but where is your companion?"

She did not meet his gaze. "Matty is still abed, sir. Although I frequently rise early, she is not quite so eager to leave her bed with the dawn. I shall awaken her if you feel it necessary for her to be present during this interview."

Pushing up his spectacles, Malcolm studied Phoebe silently. She was pale. Her reddened eyes were not filled with laughter, as in his daydream, but with chagrin. She looked, in fact, almost ready to burst into tears. If the paleness of her complexion was any indication, she had also passed much of the night in that unpleasant activity.

He frowned. He had expected his first duty this morning would be to deliver a severe dressing-down for Phoebe's unwise foray into impolite society. He had thought her resulting shame would relieve him, somehow absolve him for nearly losing his self-control, somehow give him an indication that she had finally learned not to leap before she looked. Obviously, she *was* regretting her actions. And she knew, without his explanation, that going to Lord Deauville's bachelor fete had been imprudent.

What puzzled him was why the contrition in her eyes did not satisfy him more. Instead he felt an aching need to take her in his arms and comfort her, to tell her that it didn't matter and that everything was all right. But it *did* matter. And everything was *not* all right..

The next time—and there would be a next time; with Phoebe's adventuresome nature that much was inevitable—she might not escape unscathed.

He flushed warmly, remembering that in actuality she had not escaped completely unscathed from the previous night's fiasco. "That will not be necessary," he said gruffly. "What I have to say is for your ears only."

She raised her gaze, then lowered it quickly. She said softly, "Please, be seated. I will listen to anything you have to say. Even though you are not a member of my family, I realize that you are my friend and have my best interests at heart. Thus, knowing I deserve the worst, you may say what you like.''

Malcolm cleared his throat. ''I hope you will not find my words too horrible.''

Phoebe settled herself onto a sofa. Her yellow gown contrasted beautifully with the burnt-orange brocade cushion on which she perched, making her look remarkably like a lovely, delicate swallow-tailed butterfly alighting on a blossom.

Ignoring the appealing picture she made, Malcolm sat on the edge of a cinnamon velvet armchair, leaned his cobra-headed cane against his leg, and set his gloves and beaver hat beside him. A thick rug with an intricate sunflower pattern lay at his feet. His new Wellingtons sank deep into its pile. Sunlight, streaming in through the cutwork linen draperies, scattered abstract patterns across the floor.

''Thank you for considering me your friend, Miss Lawton,'' he said, feeling humbled. ''I am honored that you would bestow such a precious gift upon me. And you may relax, for I am not going to scold you.''

Phoebe looked up again. Her eyes regained a flicker of their formerly happy shine. Her hair, gleaming like ripe wheat, was wrapped atop her head in a thick braid, a style Malcolm had not seen her wear before, but which became her immensely.

A wan smile curved her lips. ''Would it be impertinent of me to say I am glad?'' she asked. ''I assure you, Sir Malcolm, I am completely aware of the witlessness of my behavior.''

''And I of mine.'' He dropped his gaze. His cravat seemed too tight. He tugged at it uncomfortably. ''I hope you will forgive me.''

''Of course.''

For a moment Malcolm's mind reeled with the memory of Phoebe's breast in his palm and her soft lips pressed, achingly sweet, against his. He shook his head and forced a breath deep into his lungs. He tried not to think of how velvety her skin had felt, or how delicious she had tasted.

Though he could not say it, he had found nothing at all wrong with her behavior, given the fact that she'd been responding to his touch. No, it was her going to the bachelor fete at all with which he took issue.

"Sir Malcolm?" Phoebe asked at length, when he did not speak. "What was it you wished to say to me?"

Malcolm looked up and felt as if he were tumbling deep into her bottomless blue eyes. Desperately he tried to remember the plan he had concocted the night before, tried to formulate the phrases he'd practiced before she became convinced he was a witless fool. "I ... I believe ... That is ... I think ..."

Her beautiful mouth slipped upward again in an irrepressible grin. "Sir Malcolm, I do not think I have ever known you to be at a loss for words. Whatever you have to say to me, it must be truly terrifying."

Malcolm gave himself another fierce mental shake. When he felt composed, he said quickly, "What I have to say to you may come as a shock, Miss Lawton. Please do not be alarmed, for I have given the matter careful consideration."

Her smile faded, and her expression grew serious. "I shall. While we may not always see eye to eye, I assure you that I have always respected your opinions."

"Thank you." He drew a breath. "I know how badly you wish to be a part of my search for the Eye of Horus."

She went very still. She clenched her hands, which rested in her lap, so tightly they turned white, but she remained silent.

"I believe there is a way you can do so."

Her face lit up. She opened her mouth, obviously overcome with curiosity and delight.

Malcolm held up his hand. "One moment, Miss Lawton. Give me time to explain before you say anything."

She clamped her mouth shut, but her brilliant blue eyes still danced with excitement.

He suddenly froze, unable to continue. His voice

seemed trapped in his throat. His mouth went dry. "May I have a drink of water?" he croaked at last.

"Of course. Would you prefer brandy?"

Although it was still very early in the day, Malcolm felt no compunction at accepting. "Please."

Phoebe moved gracefully to a long cherrywood sideboard, withdrew a large crystal decanter, and poured out a generous amount of its contents. She carried the brimming glass over to Malcolm and placed it in his hand. He tossed off the brandy in two large gulps, then handed the glass back.

Phoebe carried it back to the sideboard and returned to the settee. "Now, sir, please tell me your plan."

A fiery burn, which he attributed to the alcohol, rose from Malcolm's chest, ran up his neck, and made his cheeks prickle. He had not known this would be so difficult. Irritated with himself, he pushed his spectacles up firmly and almost growled his next words. "Will you agree to be my fiancée, Miss Lawton?"

Phoebe's entire body went rigid. She pressed one hand to her chest. Her eyes flew open to an astonishing size, and her mouth formed a perfect O. "I beg your pardon? I do not believe I heard you aright."

Now that the words were out, Malcolm's reticence faded. "I feel it would be best if you acted as my betrothed during our search."

"Acted?" Her mouth drooped.

"Yes. It would be a mock engagement. Until we have solved the mystery, you understand. Then you would print a retraction in the *Times,* and we—you," he amended quickly, realizing that, since he was still doomed by the amulet's curse, he would be lucky to survive long enough to complete his quest, "will go on with your life as before."

Phoebe's silence seemed to stretch into eternity. "Perhaps you might tell me why you think such a drastic step necessary," she said at length. "I do not see why we could not work together without pretending to be promised."

Malcolm felt a heaviness in his chest. He should have

known she would want nothing to do with a crippled fool such as he. She would undoubtedly be embarrassed by such a masquerade. He looked away and tried to ignore the sickness he felt in the pit of his stomach. "Forgive me. I suddenly realize it would not suit. It was an outrageous suggestion. Let us forget I ever mentioned it."

Grabbing his hat, gloves, and cane, he rose. Before he could go a step, Phoebe jumped to her feet and put a hand on his arm. "Please, Sir Malcolm, sit down. I would hear more of this plan."

Though thoroughly humiliated, he complied. "I did not wish to cause offense," he assured. "I was trying to think of a way we could spend as much time together as will be required to bring our investigation to a successful close, without causing comment by the ton. You surely must be aware that all a gentleman needs to do is take a female driving several times, or pay special attention to her during a ball or some such nonsense, for people to think something is afoot—and people are always willing to believe the worst. My suggestion that we pretend to be betrothed was primarily so that your reputation would not be harmed."

Phoebe gazed at him expressionlessly. "I see. So that is the only reason you want me to act as your betrothed?"

Though that was not true, not by a league, since Malcolm wanted nothing in the world more than to lay his heart and his hand and all his worldly goods at her feet in all sincerity, he nodded vigorously, eager to put her mind at rest.

"Most assuredly," he lied. "And you would need have no fear that I would pressure you to marry me once the search was over. You see, I am to take a voyage to Zanzibar very soon." The reason sounded lame, but was the best he could think of at such short notice. "My friend Lord Cullen and I have had the expedition planned for some time."

He watched her face intently for any nuance of emotion. He knew that, despite Phoebe's embarrassment over the previous night's events, she would be highly unlikely to cease her own investigation. Thus, he knew that unless he were present during that investigation, to keep a watchful eye on her, she would undoubtedly soon be neck-deep in danger once again.

Bowing her head, Phoebe seemed to study her deep yellow morning gown as if fascinated by its tiny flowered print. Finally, she lifted her gaze.

15

Phoebe studied the baronet gravely, hoping the throbbing pain in her heart was not visible on her face. When Sir Malcolm had first suggested their engagement, she had felt an overwhelming rush of happiness. Upon hearing his assurance that he had proposed merely until the investigation was completed, however, a polar wind had blown through her soul, freezing her heart.

Memories of the time they had spent together flashed into her mind like pieces of a montage: Seeing Sir Malcolm for the first time on the steps of the London Metropolitan Museum. Admiring his crooked grin and unruly cowlick. His stunned expression on the night of the attempted burglary, as he had seen her standing in the partially open sarcophagus. And the white-hot desire from the night before, that had made his lovely hazel eyes glow like embers.

From that experience she knew he desired her. He simply did not want to marry her.

He very likely did not want to marry a woman as eccentric and willful as she. Or as crudely passionate. Most men, she knew, preferred women who were compliant and easily molded into their idea of a perfect wife. They certainly did not want a woman who could not control her lust. Taking these facts into consideration, she could not blame the baronet for not wanting her, for she was not compliant nor easily molded nor physically cold.

Upon returning home the night before, she had doubted she would be able to sleep. However, the moment her head touched the pillow she had drifted straight into a dream. A dream in which she and Sir Malcolm had still lain on the circular bed in Lord Deauville's townhouse. A dream in which the baronet had not pulled away so abruptly, but had continued touching her, stroking her, loving her.

The dream had ended with a sudden, piercing pleasure. Phoebe had awakened gasping and drenched with perspiration. Her limbs had been drained of strength, and an exquisite lethargy had clung to her muscles for hours. She had lain awake, thinking of Sir Malcolm and wondering what scathing things he would have to say to her on the morrow.

She had not dreamed it would be this.

She looked at his face. He was watching her intently, his brow screwed up and his eyes narrowed behind the lenses of his spectacles. He had certainly made no secret of his sincere desire that the charade be short-lived. Would he be shocked to learn that she longed to be his betrothed, but in reality rather than in imagination? Would he be sorry he had ever suggested this masquerade?

Swallowing her pain, she refused to allow his roundabout rebuff to hurt too badly. The thing that mattered, she told herself firmly, was that if she accepted his offer she might still have a chance to obtain the Eye of Horus, and to keep it from being destroyed. And that was really why she had started all this nonsense to begin with.

Thus, both her, and Sir Malcolm's, feelings (or lack of them) were not to the point. She looked him squarely in the eye. "I accept your plan."

The drawing room door opened. Matty strode into the room like an avenging angel. "Phoebe! What are you about, being in here like this, unchaperoned, with a gentleman? I was unable to sleep and rose rather early this morning, and was just coming down the stairs when

Mames informed me we had company. You should have called me, immediately. This is most improper.''

As Phoebe opened her mouth to object, Sir Malcolm stood and bowed over Matty's hand. Phoebe clamped her mouth shut again, more than willing to let the baronet explain the situation.

"It is all right, Miss Stoat," Sir Malcolm said smoothly as he straightened. "A bit of privacy was necessary for what I needed to say to . . . to Phoebe."

He glanced in Phoebe's direction. She felt a quick thrill at hearing her Christian name on his lips. He made it sound so special, so beautiful. She remembered hearing him say it during that intimate moment on Lord Deauville's bed, and shivered with recollected pleasure.

"What?" Matty's eyes grew round with sudden comprehension. "What?"

Phoebe also stood. "Sir Malcolm has asked me to marry him, Matty. I have accepted his offer."

Matty beamed. Clapping her hands together like a child at Christmas, she said blissfully, "Oh, Phoebe!" Then she reached up and kissed Sir Malcolm on the cheek. "Oh, sir! How wonderful! When is the happy day?"

"We have not yet decided," Sir Malcolm replied lightly. "We want to give ourselves a bit more time to become better acquainted."

Matty's smile faltered, but then she nodded. "And so you should."

"I was thinking, Phoebe," Sir Malcolm said then with a pointed glance, "that we might attend the earl of Bumstead's house party, two days hence. He has an estate some ten miles out of town. The party is only for two days—half a day coming and going, and a full day there—so we would not miss much of the remainder of the Season." He looked back at Matty. "Naturally we would also want Miss Stoat to attend. My uncle Thomas wishes to go, as well."

"Lord Bumstead," Phoebe said, catching on quickly. "He is one of the board members of the London Metropolitan Museum, is he not?"

"Precisely. That is part of the reason I thought you might find his house party interesting. He has a superb collection of antiquities. It would be interesting to see if he has added anything . . . new, lately."

"Yes, it would." Phoebe smiled. "I think attending his house party is a splendid idea. What say you, Matty?"

"I would be delighted. Oh, my dears," the older woman gushed, "I am so happy. Possibly even as happy as the two of you."

Phoebe gazed at Sir Malcolm. Was she happy? No. But she would enjoy the baronet's company for as long as she could. And hopefully by the time their mock betrothal ended, the Eye of Horus would be in her possession. That should do something to assuage her grief at losing Sir Malcolm. And even if it did not, at least the amulet would be safe.

The officially betrothed couple left London two days later. During the last two nights they had been wined and dined and feted at fully nine different entertainments, until both were heartily sick of hearing the words "you are just perfect for each other" and "I just know you will be so happy," since both knew this would not be the end result of their engagement and both, though ignorant of each other's true feelings, regretted this fact bitterly.

Phoebe and Matty rode in Sir Malcolm's luxurious carriage with his uncle, Lord Thomas, during the two-hour journey. Their maids and the two men's valets rode in a smaller vehicle behind.

Phoebe quickly found riding with Lord Thomas tiresome. That gentleman, already deeply asleep when the two ladies stepped into the carriage, had roused just long enough for a greeting and then slipped right back into dreamland. No sooner had his head tipped against the seat than he had begun snoring, great strident peals that Phoebe was sure must have been louder than all the cannons fired at Waterloo.

She desperately wished she and Matty had taken the Lawton carriage, but Sir Malcolm had rightly suggested that Lord Bumstead's other guests would no doubt be expecting the newly betrothed couple to arrive in the same party. And Matty did not seem to mind Lord Thomas's snoring, anyway.

Sir Malcolm rode alongside the carriage on a spirited black mare with a white blaze on her forehead and one white sock. Phoebe envied him this masculine freedom, for the day was bright and warm with a balmy breeze from the south. She suspected, however, that he had ridden his horse merely to avoid riding inside the carriage with her.

Though she could not help being miffed by his unwillingness to travel inside the vehicle, she could not completely blame him. Due to one of the celebratory entertainments, she had not reached her bed 'til 4 a.m. the previous night, and even though she was exhausted, she had been unable to relax. After much tossing and turning she had finally nodded off at 6 a.m. only to awaken again at eight. As a result, she had been markedly snippy all morning.

She gazed at Sir Malcolm out of the carriage window, admiring his seat on the black mare. He had no trouble controlling the lively horse, his fine, supple hands, covered by gloves of the finest tanned leather, tightening almost imperceptibly on the reins whenever the mare grew contrary.

The baronet's cane hung, suspended by two leather loops, alongside his saddle. His long, muscular legs were encased in supple buckskin leather breeches and black top boots, and his shoulders seemed as broad as a mountain beneath his new coat of hunter-green superfine wool. A high-crowned hat tipped over his eyes, shading them from the bright morning sun.

At that moment Lord Thomas woke briefly, grunted, changed position, and resumed snoring even louder than ever. Phoebe rolled her eyes and tried to tune him out by contemplating the past two nights, and the subsequent public launching of her and Sir Malcolm's mock betrothal.

Much of the two evenings had been spent dancing at

everything except the waltz, which they had not repeated after their single, exhilarating attempt at the Simmons's ball. But no matter what activity they were participating in, each time Phoebe had looked at Sir Malcolm she had found herself recalling the way he had held her in his arms at Lord Deauville's, and the scorching desire in his sparkling hazel eyes.

Finally she drew her attention away from the baronet and tried to concentrate on the shred of needlework she had brought along. She picked through her assortment of brilliantly colored silk threads, but could not concentrate on them. How, she wondered exasperatedly, could she concentrate on anything while being assaulted by Lord Thomas's stentorian snores?

Putting the embroidery away she allowed her gaze to wander back to Sir Malcolm. The baronet had crossed one leg over the pommel of his saddle and appeared deeply interested in a book. The slender volume was bound in burgundy leather and had a long braided bookmark. Now and then Sir Malcolm turned a page.

Phoebe sighed and wished she could be as oblivious to his presence as he was to hers.

Contrary to Phoebe's impression, Malcolm was having a dashedly difficult time concentrating on his book. He was not a little annoyed at himself for the way his gaze continually strayed over to the carriage. Though he held his neck rigid, at times his gaze skimmed across a line, flew right off the page, and landed inexorably on Phoebe, who seemed totally heedless to his presence.

He growled softly and concentrated harder.

She walks in beauty, like the night of cloudless climes and starry skies.

Beauty. Yes, by God, she did walk in beauty. Again he found himself staring at Phoebe. He jerked his errant gaze back to the page.

And all that's best of dark and bright meet in her aspect and her eyes.

Her eyes. Her lovely, forget-me-not blue eyes. As he

watched she brushed a stray golden curl away from her face, exposing her perfect, patrician profile. He sighed softly, then looked back at his book.

Thus mellowed to that tender light which heaven to gaudy day denies.

Instantly he remembered almost kissing her beneath the starry sky at Lord Simmons's ball. How her eyes had sparkled in the moonlight.

He supposed he could always inquire as to the ladies' comfort. His lips tightened as he hastily discarded this notion. He had already inquired several times. Any more and both the women and Lord Thomas would begin to think him daft.

Without finishing Byron's poem, he turned the page with an annoyed snap. Though the muscles surrounding his eyes ached with the strain of keeping his gaze from drifting back to Phoebe, he managed to keep his attention on the printed sheet—but did not comprehend a word.

He reached out, massaged his knee, crossed in front of him to relieve the pressure on its joint. It throbbed quite painfully this morning, due to the previous two nights' entertainments. But he would not have missed a moment of that time. The chance to stand at Phoebe's side and be congratulated on their betrothal, sham though it was, had seemed like a wonderful dream. And dancing with her, even though his knee was now presenting him with the consequences, had been truly delightful.

Clearing his throat and shaking his head, he blinked and then read on.

The time I've lost in wooing, in watching and pursuing the light, that lies in woman's eyes, has been my heart's undoing.

That was God's truth, he thought wryly. His heart would never be the same again. It was almost a relief to realize that he did not have long to live, and thus did not have long to miss Phoebe once their false betrothal was at an end.

And are those follies going? And is my proud heart growing too cold or wise for brilliant eyes again to set it glowing? No,—vain, alas! th' endeavor from bonds so sweet to sever;—poor wisdom's chance against a glance is now as weak as ever.

By the time he finished the poem his heart was throbbing with such an aching loneliness that he could read no more. This morning in his library the poems had seemed inane, simple enough to be read without much concentration. Even they, however, proved too much for his addled mind, especially since they babbled on endlessly about love, so that when he finally managed to complete a poem, its words inevitably called up images of Phoebe. Her hair, her skin, her eyes. The velvety softness of her breast in his palm and against his lips—

Stop thinking about her, damn it! She'll never belong to you! You're a dead man! And even if you weren't fated to lose your life, she would have no use for a crippled bookworm.

Ignoring the pain in his heart, he hauled his thoughts away from Phoebe for what must have been the thousandth time. Lowering his leg stiffly, he carefully laid the braided bookmark in the center of his book and placed the slim volume in his coat pocket. Forbidding himself a backward glance, he urged his mare into a canter and rode fifty feet ahead of the carriage for the remainder of the trip.

They arrived at Lord Bumstead's estate at just after 2 p.m. After Sir Malcolm had ridden out of sight Phoebe had stuffed her ears with silk threads and thus managed to ignore Lord Thomas's thunderous snoring long enough to doze off herself. She awoke when the carriage drew to a halt on the circular, pea-graveled drive. She was faintly aware that the vehicle containing the maids and valets had driven on around to the side of the house, probably to unload its occupants at the servants' entrance.

Rubbing her eyes, Phoebe studied Lord Bumstead's country estate. It was a lovely house, constructed of dark gray stone—two stories and a ground floor. Four broad columns, and at least twenty wide, gleaming windows graced its front. A man and woman stood on the half-

moon-shaped limestone steps. Phoebe assumed they were
the master and lady of the manor.

The man wore a dark blue coat, pristine white shirt
and cravat, and buff pantaloons tucked into glossy black
Wellingtons. The lady at his side, with rose-colored ribands threaded through her dusky curls, was beautiful in a
frock of pale, minty green with tiny roses embroidered
along its hem and web-fine lace at its sleeves and
neckline.

Then Phoebe's gaze was drawn to the couple's feet. She
leaned forward, eyes wide with astonishment.

16

Phoebe blinked in amazement as sixteen toy poodles dashed round and round Lord and Lady Bumstead's legs, barking frenziedly. Each of the tiny dogs, standing not more than ten inches high at the shoulder, had been dyed a different color. Intricate designs had been cut into their curly hair: rainbows, clouds, sunbursts, moons, and stars. One of them had even been dyed red, white, and blue, and was adorned with an excellent rendition of the British flag.

The carriage gave an abrupt jerk as the horses drawing the vehicle objected to the dogs' presence. Phoebe caught her breath as she was thrown back against the leather carriage squabs, and Matty emitted a surprised cry as her novel flew out of her hands and landed on the seat beside Lord Thomas.

Sir Malcolm's uncle had awakened at the same time as Phoebe, and unlike the way she felt, he looked rested and refreshed. He handed the book back to Matty, along with a smile. Then he opened the carriage window and thrust his head out.

"My, what lovely animals," he said cheerfully. "Just see that pretty lavender one. It would match my new suit of evening clothes to perfection. I wonder if its owner would consider loaning it to me. I have always been fond of purple.''

Matty beamed at Sir Malcolm's uncle, whose bald head shone in the mid-afternoon light. He was garbed in a suit of lime-green superfine, with a waistcoat of embroidered puce silk. ''Really?'' Matty exclaimed. ''So have I!''

Phoebe glanced back out of the window as Lady Bumstead snapped her fingers. Most of the dogs returned to the countess's feet and lay down obediently, though each looked ready to spring to action at a word from their mistress.

''Mimi, Fifi, Pippi, come here,'' the lady of the manor said sharply to those animals that had not obeyed her command. ''Gigi, Lili, side. You too, Dizi, come now. Dizi! I said *now!*''

A footman in white and gold livery ran forward, opened the carriage door, and lowered the step. As Phoebe and Matty were gathering their belongings, Lord Thomas preceded them out of the vehicle. Then the footman stepped forward and offered his arm to Phoebe, who gripped it and stepped down to the ground. Before the servant could offer his services to Matty, however, Lord Thomas hurried to help the older woman.

Phoebe looked around for Sir Malcolm. The baronet was dismounting from his black mare. After withdrawing his cane from its sling, he affectionately rubbed the horse's face. Then he turned and walked, limping slightly, toward his three traveling companions. Tipping his fine beaver hat back on his head and pushing up his spectacles, he smiled at Phoebe crookedly, as if faintly embarrassed at having been observed while petting his mount.

Phoebe felt a fond glow in her heart, and, at the same time, a sudden pang of sorrow that made her swallow and blink back tears. What a fine man he was, she thought ruefully. Someday he would make a lucky woman a superb husband. A chaste, compliant, nonimpulsive woman.

The poodles, seeing Sir Malcolm's approach, again jumped to their feet and began barking stridently. Several ran forward, teeth bared like gleaming white needles, their bulging eyes blazing with fury. The designs carved into their fur stood on end. While not terribly frightening, they were nevertheless as menacing as toy poodles could be.

Visibly taken aback, Sir Malcolm stopped, looking surprised and uncertain. The countess smiled apologetically and brought the dogs back to heel. The baronet resumed his approach as the countess and the earl moved down the manor steps. Sir Malcolm and Lord Thomas shook the earl's hand.

"Lord Bumstead," Sir Malcolm said amiably. "It is so kind of you to include us in your house party. We have been looking forward to it. And thank you for not allowing your dogs to eat me. Rather ferocious, for such small creatures, aren't they?"

Lord Bumstead laughed. "They belong to my wife, the little wretches. Don't be offended by their bad tempers. They dislike me even more than they seem to dislike you. One never knows who they will accept.

"I made the mistake of purchasing the first pair as a wedding gift for Madeline four years ago, and the flock—don't you think they look like tiny, exotic sheep with all that curly hair?—keeps expanding. Every time one produces a litter I mean to insist my wife get rid of some of them, but each time I see her cuddle the tiny newborn monsters in her arms I cannot bring myself to enforce my intentions.

"But welcome to The Meadows. I am pleased you could come, since the party was such a spur-of-the-moment idea. Madeline," he said fondly, taking his lady's hand, "is plagued with sudden fits of enthusiasm."

"Is she?" Sir Malcolm said interestedly. He glanced at Phoebe. "I know someone who fits that description exactly."

Phoebe blushed and turned her attention to Lady Bumstead. The countess looked much younger than her husband. The earl appeared about forty-five, while his wife could not be much above Phoebe's age.

Lady Bumstead smiled. "Welcome," she said, taking

Sir Malcolm and Lord Thomas's hands and then kissing first Phoebe, and then Matty, on both cheeks.

The poodles tipped their heads as one and watched this interaction for a moment with glittering black eyes before turning their baleful glares back to Sir Malcolm. Lord Thomas, on the other hand, was readily accepted by the dogs. He bent down to distribute pats on each colorful head, lingering over the lavender one, which had flopped onto its back to have its sensitive belly scratched by anyone who would oblige.

"We are so pleased to have you here," Lady Bumstead said sincerely. "We have planned many entertainments—probably far too many for a mere two-day visit."

Phoebe liked the countess immediately, and found herself hoping Lord Bumstead had not stolen the Eye of Horus. "Your home is very beautiful," she said. "My own family estate was sold years ago. Since I am the last of my line, I had not troubled myself with buying a replacement. But, seeing The Meadows, I am nearly convinced to dash out and purchase one just like it."

Lady Bumstead looked surprised. "There is no need now, surely, for you to purchase an estate."

"Why is that?"

"Surely Sir Malcolm already owns several."

Phoebe flushed hotly. "Oh. Yes, I suppose he does."

One of the poodles, with daffodils shaved into its curly, saffron-yellow fur, put its paws up on the countess's mint-green skirt and yipped shrilly until she picked it up and tucked it beneath her arm. Then Lady Bumstead said, "I was so pleased to hear about your happy news."

Phoebe nodded, feeling angry with herself for going along with the betrothal hoax. Somehow it did not seem right to fool this charming lady. It seemed to Phoebe as if she were a fly caught in a web, and that each time she answered another curious question or comment, she entangled herself still further. She could not imagine how she would word her retraction to the *Times*, when the time came to back out of the betrothal. She hoped Matty, or even Sir Malcolm, would know how to phrase it.

"Thank you, my lady," she stammered. "Malcolm and I are fortunate to have so many friends to wish us well."

"Please, you must call me Madeline. And I shall call you Phoebe and Matty—we are all on a first-name basis here."

"We will be honored," Matty replied.

The countess took both women by the arms. Sending a tenderly scolding glance toward her husband, who was discussing the Roman ruins on the estate grounds with a deeply interested Sir Malcolm and a rather vapid-looking Lord Thomas, Lady Bumstead shrugged and led the ladies into the house.

"Since it appears we have been forgotten," she said, "let us go in out of the sun before we ruin our complexions."

As if on cue the sixteen toy poodles jumped up and scampered through the door. They seemed to know exactly where their mistress was headed. As Lady Bumstead led the way into an aqua and gold drawing room, the dogs scattered about on the floor like brilliantly colored confetti.

Seeing Phoebe's amused grin, Lady Bumstead remarked, "I am very fond of my dogs, but I maintain firm control over them at all times. It is necessary since there are so many of them. It would be impossible to allow all of them indoors, if they were not well behaved. They are not allowed on the furniture, so if you see them on a chair or settee, please push them off, and tell Sir Malcolm to do the same."

Phoebe tried to imagine the baronet bullying the little beasts, but could not. Somehow Sir Malcolm did not seem the kind of man who had a power complex and a need to lord his superiority over simple beasts. She thought about him stroking his mare's nose, and smiled. "I shall."

Lady Bumstead led Phoebe and Matty over to a small cluster of women who were chattering amongst themselves like a troop of monkeys. "Our number is now complete, ladies," she said convivially. "For those of you who are not acquainted with them, please allow me to present Miss

Phoebe Lawton, newly betrothed to Sir Malcolm Forbes, and Miss Mathilde Stoat, Phoebe's cousin.''

After they spent a few minutes getting acquainted with the other female guests, the countess escorted Phoebe and Matty to their rooms. Matty was in the suite next to Phoebe. The other unmarried women were also in that wing, while the married couples and single men were in another wing altogether. Phoebe frowned at this, wondering where she would meet Sir Malcolm that night, so they could go forward with their investigation.

After tea, all of the women retired to their rooms for naps. Phoebe was unable to sleep, and quickly found herself getting bored. Rising, she pinned her hair into a loose bun at the nape of her neck, dressed herself in a cerulean-blue afternoon gown of butterfly-soft muslin trimmed with white Russian lace, a small, stylish bonnet with a white feather, white, ankle-height walking boots and matching kidskin gloves, and went back downstairs. Finding no one to talk to, she walked through the outer salon doors, intent on exploring the estate's lovely formal gardens.

She wandered down gravel pathways, enjoying the multitude of colors and smells, for three quarters of an hour. Lord and Lady Bumstead, she decided at length, surely must have the finest gardens (and obviously gardeners) in all of England.

Once, in a distant clearing, she saw a group of the gentlemen playing cricket, and several times she saw flashes of color that turned out to be Lady Bumstead's ''flock'' of poodles. They approached Phoebe, wagging their tails and begging for pats, and then ran off again. She hoped Sir Malcolm did not happen upon them as she doubted that, since the dogs seemed to have taken an immediate dislike to him, his unescorted presence would be so readily accepted as hers.

Soon thereafter she discovered a boxwood maze. As she meandered through the lush corridors, she marveled at the size of the bushes. They were nearly twelve feet high and, since Phoebe knew that boxwood grew so slowly it almost seemed motionless year after year, she decided the bushes must have been over a hundred years old.

Leaving the maze, she turned left and unexpectedly found herself in the middle of a huge wildflower garden. It had been left quite untamed, and sprawled across several acres in a profusion of hues and scents. Widely interspersed with willow, ash, and dogwood trees, it was quite the loveliest garden she had seen all afternoon.

She was so engrossed in exploring it that she almost stumbled over Sir Malcolm where he knelt on one knee beside a bunch of forget-me-nots. His sandy-brown hair was ruffled by the breeze, and he was studying the bright blue flowers with an oddly poignant expression. His hat, gloves, and ebony walking stick lay on the grass beside him. The cane's cobra head gleamed in the sunlight.

Phoebe felt a quick burst of pleasure at finding him there. "Sir Malcolm," she exclaimed. "How delightful to find you here. You quite took me by surprise."

Hearing Phoebe's melodious voice, Malcolm thought the sound must have been a continuation of his daydream. His mind registered that the voice had come from slightly behind and to the right, so he turned his head in that direction. He gazed up into the same eyes he'd been dreaming about, once again acknowledging their similarity to the flowers in front of him. Then his gaze wandered blissfully to the utter perfection of Phoebe's gently curving shape, garbed in soft blue muslin and framed against the background of the clear sky. The feather in her flirtatious bonnet fluttered in the breeze.

When the vision moved and cleared its throat, Malcolm started violently, realizing that this was no figment of his overly active imagination. "Phoebe!" he burst out. "I did not hear you come down the path."

She smiled. "I could see that. You seemed quite enthralled with your thoughts."

He grinned crookedly and pushed his glasses up with one forefinger. He brushed a hand through his hair to smooth it, in case his cowlick was standing up. Then, putting his hands on his knees, he raised himself to his feet. "Of that, dear lady," he replied, "I can assure you."

Phoebe's brows drew together as if she wondered what he meant. Then she seemed to dismiss her curiosity, and looked around. "What are you doing here? It seems an odd place to find a gentleman. Especially on his knees. I would have thought you would be with the other guests."

"I have always been fond of gardening. I have a fine perennial flower garden at my townhouse, and was interested to see what varieties the Bumsteads grow here. However, do not think me antisocial. I spent several hours playing cricket. My uncle is still playing, I believe. I simply grew bored with the game and decided to explore."

Phoebe nodded. "I know precisely what you mean. The other ladies were entertaining for a time, but gossip and cards and needlework is interesting for just so long. And then they all wanted to take naps, and I could not sleep." She added dolefully, "Just another of my undesirable traits, I suppose."

"Undesirable? How so?"

"Oh, it just seems rather unfeminine, or at least improper, not to need a nap when all the other ladies are spending the afternoon languishing on their beds."

Malcolm laughed. "Well, I do not know about that. It would seem rather foolish to lie there staring at the ceiling when you could be outside enjoying this lovely summer day." He thought she brightened visibly. "But are you not even slightly tired? I'd have expected you to be weary after journeying here this morning."

"Not particularly. It was a short ride. I noticed you read during much of the trip. What was it that held your attention so firmly?" As the words left her mouth, her cheeks blushed rosily.

He wanted to tell her that it was she, not any book, that had occupied his thoughts during the ride. But he answered, "A copy of Byron's poems. Would you like to read it?"

"Yes, I would," she replied. "In case I have another

bout of sleeplessness and am unable to escape to this beautiful garden.''

"I shall give you the book this evening. The poems are lovely, if you like that sort of thing, as I do. Almost as lovely as—'' He broke off and cleared his throat. ''Almost as lovely as this garden.''

"Thank you. Actually," she confided then with a little smile, "I did not try very hard to nap with the other ladies. I cannot imagine sleeping away such a glorious afternoon. And I am so glad I found you. I was wondering where you were, as well as how to get you alone to discuss this evening's search plans. We had not discussed where we were to meet tonight, after everyone else is abed.''

Malcolm studied her smiling face for a moment, concluding that he liked her in blue more than any other color. "I planned to take you aside this evening, after supper. I am assuming that if the earl has the Eye of Horus, he will very likely be storing it with the rest of his Egyptian collection, which is housed in a building here on the estate grounds. However, in case he is not keeping it there, while my fellow visitors played billiards I searched most of the house, including his lordship's library safe. I found nothing.''

Phoebe shook her head in obvious amazement. ''Are you certain you are not a professional jewel thief, Sir Malcolm? You seem to have a remarkable knack for sneaking in and out of locked places.''

"At the risk of disappointing you," he replied with a disparaging chuckle, "I must admit that I am nothing more than an archaeologist and a scholar with a penchant for exploring places that are often off-limits. You know, like tombs, or other historical areas that are not open to the general public—although I have not indulged in that particular pastime for well over a year. As for where we shall meet this evening, I do not think it wise for you to be walking about unescorted after dark, so I will come to your room.''

"At what hour?''

Malcolm gazed at Phoebe's face, struck by the rosy

flush on her creamy cheeks and the excited glow in her
eyes. Then he caught his wandering thoughts and forced
his mind back to the topic of conversation. "Two a.m.
That should give everyone a chance to get to sleep"—he
paused—"or to get wherever they plan to spend the
night."

Phoebe's brows lifted. "Whatever do you mean?"

He cleared his throat, deciding it was best not to say
anything that would remind her of their near-tryst in Lord
Deauville's bedroom. "Nothing." To change the subject,
he added, "Wear the darkest gown you own. Just in case
we run across someone else up at that hour, we want to
be as inconspicuous as possible."

As intended, she was instantly diverted. "Yes, most
assuredly." Her blue eyes twinkled. "Sir Malcolm, I must
confess I was having misgivings about our masquerading
as a betrothed couple. But even though there have been a
few uncomfortable moments, I would not have missed this
for the world."

Malcolm's mouth tightened as he wondered why she
found it uncomfortable posing as his fiancée. Possibly she
felt embarrassed at being paired with such an eccentric,
crippled man as he. But he was determined not to wallow
in self-pity; he wanted, rather, to enjoy the time he had
with her. Though she would not be his for long, he intended to savor every moment they were together.

"I am glad, Phoebe." He loved the way her name rolled
off his tongue. While he knew he should call her Miss
Lawton when they were out of earshot of those they were
hoaxing, he could not deny himself this innocent pleasure.
"I remember your complaining about how women are always left out of life's adventures. I hope by the time our
investigation is over, you will have something grand to
look back upon in future years."

Then, before he could stop himself, he stooped and
broke off a spray of forget-me-nots and tucked it just
above her left ear, between her silky blond hair and her
bonnet. He grinned as he noticed how the low bun at the
back of her neck had come loose and her golden hair was

spilling past her slender waist in a gleaming honey-gilt wave. Then his smile faltered.

Phoebe was gazing at him, the color in her eyes echoed by the sky-blue flowers in her hair. She looked strangely sad. She stared, unsmiling, into his eyes.

Malcolm hastily suppressed an urge to take her in his arms, to hold her close, to ask her what troubled her, to kiss away her forlorn expression. Instead, needing something to do with his hands, he picked up his hat and gloves and cobra-handled walking stick from where they lay in the grass.

"Come," he said gruffly, pulling on his gloves and setting his beaver hat on his head. "Let us go back to the house. It will soon be time to change for dinner. I don't know whether or not you are aware of it, but we've come quite a distance from the manor."

Phoebe did not reply, but laid her gloved fingers on his forearm and let him lead her up the gravel path. As he hung his cane over his other arm, Malcolm could not help noticing that she did not remove the flowers from her hair, even when they saw Lord and Lady Bumstead strolling toward them, or when that couple glanced at the blossoms and smiled. And though he knew his happiness would not last forever, he did not even try to squelch the warm glow that kindled around his heart.

17

Phoebe and Matty walked down the main staircase toward the drawing room where the guests were to meet before dinner.

Sir Malcolm had, as promised, delivered the slim, leather-bound volume of poetry into Phoebe's hands before she had gone to her chamber to dress for the evening meal. The poetry was beautiful, although it had a distressing tendency to call the baronet to mind. Finally, because the rhymes made her heart ache so, she had been forced to put the book away, but not before tucking the spray of forget-me-nots Sir Malcolm had placed in her hair between the volume's pages.

Matty, Phoebe noticed as they continued toward the drawing room, must have discovered a new shade of purple at one of the milliners. The color of her gown fell somewhere between mauve and fuschia. The hue looked very well with Matty's fine eyes. Phoebe said as much and the older woman blushed becomingly, which made Phoebe wonder if perhaps Matty had met someone interesting at the house party.

After a great deal of consideration, Phoebe had worn a new dinner gown of teal-blue watered silk. Edged with tiny silver beads, its skirt was banded by three wide rows of lace that matched the silver shawl slung over her arms.

Long silver gloves covered her arms, and were in turn covered with numerous bracelets inlaid with Chinese turquoise. More of the gems, mounted in platinum, were placed around her throat and also dangled from her earlobes. A large stone nestled at the center of her bodice, just between her breasts.

Tribble had dressed Phoebe's hair a la Aphrodite, so that the long yellow curls were caught up with a blue bandeau but draped down her back in a stream of gold. Small ringlets fell over her brow and around her ears. On her forehead rested a dainty tiara, studded with tiny diamonds and turquoise chips.

As they entered the drawing room, Sir Malcolm, standing near the fireplace and speaking to Lord Bumstead, turned and smiled at Phoebe. Behind his spectacles his hazel eyes darkened approvingly. Excusing himself, he left Lord Bumstead and walked toward her. Phoebe was relieved to see that he was limping less than earlier. He had apparently left his walking stick in his room, for it was not with him.

Matty had wandered off; Phoebe noticed that the older woman did indeed place herself strategically near a gentleman—Sir Malcolm's uncle, Lord Thomas! Astonishingly, their clothing was almost a perfect match. Matty wore her mauve and Lord Thomas was garbed in what could only have been the lavender ensemble he'd mentioned upon first seeing the rainbow of poodles.

"Phoebe," Sir Malcolm said softly as he took her hand, drawing her attention back to him, "you look utterly stunning."

The warmth in his expression made Phoebe want to laugh with joy, but she contented herself with a smile. Glancing at the baronet's clothing, a coat of black wool that fitted his broad shoulders like a second skin, a shirt and cravat so white as to be almost blinding, pantaloons of pale gray, clocked stockings, and leather slippers, she replied lightly, "Not nearly so stunning as you, sir."

To her delight Sir Malcolm smiled his familiar crooked

grin and flushed. "I do?" he asked with ingenuous plea-sure. "No one has ever said that to me before."

Phoebe was pleased she had been the first. Glancing toward a green and gold brocade settee, liberally covered with poodles, she said, "Shall we sit down? I believe we have ten minutes before dinner. Madeline told me that we were to keep the dogs off the furniture, so she will not think us rude if we appropriate their chair."

Sir Malcolm nodded. As they neared the settee, he put out a hand to push the dogs away. The poodle with the British flag carved into its fur reared up, jowls pulled away from its needle-sharp teeth in a miniature snarl. It sank its fangs deep into Sir Malcolm's palm. The baronet jerked away with a curse that made several ladies blush. Then he looked around, mortified.

"Oh, I am sorry," he said through gritted teeth. "Pray forgive my language."

Phoebe glared at the offending dog and shoved it off of the settee. "Shame on you! Get away, you hateful thing!" she scolded. Then she took Sir Malcolm's hand and in-spected the bite.

Lady Bumstead, who had just entered the room, rushed toward them. "I am so sorry, Sir Malcolm," she said in a distressed voice. "I cannot believe Dizi did that to you. He has always been such a little darling. Of course, he does dislike my husband more than any of the others do. Please, come with me and I will tend to your wound."

Phoebe forced a smile, though she felt like clubbing Dizi over his small head. "Apparently he took an instant dislike to Malcolm, too. You remember how he growled when we arrived. Animals do that, sometimes. Take an instant dislike, I mean." She followed closely on Lady Bumstead and Malcolm's heels as they left the room.

When the countess had dressed the baronet's wound with a special ointment she had made with herbs from her personal herb garden, the three of them returned to the salon and everyone went in to dinner. Despite the unpleas-ant occurrence, the meal, with its vast array of delicious removes, was a splendid affair.

Everything glittered and sparkled in the candlelight: the ladies' gems, the gentlemen's tie pins and cufflinks, the full-length mirrors that ran the entire length of the chamber as well as the ceiling, the Irish leaded crystal, the gleaming gold flatware. Even Lady Bumstead's poodles had exchanged their everyday collars for gold links encrusted with gems that matched the colors of their fur. The dogs hovered around the countess's chair, neatly catching the scraps she tossed down when the earl wasn't looking.

After the meal and a short chat, Phoebe retired early in order to sleep for a few hours before she and Sir Malcolm searched Lord Bumstead's Egyptian gallery. When Matty asked if she felt unwell, Phoebe remarked that she must have been especially tired because she had missed the nap the rest of the ladies had enjoyed that afternoon.

She rose again at one o'clock in the morning and, after pinning her hair atop her head in a thick braid, dressed in the ensemble she'd gathered earlier. Several times she heard an odd scuffling sound outside her door. Finally, hearing it yet again, she unlatched the door and peered out into the hall.

Her visitor was the same poodle that had bitten Sir Malcolm. "Get out of here, you nasty thing," Phoebe hissed. The patriotic-looking dog wagged its tail so wildly she thought he would shake it off. Unable to resist his delight at seeing her, she smiled reluctantly. "Please go away, Dizi. Sir Malcolm will be here soon, and I do not want you and he to have another altercation."

Upon hearing the baronet's name, the little dog snarled and emitted a high-pitched yip. Then he turned and dashed off down the hall. Laughing reluctantly, Phoebe closed her door.

Shortly before 2 a.m. there was a light knock on the bedchamber door. She hurried to open it. The hallway was lit by wall sconces, spaced every twenty feet or so, that illuminated Sir Malcolm's tall figure. He held his cobra-handled cane in one hand, wore no hat or gloves, and, from his linen shirt, his low leather shoes, and his snug leather breeches, was dressed entirely in black.

"You are early," Phoebe said softly so those in the nearby suites would not overhear. "I am so glad. I have been so excited for the last hour that I have been unable to sit still."

The baronet did not reply. His gaze skimmed rapidly up and down her body. Then he pushed past her and closed the door firmly behind him. His mouth was a tight, disapproving line. "Where the devil did you get those clothes?" he demanded.

Phoebe's smile faltered. She glanced down at herself.

True, her dark gray homespun shirt was a bit tight across her breasts, her black breeches were somewhat snug around her thighs, and her slippers were a bit tattered, but she had thought she looked rather well. She had even dared to hope Sir Malcolm would consider her attractive. Apparently she had been horribly wrong.

"You told me to wear something dark, but I had nothing suitable," she said anxiously. "So while everyone else was chatting or playing cards in the salon, I slipped out to the stables and borrowed some clothing from one of the grooms."

"And what if the boy finds them missing before our search is completed? Do you realize that most grooms have only one set of clothes, and that a second is a luxury? Do you think he will just shrug and forget about their loss? And did you even pause to think that sneaking into a male servant's sleeping quarters might have been dangerous?"

"I—"

He cursed. "Of course you did not," he finished for her. "Woman, you are no end of trouble."

Phoebe swallowed the lump in her throat. "I left a guinea in the clothes' place. I thought that even if the groom did find them missing he would say nothing but merely think it was a guest's prank and thank his lucky stars for the gold."

"Let us hope so. Damn! I should never have let you coerce me into allowing you to join this endeavor," Sir Malcolm muttered. "But I suppose if I left you here tonight you'd just go off on your own search and get into more mischief. Without my protection, God knows what you'd get involved in.''

Stung, Phoebe retorted hotly, ''I did not coerce you into anything, sir. 'Twas not I who insinuated myself into your plans. 'Twas not I who insisted you'd make a mess of things. You call me impulsive, do you? Well, sir, if I am impulsive, then you are a staid, overly conventional, ridiculously restrained prig. I'll have you know, I have survived for twenty-five years perfectly fine without your 'protection.' Perhaps we should call off this horrid mock-betrothal, here and now.''

Malcolm felt himself go red in the face. When he'd looked down at Phoebe's shapely figure wrapped tightly in a male servant's clothing, his heart (as well as a few solely male anatomical parts) had pounded and throbbed so violently he'd thought he was going to be ripped apart by its quaking. He had had to clench his hands to keep from running them over her entire luscious length.

To his experienced eye—experience acquired during the countless times he'd viewed harems and dancing girls in his lifetime—Phoebe had the most perfect body he'd ever seen. Truly divine. And, God knew why, but somehow the dingy stable-boy's garb was even more enticing than the miniscule black dress she'd worn at Lord Deauville's bachelor fete.

Her waist was small enough to be spanned by two hands, her breasts high and firm beneath the form-fitting homespun shirt. Her bones were slender and delicate. In short, her shape was enough to drive a sane man mad, and an insane man even more crazy with lust.

She had no business dressing thus, enticing him like Eve had tempted Adam. If he were a different sort of man, she would already have lost more than she could afford, during one of her past impetuous sprees.

But *this*—this was sheer madness. The woman had no more sense than a plump house mouse blithely parading itself before a wraith-thin alley cat.

Nevertheless, still feeling responsible for her welfare

and, if the truth be known, loathe to deny himself the opportunity of seeing her garbed so deliciously, after a struggle he managed to hide his overset emotions and shook his head. "I do not think that would be a good idea. I . . . I apologize. I should not have spoken so hastily. Your clothing is . . . it is fine." Certain that if he kept looking at her he would also touch her, he turned on his heel, opened the bedchamber door, peered out to make certain the hallway was deserted, and moved out of the room.

Phoebe scampered after him. She caught up in a few steps, although she had to trot to keep from falling behind as he walked swiftly through the quiet house. They went up and down several halls, climbed and descended innumerable flights of stairs, and finally paused beside a small, unimposing wooden door. A single candle burned in a plain sconce on the wall.

"Where . . . are . . . we?" Phoebe gasped, pressing the flat of one hand against her chest. Her braided hair seemed to glow in the faint candlelight. It looked like an intricately designed crown, the way it wrapped around her finely shaped head.

Malcolm felt a twinge of remorse. Phoebe's legs (those superbly shapely limbs) were much shorter than his. He was being a beast, and all because he was having trouble controlling his normally sanguine nature. But it was so damned hard not to pull her into his arms, sweep her off to his rooms, and make mad, passionate love to her.

God knew why, but with Phoebe he constantly seemed on the verge of losing all sense of perspective, every shred of his usually abundant self-restraint.

He stood still for a few moments to give her a chance to catch her breath. "On the western side of the manor. This door leads directly outside. I discovered it during my explorations this afternoon. It is fortunate that The Meadows is such a huge place, for all day I saw only two servants and easily evaded them.

"From this door we will go directly to Lord Bumstead's Egyptian gallery. You may have seen the edifice during your walk this afternoon.'' He chuckled suddenly. ''You know, Lord Bumstead offered to show us his collection the next time we visit The Meadows, since, as his lordship apologized, we will not have an opportunity to see them during this visit, due to all of the countess's planned entertainments.''

Phoebe grinned. Then her brow puckered thoughtfully. ''Is the gallery the building shaped like a Steppe pyramid?''

''That's right.'' Glancing at her, he noticed she was no longer panting. ''You have a good eye. I can tell your knowledge of history is quite extensive. I'll wager you'd do very well on an expedition.''

Her eyes shone at his approbation. ''Truly? I *have* read a great deal. Especially about different building styles, as they seem such an important part of correctly deducing archaeological dates.''

''They are, indeed.'' Malcolm opened the small door and they walked through, closing it firmly behind them. He already knew the door locked automatically from the inside, but was confident he could open it again when they were ready to return to their rooms. ''The gallery is this way.''

A full moon shone down through the limbs of tall trees, casting strange shadows on the grass. A fierce wind swept through the gardens and made the trees sway eerily. It sounded, Malcolm thought uneasily, like an old man moaning his last breath.

He and Phoebe moved speedily across the lawn, then walked through an extensive topiary, filled with trees and bushes cut in the forms of deer, rabbits, chess pieces, and one very real-looking, menacing wolf. As they passed this last figure, Phoebe moved closer to Malcolm. Given her previously mentioned ideas about needing no man in her life, he felt a warmth flow through his limbs at the realization that she had turned to him for comfort, albeit of the mildest kind.

When they reached the Egyptian gallery, which was indeed shaped like a steppe pyramid, with smaller blocks piled on increasingly larger ones, Malcolm removed a small, golden object from his pocket and inserted it into the gallery's lock.

"What is that?" Phoebe asked softly.

"One of your hairpins. You dropped it in my library. I was going to return it, but then I thought 'finders-keepers.' It has come in very handy during my other explorations, both here and at Lord Deauville's."

She watched, looking suitably impressed when the lock gave a faint click and the door handle turned in his fingers. Replacing the hairpin in his pocket, he removed two beeswax candles from the same place and handed one to Phoebe.

He smiled. "After you, my dear."

Putting a hand against her warm back, he urged her into the building. When he had closed the door behind them, he proceeded to light both of their candles, then raised his above his head.

18

"My God." Phoebe also held her candle aloft. "I thought my own collection was extensive, but this is absolutely amazing!"

Malcolm glanced around and nodded. "Quite impressive. I've only seen one collection to top it. And that one got so large its owner began donating any objects he discovered to museums."

Phoebe, gaping at the magnificence around her, did not seem to hear. She walked to the center of the room and turned in a complete circle. With difficulty Malcolm kept his gaze off of his lovely companion's backside, but not before noticing that her bottom was almost a perfect inverted heart. Exercising an iron will, he looked away.

Flickers of light fell upon piles and piles of ancient treasure. In one corner of the room, a complete Egyptian chariot stood ready, as if all it required to dash along the Nile were a pair of plumed horses and one royal prince. Hanging on the walls, huge gold funerary masks glittered and sparkled, embedded with jewels. Sarcophagi, these of stone and much heavier than the imitation coffin at the London Metropolitan Museum, were arranged row upon row. They were unopened and, Malcolm knew, undoubtedly still contained their mummified occupants.

Intricately wrought thrones from which pharaohs had

judged their subjects, lapis-inlaid statues of men, women, children, and animals, polished bronze hand-mirrors, solid gold chest pieces and wide bracelets of the same precious metal, huge frieze-painted chunks no doubt removed directly from the walls of ancient tombs, animal-shaped beds with high, uncomfortable-looking headrests, all this and more lay strewn artfully about the chamber in royal splendor.

When Phoebe's glazed eyes finally locked with Malcolm's, he smiled tenderly. "I'd love to see your face during a tomb opening," he said. "That is, if you didn't pass out cold after one glance. Shall we begin searching?"

She nodded.

After leaning his cane against the door, Malcolm pointed to the other side of the chamber. "You start over there. We'll work our way toward the center of the room."

They examined the treasure carefully, going over every square inch of the gallery, but finally met in the middle of the pyramid empty-handed. Phoebe sighed and blew out her candle. She handed it to Malcolm, who put it back in his pocket.

"Well," she said ruefully, "I am sorry we did not find the Eye, but I am glad Madeline's husband is apparently not the culprit. I like her very much and would have hated to cause her pain by exposing Lord Bumstead as a thief. Still, as you said earlier, I suppose the earl could have the Eye hidden elsewhere. Have you given any thought to what we will do if we search all three of the suspected board members' homes and find nothing?"

"I have tried not to." Malcolm led the way back to the main door. There, he blew out his own candle and placed it, too, in his pocket. Opening the door, he adjusted his spectacles and, unable to resist, watched Phoebe start across the lawn. Her shapely hips swayed from side to side in an innocently provocative manner.

Grinning appreciatively, Malcolm picked up his cane and hung it over one arm. Then he followed, catching up and tucking her arm through his. She looked up and smiled wearily. "You look tired," he observed.

"I am. But it was wonderful exploring Lord Bumstead's collection, was it not? I never thought to see so many artifacts in one place. And all of them in such unspoiled condition."

He nodded, thinking of his own collection. "It is true that the earl's collection is magnificent. But, you know, I have changed my opinion about endless gathering of artifacts for one's personal gratification. I used to think it perfectly acceptable to bring so many wonderful things home and lock them away for my own delectation. I no longer do."

"What do you think should be done, instead?"

"I think the treasures should stay in their own countries unless sold by their countries' governments. The people of Egypt should decide whether a certain piece leaves their native land, not a few privileged souls. And those artifacts that do come to England should be shared with our countrymen in museums or such."

Phoebe looked uncertain. "How can you feel that way and keep your own collection private? You say it is quite extensive."

"It is. I plan, when I have time, to catalogue my pieces and allow the English government to put them on display at various museums around Britain. Also, I think digs should be run by professionals, not greedy bastards who are in such a hurry that they ruin a hundred exquisite pieces for each one they excavate successfully."

Phoebe winced. "My God. I did not know."

"Few people do. It is hardly a fact the guilty parties want to have spread about London. However, you need not worry about Lord Bumstead's collection being gathered that way. I know for a fact that he is one of the most dedicated archaeologists in England. Those who have worked with him in Egypt say he is excruciatingly meticulous."

"That is a relief. But, all the same, I shall never look at another artifact in the same manner again."

Lowering his eyebrows, Malcolm said regretfully, "I should have said nothing. I hope I have not ruined museums for you. Although I like to think of myself as cautious and restrained, sometimes I speak with a sad lack of forethought.''

She smiled faintly. ''Do not worry, Sir Malcolm. You could not ruin my love of exhibits. Although I understand and share your desire for safer excavating conditions, I fear I enjoy seeing artifacts too much to stop going to museums simply because something truly unfortunate happened when the pieces were collected. Does that make me sound hypocritical?''

''No. It makes you sound honest. Most women of my acquaintance would have said exactly what they thought I wanted to hear—trading honesty for my own gratification.''

Phoebe's smile faded as if she were considering his words and found herself lacking because of them. They had reached the topiary and were passing through its fancifully carved bushes when she paused, tilted her head to one side, and squinted as if listening intently. ''Do you hear something?''

Slowly Malcolm also became aware of a peculiar sound. At first faint, then louder, the shrill baying of dogs grew louder with each passing second. A pale shadow streaked toward them, across the wide lawn.

Phoebe stifled a cry. She raised her gaze. ''Dear God. It's Madeline's poodles! What are we going to do?''

The dogs drew ever nearer. Despite their diminutive size, Malcolm knew that so many of them together could be quite dangerous. In the back of his mind he remembered hearing tales of old women who kept large numbers of small dogs as pets. The dogs, through some odd set of circumstances, became overexcited and killed their owners. It sounded impossible, but it was solid fact that the events had truly taken place.

While he and Phoebe could undoubtedly evade most of the poodles, some would surely manage to inflict damage. And, though he knew the animals would primarily attack him, they would very likely also attack Phoebe if only out of the frenzy of the moment—like those poor old women.

He had to protect Phoebe.

Heart racing, he looked from right to left for cover. "We can't go back to the gallery, because they'd catch us before we got halfway. And none of the nearby tree branches look low enough to climb." Then he pointed with the tip of his cane. "Over there. See that wall? We must reach it."

Catching her hand in his, he began running. His legs were far longer than hers, and he knew it was hard for her to keep up with his long strides. She stumbled and almost went down, but he pulled her back to her feet. For her own sake, he dared not slow his pace.

Behind, the barking peaked 'til it was almost deafening. The high-pitched yelps stabbed against Malcolm's eardrums like shards of glass. Phoebe laughed hysterically. On the heels of laughter came a frightened sob. Malcolm knew her laughter was more from terror than hilarity.

"We are not going to make it." Tears streamed down her cheeks. "My God," she panted, "we are going to be killed by *toy poodles!* Sweet heaven," she gasped, "if we do manage to get out of this, no one will ever believe our tale."

To his relief, he saw that they were almost to the wall. "We'll make it. Keep running."

Then his heart fell. The wall looked much higher than it had from a distance. He was glad he had worn the same low leather shoes, with ultra-thin soles, that he'd worn during previous midnight adventures all over the world, as they made it very easy to grip rough surfaces and cracks and thus simplified climbing over obstructions.

But would Phoebe be able to climb the wall, since, to the best of his knowledge, she had no experience at this kind of thing? He could not leave that to chance, even though in helping her he might be savagely bitten. He would have to see that she got up first.

When they reached the wall he once more tucked his cane under his arm. Putting his hands around Phoebe's waist, he hefted her high into the air with almost super human strength. She put her hands on top of the wall and he thrust upward until her elbows lay across the top stones. Planting his hands on her firm buttocks, he shoved her up the rest of the way.

Then, taking his cane in one hand and laying his own palms on the top of the wall, he managed to lift his body halfway up just as the poodles swarmed around his legs like a hive of outraged, multicolored wasps.

The dogs snarled and yapped viciously, snapping their tiny jaws like a school of hungry piranhas he'd once seen while sailing up the Amazon River. One of the native porters had fallen into the water, and within seconds nothing remained of his body but bare bones in a blood-clouded pool. Malcolm had no doubt that the poodles' jaws could easily inflict as much damage as the fish.

Then Phoebe cried out and began searching the pockets of her gray homespun shirt. "I put a few biscuits in here in case we got hungry during our search. God, I hope I didn't drop them while we were running. No! Here they are!"

Hungry? Malcolm thought dimly. A dry laugh escaped his lips. She was hungry at a time like this? Good Lord.

But he understood as Phoebe shouted, "Here boys, here girls, get the lovely biscuits!"

Cocking her arm, she brought it forward again, forcefully hurling a fistful of small objects into the distance. The poodles hesitated in their barking, lifted tiny muzzles to the air, sniffed, and took off at a dead run in the direction of the scattered food.

Setting the toe of his leather shoe in a crack between the rocks in the wall, Malcolm began pulling himself the rest of the way up the wall. Quite abruptly he felt a stabbing pain in his left calf, and a weight hanging from his leg. Turning his head, he saw that one of the dogs had not been fooled into giving up the chase. The English flag was emblazoned across the poodle's flanks.

The tiny dog wrenched its head from side to side, suspended from Malcolm's leg like a trout from a line. With its jowels pulled back from its teeth it seemed, almost, to be grinning. Apparently it had not gotten enough of his blood earlier that evening to be satisfied, but was enjoying itself heartily now.

Malcolm lifted his cane and swung, catching the little dog across its snout. The poodle opened its mouth, let out a startled yelp, and dropped to the ground like a piece of overripe fruit falling from a tree. Malcolm swung himself up onto the wall just as the dog leapt to its feet and, apparently unharmed, resumed its frenzied attack.

With a final glare at the poodle, Malcolm jumped to the ground on the other side of the wall. Holding out his arms, he helped Phoebe descend as well.

"I heard the dog yelp," she said anxiously. "What happened?"

"Are you concerned about that little monster?" he asked incredulously.

"Do not be ridiculous. I merely want to know what happened. I was worried about *you*."

"Little bastard latched onto my leg like a damned leech," Malcolm informed her. He heard her sharp intake of breath.

"Dizi bit you *again?* Are you hurt badly?"

"Let's just say I'm lucky miniature poodles have equally miniature mouths. Had the dog been a hound I'd still be back there, most likely in pieces." He grinned down at her, quite pleased by her concern. "Nevertheless, it could have been much worse. Thanks to you, the rest of the pack was not available to help the little wretch. Tricking them into going after your food was brilliant, and extremely well timed. You have my heartfelt thanks."

Phoebe returned his smile. "You are most welcome."

"Come," he said then, experimentally putting his weight on his wounded leg. Except for a sharp stinging, it did not hurt excessively to walk on it. "We must get back to the manor before a caretaker comes to see what all the fuss was about. We've been fortunate to run into only dogs thus far."

She nodded and they began moving. In a few moments Malcolm realized that they were not far from the house at all, despite climbing over the wall. He'd thought the devia-

tion from their original route had taken them far out of
their way, but apparently he'd gotten turned around somehow in all the excitement.

The wall ended abruptly after several hundred feet.
Phoebe glanced nervously back in the direction they'd
come. "I hope the dogs do not know the wall stops here."

"I think if they did they'd have been here to meet us,"
Malcolm replied gruffly. His bitten leg had started burning
as if twenty or thirty white-hot needles had been jabbed
into his flesh. Really, though, it seemed ridiculous to allow
such a small bite to cause him pain.

Seeing his grimace, Phoebe said firmly, "I want to see
that leg. The wound could be much worse than you think.
The dog may have torn the flesh badly when he was hanging on and twisting his head back and forth."

"Thank you, but I will tend it myself when I get to
my room."

Her determined expression did not falter.

Gazing down at her, Malcolm sighed. Despite his leg's
discomfort, he felt a familiar, pleasant ache begin to throb
in his lower parts. He shifted, hoping she would not notice
how she affected him. It was simple to hide his emotions;
it was less easy to hide his body's preferences.

The thought of being alone with her in her bedchamber
was almost too wonderful to resist, since their betrothal
would soon be at an end, and, shortly thereafter or possibly
even before, he would be six feet underground. He hoped
sincerely his end would come after they had recovered
and destroyed the Eye of Horus, since he wanted to know,
before he died, that the amulet could never hurt Phoebe.

"All right," he agreed at last, hating himself for his
weakness but promising himself that nothing more than a
medical examination would ensue.

When they reached the same door through which they'd
sneaked out of the manor, Malcolm fished Phoebe's hairpin out of his pocket and deftly picked the lock. They
moved back toward the private suites, seeing no one.

Idly, Malcolm wondered who from the party was enjoying the evening with whom. He forced his mind to be

blank, conscious that such thoughts would only lead to imaginings of himself with Phoebe and make it very difficult to maintain a businesslike demeanor when he had her alone in her chambers.

When they reached Phoebe's rooms she opened her door and ushered Malcolm inside. He leaned his cane by the door and stood there, watching her uncertainly as both his leg, and his manhood, throbbed. He knew he had been mad to come here. Utterly, unmistakably mad. It was just that, somehow, the thought of being alone with Phoebe had blown away his common sense like woodsmoke on the wind.

Going to the fireplace, Phoebe stoked up the coals until yellow and blue flames licked the grate. She pointed to a chair not far away from the fire. "Sit down."

While he did so, she rose from the hearth, poured water from a Sevres pitcher into a matching basin, found several towels and a bar of sweetly scented soap, and knelt by his side. Malcolm removed his low leather slippers, then tensed as her hands rose and moved toward his leg.

"You know," she said, "Dizi would not have been able to bite you, had you been wearing boots. Do your slippers serve some special purpose?"

He quickly explained.

"I see." Her fingers trembled faintly, hovering over his limb. She said then, "I do not know how to lift your pant leg without causing you pain, but must remove it in order to wash your wound. Do you have any suggestions?"

Since he knew it would be madness to completely remove his breeches for her examination, Malcolm said in a voice that sounded much too loud, "Get me a pair of scissors. I will cut the fabric away."

She nodded and went to the same sewing box he'd seen her carry onto the carriage for the journey to the Bumstead estate. Rummaging around for a moment, she pulled forth a pair of silver scissors in the shape of a heron.

When Malcolm reached for them, she shook her head. "I will do it. You sit back and relax."

He almost laughed aloud at the absurdity of her statement.

Relax, when her butterfly-soft touch was causing him far more pain than the dog's bite, simply because he knew that, very soon, he would never experience her touch again?

Relax, when shudders of desire were coursing through his body like lava streaming down the side of an active volcano?

Relax, when he wanted nothing more than to finish what he had started in the bedchamber at Lord Deauville's townhouse?

No doubt about it. He had been positively mad to come here.

His entire body vibrated with unfulfilled longing, but he tried to let his leg muscles go limp to keep Phoebe from realizing the effect she had on him. It seemed to work. In seconds she had split the fabric of his black breeches and spread the material wide.

The wound was still hidden by his stocking. Phoebe took a deep breath and pulled the silk stocking down around his ankle. Her fingers were gentle against his damaged flesh, but it stung nonetheless. She probed the wound, washing away the blood and carefully soaping and rinsing the entire area. From his vantage point Malcolm could see two ragged rows of punctures. Again he thanked his lucky stars that he had been bitten by a toy poodle, rather than a hound.

Finally Phoebe looked up. "I think you will live. The flesh was not torn too badly, although I believe you will be sore for a few days. Be certain that your valet changes this dressing every day, when we get back to London."

Malcolm's heart thudded wildly against his chest when he saw that her eyes were filled with stark longing. Dear heaven, was it possible that she wanted him as much as he wanted her? Or was she merely reacting to the stress of the situation, now that the danger was past?

Firelight danced over the delicate bones of her face, shading and accentuating her elegant features and her long, slender neck. Her worn stable-boy's shirt gaped at the throat. He could just see the gentle swell of her bosom, which rose and fell with each breath she took.

It took all of his willpower to keep from lifting her onto his lap and claiming her soft lips with his own. He knew he could not touch her without carrying her to her soft bed and finishing what he had begun at Lord Deauville's townhouse. And he could not do that and still release her from their betrothal—although he wanted to make love to her more than he wanted to continue breathing.

Lifting a hand, he ran his fingers over her thick golden braid, which had come unpinned and now lay across one slender shoulder. It felt like corded silk. He'd never felt anything remotely as soft—except, perhaps, the velvety skin of her breast.

Phoebe's eyes were wide and luminous, her full lips moist and slightly parted. "It is terrible that you were bitten on the same leg as your earlier injury. Is your knee paining you, as well?"

"A bit. But I believe that is still from dancing, before we came to The Meadows."

"Oh. Well, perhaps if I massaged it, it would feel better." Putting down her medical materials, she returned her hand to his leg. Slowly, ever so slowly, her fingers began climbing his calf. When they reached his knee, Malcolm felt himself begin to shake.

His hand shot out and grabbed hers. "Thank you, but I do not think that would be advisable." Jumping up, he grabbed his stocking, pushed down his shredded pant leg, put his leather slipper back on his bare foot, and crossed the room to stand by the door.

Phoebe did not rise from her knees, but gazed after him with a forlorn expression. He longed to return to her side, but he did not dare. Though she obviously wanted him, he knew she was too innocent to be aware of what fulfilling that desire entailed. And, though he cursed his inconvenient conscience, he was not such a cad as to take advantage of her.

She did not want this betrothal. She did not want to be

married. She had made that perfectly clear during their
first conversation. And he loved her too much to force
her hand.

"Thank you, Phoebe," he said at last. "The pain is
less . . ." He broke off, realizing that he scarcely felt his
wound at all, because the agony in his heart was so in-
tense. "I can hardly feel where I was bitten," he amended
huskily. Out of sheer habit, he pushed up his spectacles.
Then he picked up his cane and retreated to the lonely
safety of his own bedchamber.

19

They left The Meadows late the following day.

Lady Bumstead, standing near the carriage, remarked how her poor little Dizi had a lump the size of a goose egg on his head. She was carrying the wounded poodle under one arm, and when she neared Sir Malcolm the dog bared its teeth and began growling and barking ferociously. The countess hastily bade her new friends goodbye and carried the beast away before it could jump out of her arms and bite Sir Malcolm, as it so desperately wanted to, a third time.

It was evening when they reached London. After Sir Malcolm and Lord Thomas had seen the ladies settled at their own home and then left for 102 Prichard Place, the women immediately sought their beds. Phoebe was extremely tired from the previous night's activities, and Matty seemed strangely quiet and eager to be alone.

When Phoebe made her way to her room, she noticed that Tribble had already unpacked several trunks, including the one in which Phoebe had placed Sir Malcolm's copy of Byron's poems. She had forgotten to return the slim volume, but promised herself she would do so as soon as possible. Thus, the day turned into night.

* * *

The following morning at the stroke of ten, Malcolm knocked on Phoebe's townhouse door with enough fervor to wake the dead. The butler, Mames, granted him entrance, and Sir Malcolm, after hanging his cane over his arm, moved into the hall.

As Mames was conducting him to the salon, a sound caused Malcolm to look to the left, where he saw Phoebe descending the main staircase. She was patting her hair into place, and her raised arms brought the fullness of her bosom up for Malcolm's inspection. He sucked in his breath appreciatively, then forced his rapt gaze to leave her lush endowments and rise to her lovely face.

"Phoebe," he said, "good morning. Dressing your own hair again? Is your maid ill, like my poor coachman and tiger?"

"Yes," she replied, looking quite astonished at seeing him standing in her hall at such an early hour. She also seemed a bit nervous to see him; probably, Malcolm realized, because of their near-intimate encounter in her bedchamber at The Meadows.

"It must have been the fish they all ate when we stopped for luncheon at the Golden Quail yesterday morning," she added. "Matty is feeling a bit queasy, as well. I am glad you and I did not eat it. How is Lord Thomas?"

"Well enough. The roast duck we three dined upon seems to have been quite fresh," Malcolm said impatiently, slapping his leather gloves against his thigh and fiddling with the brim of his hat, which he had removed immediately upon seeing Phoebe. He was eager to get the niceties out of the way in order to progress to the matter that had brought him to her side so early.

When she appeared satisfied that her hair would stay in its chignon, Phoebe lowered her arms and daintily brushed out the green and white floral print skirts of her morning dress. Her hands were very white, and looked as soft as the wing of a dove. Malcolm wished he could touch her, but satisfied himself with gazing at her fresh loveliness.

"What brings you here so early, sir?" Phoebe asked then.

Mames seemed to have become accustomed to the baronet's presence in the townhouse at all hours and thus did not bat an eye at seeing that gentleman conversing with Miss Lawton at what most reasonable souls would conceivably consider an ungodly hour. He reached for Malcolm's tall beaver hat, his gloves, and his ebony cane. Malcolm relinquished them absently, still concentrating on Phoebe, and the servant disappeared without a word.

Malcolm took Phoebe's arm and led her into the drawing room. "We must find costumes," he said abruptly. "I have been racking my brain trying to figure out how to get us both into Mr. Montgomery Milhouse's residence. As you know, he is not a member of the ton, and thus entertains a different set of people than we."

Phoebe settled herself on the embroidered cushion of a cross-backed Chippendale chair and eyed him expectantly.

"As luck would have it," he continued, "Mr. Milhouse is giving a masquerade ball this evening. Since he is the last of our suspects we absolutely must gain access to that ball. Mr. Milhouse, while as rich as Croesus, is in trade, and thus neither of us are likely to receive invitations. But I believe we may sneak in if we wear masks and proper attire."

Phoebe tipped her head back and laughed melodiously, but her chuckles, rather than mocking, were laced with good humor. "Good gracious, Sir Malcolm. Have you come here this early just to tell me that? Could it not have waited until later? After all, how difficult could it be to obtain masks and dominoes?"

Malcolm flushed hotly and wondered if she found him entirely obvious in his affection for her. He wanted to tell her the truth, that he had felt compelled, by an overwhelming need to see her smiling face, to rush to her side at the break of dawn, but that he had managed to suppress the desire until ten o'clock.

He said instead, "I thought we should plan our mode of attack, and did not want to waste a moment. Regular dominoes will not suffice, since the ball is to be a full costume affair.

"I confess I have absolutely no idea where Mr. Milhouse might be hiding the Eye. With Lord Deauville I knew that, if he had the amulet, it would most likely be in his safe—an entire room whose only access is a large iron door—since I have often heard him speak of entering it to ponder his treasures." He grinned briefly. "His lordship should replace his safe's lock. It took me nary ten seconds to open it, using only your hairpin. At any rate, the amulet was not there and I ended up searching the entire townhouse, to no avail.

"As for Lord Bumstead, it is common knowledge that he keeps that magnificent Egyptian gallery. If he had had the amulet, it would most likely have been there—although, as in Lord Deauville's residence, which I searched after escorting you home, I again examined the entire house rather than concentrating solely on the gallery."

"So Mr. Milhouse is our last chance," Phoebe said softly.

"Yes." Malcolm sobered. "Since the Eye was not at either house we must assume that either Mr. Montgomery Milhouse is the thief, or that we have nowhere else to look and must give up."

"God willing, that will not be necessary." Phoebe chewed her lower lip. Finally she nodded. "Sneaking into the masquerade ball does seem to be the only available avenue of attack. Where shall we meet this time?"

"I shall have my carriage at the end of your street at ten o'clock this evening. I will be standing in the bushes at your front gate, so you need not walk all that distance alone." He grinned, crookedly. "I cannot believe I am asking this, since until I met you I was a rigid stickler for propriety, but how do you plan to get away without Miss Stoat being aware of your departure?"

"I shall plead a headache." Then Phoebe frowned, thoughtfully. "Now that you mention it, speaking of changes in our basic personalities, I seem to be losing a bit of my impulsiveness and becoming a bit more cautious. For example, I am oddly nervous about tonight's endeavor, rather than excited, as I was during my own attempt at

Lord Deauville's, and our joint effort at Lord Bumstead's.''

Malcolm wondered why Phoebe's newfound prudence did not please him more. Now that he thought about it, he was not sure he wanted to change anything about her. She was so splendid, just as she was.

Before, he had been worried about her safety, and that was why he had wished she would learn more circumspection. But, he could not help thinking that, with a man at her side, she need never be in danger, even if she continued to hurl herself headlong into new experiences with the eager delight of a child.

"Cautious? How do you mean?" he asked uncertainly.

"I keep thinking about what will happen to us if we get caught. In the past, such thoughts would never have occurred to me. I felt invincible. Now I find myself carefully considering my actions.'' She laughed and amended hastily, "Some of the time, that is.''

"I suppose your newfound discretion could have something to do with nearly being eaten by a pack of poodles,'' Malcolm replied with a wan smile.

"Yes. Perhaps we are rubbing off on one another. Who knows but, given enough time, we would not become almost identical in nature.''

She frowned, and Malcolm asked, "Are you all right?''

"Yes. Or, at least, there is nothing wrong with me that will not mend itself over time,'' she answered quietly. Then she forced her lips into a weak smile. "You know, if you were to ask Lord Thomas to escort Matty to the theater this evening, as she and I were planning to see Keane play Iago, I am sure Matty would be delighted by my absence. She seems to be growing quite fond of his lordship.''

"So there is smoke coming from her direction, also,'' Malcolm said. "My uncle has spoken of little else but the wonderful Miss Stoat ever since the Bumsteads' house party. Do you smell a match in the offing?''

"One never knows. They have only known each other for four days, but I do think Matty is somewhat enamored of him." Phoebe gazed at Malcolm intently. "She is a gentle-hearted creature, Sir Malcolm. I would not want to see her hurt."

"I do not think it likely. My uncle is a fine gentleman, though not plump in the pocket. I will be more than happy to settle an income on them, if they decide to set up house. I shall tell my uncle that Miss Stoat has unluckily found herself without an escort to the play, and I make no doubt but that he shall rush to her rescue.

"So," he said then, removing his spectacles to polish their lenses, and then resettling the glasses on the bridge of his nose. "How shall we dress so that we do not lose track of each other at the masquerade ball? It's bound to be a real crush. The merchant class is enormous."

"I know just the thing," Phoebe said. The aura of sadness surrounding her seemed to vanish, and her beautiful face was illuminated by the brilliance of her smile.

As she made her way down the walk toward the road in front of her townhouse, Phoebe felt like Cleopatra going to meet her Marc Antony.

Her costume, though hastily gathered together, was nonetheless quite exquisite. At a shop in Mayfair she had found a length of gossamer-fine ivory silk, shot through with metallic threads in every color of the rainbow. She had wrapped the fabric around her body, leaving one shoulder bare. Her undergarments were faintly visible through the sheer fabric, though the silk was not so transparent as to be indecent. Along the hem of the gown she had sewn minute gold bells that tinkled musically with each step.

Her hair was covered by a shoulder-length wig of blue-black horsehair that shone beneath the gaslights lining the street. Only her eyes were visible through the gold mask that hid much of her face. Though she had no jewelry suitable for the evening, she had found a pair of gold sandals. She had also located some gold paint, and had painted her toe- and fingernails.

At her waist she wore a wide gold belt and a gold

reticule in the shape of a cat's head. Within the handbag she had placed two of Cook's apricot tarts and a few lemon candy wedges, just in case Sir Malcolm became hungry.

A slight breeze, smelling faintly of rain, rustled the bushes in front of the townhouse. Phoebe hurried down her walkway, peering nervously into the foliage. "Sir Malcolm," she called softly. "Are you there?"

She smiled as the baronet stepped out of the shadows and held out a hand. She placed her fingers in his firm, warm grip, and they walked swiftly to the end of the street, staying in the shadows to avoid curious eyes. Reaching the carriage, they climbed inside. Then both relaxed and took a few moments to study each other's attire.

Behind his own gold mask, the baronet's eyes widened. "You look magnificent, Phoebe," he said softly. "Truly like an Egyptian queen."

"Thank you, sir," Phoebe replied with a light laugh.

Sir Malcolm, too, had found gold sandals, though his shoes had slender leather straps that wrapped around his bare calves. Around his waist he wore a white linen skirt, pleated in front. His chest, deeply tanned as if he were in the habit of leaving his shirt off during excavations, was bare save for a genuinely ancient, solid-gold chest piece featuring a kneeling Isis with outspread wings. Wide golden cuffs wrapped around each of his wrists, and he had colored his hair with something that made his curls gleam like ebony satin. His cobra-headed cane lay on the seat beside him.

The only thing that did not appear genuinely ancient was his spectacles. Their lenses shone momentarily as he moved his hand to push the glasses more firmly onto his mask. But even they did not make him look ridiculous. He looked, rather, utterly majestic.

Phoebe's gaze drifted to Sir Malcolm's bare chest, which was covered by a thick mat of curly black hair. Phoebe's heart pounded so fiercely that she thought it would leap out of her body. She had never seen a man's bare torso before, but knew that if she ever did again it could not possibly be so superb as her mock-fiance's. She longed to touch his black curls, and was hard-pressed to keep her hands at her sides.

After several moments Sir Malcolm said in an edgy voice, "Do you find my attire acceptable? I hope the bare chest is not too excessive. I hear these Cit affairs are much more relaxed than tonnish gatherings. And I hope my spectacles do not look ridiculous."

"They do not," Phoebe said honestly. "You look splendid. Also, I have never seen such fantastic jewelry."

Sir Malcolm looked pleased. He reached toward the seat beside him and drew forth a flat box. "Good. I took the liberty of gathering a few more pieces and bringing them along, just in case you had none of your own to wear with your costume." He opened the case and held it toward her.

As Phoebe's gaze fell upon the glittering pile he offered so casually, she drew in her breath so sharply she coughed violently for some moments, while Sir Malcolm patted her on the back.

When she had recovered, she took the flat box and gazed at the ancient jewels, speechless. At last she closed the container regretfully and handed it back to him. "I cannot wear these things."

"Oh." He looked disappointed. "You do not like them?"

Phoebe laughed at the absurdity of his statement. "I *love* them. I have never seen anything so beautiful in my entire life. But if anything were to happen to them, I should simply die."

The baronet waved her worries aside. Reopening the box, he studied her costume for a moment, then lifted out several pieces. Raising his hands, he placed a golden circlet, from which a large cobra's head reared, onto her head. Then he drew forth earrings strung with midnight-blue lapis-lazuli beads and set them on her ears. One of the long earrings brushed her bare shoulder sensuously, and Phoebe shivered with delight.

Next he picked up a necklace much like one Phoebe had seen and lusted after at the London Metropolitan Museum. It was crafted of carnelian chips, but also contained chunks of lapis and innumerable gold beads strung on seven or eight strands. Sir Malcolm clasped it around her neck, then adjusted the strands carefully. Lastly, he set two ornate gold bracelets, much like his own although more feminine in style, on her wrists.

Then he sat back and smiled. "Perfect. You look most royal. Those jewels could have been made for you."

Phoebe's hands fluttered up to touch the necklace, but she jerked them back to her lap before they could disarrange the dainty strands Sir Malcolm had so carefully placed.

As the carriage slowed and stopped in front of Mr. Montgomery Milhouse's townhouse, Sir Malcolm climbed out, hung his cane over his elbow and offered his other arm to Phoebe. She took it, and they walked inside to the masquerade ball.

The noise inside the house was thunderous. As Sir Malcolm had suggested, many of the people at the ball were dressed in far more outlandish, and frequently more revealing, clothing than would have been found at a tonnish gathering of the same type. And, although there were a few other Egyptian nobles, none had such fantastic jewels as Phoebe and Sir Malcolm. Phoebe felt like a genuine queen, and knew her frame of mind showed in her demeanor.

They spent much of the evening wandering around the house. It was not difficult to search the residence, since there were amorous party-goers moving in and out of every room, and Phoebe and Sir Malcolm's presence was never questioned.

They found nothing, and decided to look for a safe in Mr. Milhouse's library. They found one. While Sir Malcolm opened the vault, Phoebe successfully intercepted each would-be intruder. At last the baronet came out of the library, his cane drooping dispiritedly over his arm. Phoebe immediately knew his search had not been fruitful.

Heavy of heart, they were preparing to leave the ball empty-handed when a trumpet blared. Mr. Milhouse, his

golden hair shining and his youthful eyes aglow with excitement, jumped up onto a chair to address the crowd.
He was dressed in medieval garb, and wore a doublet,
woolen hose, and had a large, starched ruff around his
neck.

"Ladies and gentlemen," he shouted over the din. "I
am delighted to have you here this evening. I hope you
are enjoying yourselves." A loud roar from the masked
party-goers made him laugh with boyish glee. "Good! I
have a surprise for you. This evening I invite you all
to inspect my newest acquisition. I recently employed a
gentleman from Bavaria to create my own waxworks. I
am told it rivals even Madame Tussaud's. If you will all
follow me, I will take you on a guided tour."

Leaping off the chair, he ran directly past Phoebe and
Sir Malcolm. Rather than be crushed by the mob swarming
after the young man, Phoebe and the baronet followed
closely on Mr. Milhouse's heels.

Their host led the way out the back door of the townhouse toward a large building. Two burly footmen, holding
flaming torches, stood beside the structure. As their master
arrived they flung open the building's large doors. Waving
his arms for his guests to follow, Mr. Milhouse vanished
inside. The crowd, including Phoebe and Sir Malcolm,
complied eagerly.

Inside, Phoebe blinked in astonishment. Although she
had visited London's public waxworks, she had never
viewed such lifelike creations as those staring back at her
now. It seemed that every famous face she'd ever seen was
present, from Marie Antoinette to the Duke of Wellington.
Princesses Caroline and Charlotte were there, as were
Beau Brummell and Lord Byron. Even a lifelike depiction
of the regent, mockingly fat, gazed down his nose at the
crowd as if he were addressing them from the balcony
at Windsor.

The crowd passed through several rooms filled with wax
figures of people from other countries, other times. Nubi-
ans, Indian swamis, red Indians, Chinese aristocrats in rich
silks, these and more were present. And when they passed

within inches of two statues that looked disturbingly like Phoebe and Sir Malcolm, dressed in Egyptian garb, Phoebe almost cried out.

There, nestled amid the folds of the beautiful Egyptian queen's wax bodice, lay the Eye of Horus.

Before Phoebe could say a word, the crowd pressed forward and the Egyptian statues were left behind. Shortly, the tour was over and Phoebe and Sir Malcolm stood outside in the cool night air. The rest of the group disappeared immediately back into Mr. Milhouse's townhouse, leaving them alone in the darkness.

"Did you see it?" Phoebe demanded.

A slow, deliciously smug grin curved Sir Malcolm's lips. "See what?" Reaching into a hidden pocket in his linen skirt, he pulled forth an object that flashed in the moonlight. "This?"

Phoebe gazed at the object silently. The Eye of Horus gazed back.

20

Before Phoebe could voice her delight, Sir Malcolm grabbed her hand, hurried along the dimly lit path, skirted the house, and made his way back to the carriage. When they reached it he paused and glanced left and right as if to be certain they were unobserved. Then he tucked his cane under his arm and held the newly recovered Eye of Horus up to the carriage lantern.

After a moment he frowned. "Something's wrong," he muttered, turning the Eye over in his hand. "Something just doesn't feel right about this amulet."

Phoebe's gaze ran the length of the shiny gold chain that glittered as if studded with diamonds. Then she studied the Eye itself. At first she noticed nothing, and when she finally did, she thought her eyes were playing tricks on her.

She removed her mask and rubbed her eyelids carefully, not wanting to smear the black kohl outlining them. When she pulled her fingers away from her eyes, the amulet still looked peculiar. Briefly she wondered, tensely, if the amulet were invoking its ancient, deadly curse, and if that could be why it appeared to waver oddly in the lamplight. She quickly dismissed this fanciful idea.

"What is wrong with it?" she demanded fretfully.

Sir Malcolm stopped squinting. To Phoebe's astonishment, given his previous terror of her touching the amulet and being stricken by the Eye's curse, he handed the necklace to her. As soon as she took it she realized why it had seemed to be shifting like the evening shadows.

She gasped. "Sir Malcolm, it's wax! Wax with glass stones and a cheap tin chain! 'Tis nothing but an imitation!"

The baronet nodded wearily. He shook his head when his postboy began descending from the carriage boot to open the door for them. Instead, he performed this service himself, then handed Phoebe, who was still gazing at the fake amulet, into the vehicle.

"It is wax," she said again, her voice trembling with shock and disappointment. "Nothing but a fake!"

"So it is." He smiled now, feebly. "Come, Phoebe. Did you really think I would hand you the genuine article?"

She shook her head. "I did wonder what you were about." A drop of blue wax, melted by the combined warmth of the carriage lanterns and human fingers, fell unheeded onto the skirt of her Egyptian costume. In a fit of pique, Phoebe opened the carriage window and threw the rapidly disintegrating amulet out into the darkness.

"Bloody hell," she whispered brokenly, absurdly close to tears. A few spilled over her eyelids and trickled down her cheeks.

Sir Malcolm removed his spectacles and his mask and dragged one large hand over his face. "God, but I'm tired. I'm tired of all of this. I wish I'd never even seen the Eye of Horus. I wish I'd never seen Pharaoh Setet II's tomb." He halted, shook his head, then continued. "No. I do not wish that. But I do wish I had not requested the amulet in return for discovering the burial site."

"Were the other artifacts not cursed, as well?" Phoebe asked tearfully.

"Not that I am aware of." He sighed, looking older than his thirty-two years. "It begins to appear that we will never recover the amulet, Phoebe. Perhaps it is time to give up our search."

Phoebe sniffed. "I was so certain this necklace was real. I was so sure we had finally found it. It would have been so brilliant to have hidden it in a wax museum. No one would have suspected it to have been genuine." She laughed harshly and wiped away the last of her tears. "No one but a pair of fools."

Sir Malcolm did not reply.

At length Phoebe asked, "What do we do now? Have we really nowhere else to look?"

Sir Malcolm gazed out of the window, apparently surveying the passing scenery although Phoebe knew this was not possible; it was too dark to see anything outside and, even if it had been daylight, the baronet still held his spectacles in one hand.

"I wish I could tell you I had some brilliant plan of action, my dear," he said dully. "But I do not. Mr. Milhouse's masquerade ball was my last hope. Since we failed to find the Eye there, I do not have the slightest clue where it might be."

"So we just give up?" Phoebe shook her head fiercely. "No. I won't. I can't. Not after all this."

Suddenly Sir Malcolm turned to look at her. His eyes, not hidden by his spectacle lenses, seemed to flicker. They narrowed to mere slits. "You know," he said slowly, "I do not think it has occurred to me until just now to wonder exactly why you are here, Phoebe. Much like I did not wonder, until the end of the day, why you had been at Mr. Grundle's office the morning he died."

She swallowed, nervously. "I am sure I do not know what you mean. I am here to help you find the Eye. I told you that I felt responsible for Mr. Grundle's death, and wished to help you recover the amulet."

"Yes, I remember that," he said softly, running his fingertips along his lips. "But I am suddenly curious. I am wondering though, if we had found the genuine Eye, would you have watched me destroy it without lifting a finger to save it? Knowing you as I have come to, I do not believe you would have allowed its destruction without a fight. Am I wrong?"

Phoebe opened her mouth to lie, but found she could not. Cheeks burning with shame, she said after a long silence, "No. You are quite correct. I intended to steal the Eye from you before you had the opportunity to destroy it. I am sorry to have misled you. Truly, I am. I am completely ashamed of returning your trust with duplicity."

"And the curse?" Sir Malcolm's gaze remained steady. "What of that?"

"I decided that even if the amulet was cursed, I was more than willing to risk my life in order to possess it. And if you were wrong, and the curse was not valid, how could I allow it to be destroyed? Oh, Sir Malcolm," she continued earnestly, "have you never seen something you were driven to own at any cost? Has nothing ever caught your eye that you would have given your very life to obtain?"

He looked deep into her eyes. Then he made a show of inspecting and putting on his spectacles. "Indeed I have," he said with a rueful smile. "But, like your wish to possess the Eye, my desires will also remain unfulfilled."

Phoebe leaned back against the leather carriage squabs. "Life is not fair, is it?" she asked wearily.

"No. But as I am sure you are already aware, it seldom is. So, Miss Lawton," Sir Malcolm said with false cheer, "have you brought anything edible with you, tonight? We were so busy searching Mr. Milhouse's house that I do not believe either of us got anything to eat. Pity, too, since I noticed a banquet table fairly groaning under a feast fit for King Henry VIII and his entire court."

Phoebe was unable to summon an answering smile. She didn't reply, but removed her cat-shaped reticule from her belt and handed it to him. He withdrew an apricot tart and lifted it halfheartedly to his lips. He took a single bite and then set the food aside.

Reaching out, he took Phoebe's hand and pulled her across the carriage aisle. Wrapping his arm around her, he tucked her head under his chin and held her close. "No matter what happens, Phoebe," he said softly, "I want you to know I have cherished our time together."

"As have I." Phoebe snuggled into the haven of his

strong embrace, feeling utterly desolate at having lost the
Eye and, now that their search was at an end, undoubtedly
the baronet as well. He was so kind, so dear to comfort
her like this. What would she do without him?

When they reached the street near Phoebe's house, he
released her. Leaving his cane in the carriage, he walked
Phoebe to her gate. There, he stopped, gazing down at her
with an inscrutable expression. His dyed curls gleamed in
the night, and his bare chest seemed impossibly broad.
Phoebe longed to caress those muscular planes, but she
did not dare.

Instead, she lifted her face to inquire when she would
see him again. She had a terrible fear that he would say
"never." She was utterly flabbergasted, thus, when he
took her in his arms and his lips came down on hers.
Then, without another word, he walked away.

Phoebe watched until he vanished into the shadows.
Finally, noticing that a carriage suspiciously like her own,
which Matty and Lord Thomas had taken to the theater,
was rounding the corner, she hurried into her townhouse
and made her way to her room. There she crawled right
into bed, not moving until Matty had peeped into the dark
chamber, believed her to be asleep, and closed the door
once again.

When Matty had gone Phoebe rose, washed the paint
from her face, and changed into a worn chenille bathrobe
with holes at the elbows. Pouring herself a glass of brandy
from an etched silver decanter on her bureau, she poked
the coals glowing in the fireplace grate, settled in a large
armchair, and relived Sir Malcolm's kiss until she fell
asleep with her feet curled under her.

When morning arrived, Phoebe awoke still in the chair.
She felt as if someone had bent her neck and spine into
a pretzel and then stomped upon it. Rising stiffly, she
discarded her favorite bathrobe in favor of a morning dress
in several shades of peach, which she donned without ring-
ing for Tribble.

She had hoped her gown, which had a lovely wool

underdress and a frothy gauze overskirt, would lighten her mood and give her cheeks some color. However, sitting before her looking glass and dressing her hair, she observed that even the vivid gown had failed to give her face a healthy glow. Her pale cheeks perfectly portrayed the heartsick pangs in her chest.

Tucking a final pin into her simple coiffure, she sighed and rose. There was no point in stalling. The sooner she finished the horrid task of placing the betrothal retraction notice in the *Times,* the better.

She would read the paper while breakfasting with Matty. Perhaps it would contain a notice, like the one she intended to send, which she could copy. If not, she would have to ask her cousin how one worded such a document. She felt ill when she thought about breaking the news about her broken engagement to Matty, especially now that Matty was enamored of Lord Thomas.

But she had no choice. There was nothing else to be done. No matter how much she wanted Sir Malcolm, he definitely did not want her. Aside from last night's kiss, he had never so much as intimated a change in his feelings. And, surely, if his embrace had signified a desire to truly marry her, he would have said something then.

No, there was nothing to be done but to send the retraction notice. She had known this pain would come. She had agreed to this venture. And she intended to keep her word, no matter how much it hurt or how much she wanted to do otherwise.

When she arrived downstairs she found Matty sitting at the table in the informal dining room. Rather than her usual plate piled high with delicious and extremely fattening morsels, the older woman appeared to be contenting herself with a few pieces of fruit and some toast. When Phoebe commented on this, Matty blushed an alarming shade of crimson.

"I"—Matty gabbled, "I was not hungry."

Phoebe stared. "You are always hungry. What is it, Matty? Is something wrong?"

"Oh, certainly not. Everything is wonderful. Listen,

Phoebe, I was thinking of going shopping this afternoon. I have decided to purchase some gowns in colors other than purple and gray. I am quite tired of those hues. I have been told—that is, I have decided—that something like rose or green or yellow, or perhaps even peach, such as you are wearing this morning, would suit me as well.''

Phoebe blinked. It was a man, obviously, that had Matty in such a dither. Lord Thomas, without a doubt. She sighed heavily. Best to wait until after Matty finished her scant breakfast to tell her about the betrothal retraction. No need to ruin both their appetites, what little there was of Matty's, anyway.

"And so they would," she agreed heartily, trying to smile as she poured a cup of coffee and picked up a bit of dry toast. "I have often thought you would look lovely in more colorful gowns."

Saying nothing more, she opened the *Times,* laid it beside her cup, and perused its pages. There was, she noticed glumly, no easily copied retraction notice. She had no choice but to ask Matty's opinion. Resignedly, she opened her mouth to voice the inquiry. However, as she began to speak, her gaze fell upon an article in the newspaper.

"Good heavens!" she cried abruptly. Dropping the piece of toast, she snatched up the paper. Rushing from the room she shouted, "Mames! Mames! Call for my carriage! Hurry!"

Matty jumped to her feet. "Phoebe! Where are you going? What about breakfast? What about a bonnet? Or a shawl? Phoebe! It looks like rain!"

"Rain be hanged, Matty!" Phoebe yelled over her shoulder. Grabbing up a pair of kidskin gloves from the hall table, she managed to pull one on, but dropped the other as she dashed down the hall and out the front door. She did not pause to retrieve it. "I must see Sir Malcolm!"

She was only slightly surprised when her cousin followed her outside, also without a bonnet and shawl, though Matty had managed to locate a pair of gloves, and climbed into the carriage beside her.

21

Malcolm, sitting at his desk in the library, was so sick at heart from considering whether Phoebe would print the betrothal retraction tomorrow or the day after, and whether or not she would feel even a twinge of regret when she did so, that he barely glanced up as the library door flew open hard enough to crash against the wall. When he did lift his gaze, his heart gave a leap and he jumped out of his chair.

"Phoebe!" he exclaimed. "What is it? What is wrong?"

She was bonnetless, her hair escaping the confines of its bun. Her peach-colored gown was rumpled, and she wore only one glove. In the other ungloved hand, she held a copy of what looked like today's edition of the *Times*. Briefly Malcolm wondered if she had come to show him the retraction, then dismissed this thought as he remembered that she had not had time to place it. She had obviously run through the house to reach his library, and was puffing so hard he could scarcely comprehend what she was saying.

"The Eye. The museum. Security. Still there."

Malcolm drew her to the emerald-green velvet armchair. Gently forcing her onto the cushion, he pulled a matching settee close, sat down on it, and took her hands. "Relax,

Phoebe. Steady. Take a deep breath. That's it. Better? Good. Now, speak slowly and tell me what all this excitement is about.''

He was deeply relieved when Phoebe smiled radiantly. He had been afraid something dreadful had happened, though he knew not what, and was nearly bowled over by the way the smile illuminated her face. He wanted, very, very badly, to kiss her sweetly curving lips.

"The museum is installing a new security system," she said breathlessly.

He raised a brow, still concentrating more on the bearer than on the news. "I do not mean to be obtuse, but what has that to do with anything?''

She made an impatient sound. Grinning almost foolishly, she pulled her hands from his and thrust the newspaper toward him. "Read the article.'' She bent forward to point with a bare finger. "Third column. There.''

Malcolm rapidly scanned the printed page. Then he lowered the paper and stared at the opposite wall. "My God,'' he said wonderingly. "Is it possible? Could we really have been so foolish as to keep searching for what was under our noses all the time?''

Phoebe laughed with unabashed delight. "Obviously we were.''

He shook his head. "The Eye was safe and sound at the museum all the time. I feel so foolish. I should have thought of this long before now. Or at the least, inquired.''

Phoebe lowered her brows. "I do not agree, sir. How could you have asked, when the amulet's disappearance—if it truly had disappeared, which now we see it had not—would have set up a violent outcry? As you said, men would have been searching everywhere, and all of them would have been candidates for its fatal sentence.''

"Possibly, but I was too quick to leap to the conclusion that someone had stolen it from Mr. Grundle, either before or after his death. In actuality, it seems he must have placed the amulet back in its new case the same morning he was killed. Or,'' he added, "I should have realized that if the amulet had truly vanished, the museum board would have set about making its own search, and would have alerted the police, who in turn would have alerted the *Times*.''

"Well." She laughed. "I suppose that is true. Except that if the Eye had genuinely disappeared, it is possible the other board members may have thought Mr. Grundle put it somewhere other than his safe for safekeeping. Then they would not have gotten upset about its disappearance, for it would have been considered misplaced, not missing.''

"Thank you for attempting to make me feel better, anyway. So,'' Malcolm mused, "we are back where we started.''

"Exactly. Now that we have discovered the Eye's whereabouts, we must simply break into the museum again and obtain the amulet. Where it was—or was not—until now is really of no relevance. Our previous searches were unnecessary, but under the circumstances—or what we thought were the circumstances—we could have acted in no other way.''

"I agree with the last part of that statement," Malcolm said. "But not the first.''

She looked puzzled. "I do not understand.''

"It is perfectly simple. This time I shall break into the museum by myself.''

"What?'' Phoebe cried, flushing angrily. "Absolutely not. We are partners.''

"Yes,'' Malcolm said soothingly. "But now that we are so close to completing our mission, we must be extra careful, and that means that one of us illegally entering the museum will have a far greater chance of success than two.''

"I disagree.''

"Phoebe, listen to me. The situation was different during our searches at Lord Bumstead's and Mr. Milhouse's houses, when you were standing lookout, but at the museum that will be unnecessary and even unwise, since two people stand a better chance of being spotted than one lone burglar.''

Phoebe obviously did not like what he was saying, but seemed to see the logic in his words. "Perhaps, but—"

"No buts. You forget I am now aware that you planned to obtain the amulet for your own collection, all along. Taking that into consideration, I am not about to allow you anywhere near it. You may not be convinced of the curse's validity, but I am. And I will not risk your life. You must be careful. There are so many of us who care about your well-being. You must not take any unnecessary chances."

"But Malcolm—"

He rushed on, not wanting to give her the chance to realize he had just told her she was important to him. "Besides that, with a new security system there is a grave danger that I will be caught. Better that, if I am apprehended, I go to Newgate alone. Therefore, I will go myself, and destroy the amulet immediately upon obtaining it. From your own admission I know that you would try to stop me. You simply cannot go, Phoebe."

She glared at him mulishly. "I will. You know I will go, Malcolm. With you, or without you."

"If you do," he said, removing his spectacles and gazing at her sincerely, "I will turn you over my knee. Don't you dare show up at the museum, Phoebe. I mean it. If you do, you will regret it."

She did not respond, but sat erect in her chair, glowering mutinously.

Malcolm raised a brow. "Phoebe? I want you to tell me you will not go."

Finally she turned her brilliant blue gaze toward him. "All right. I will not go with you," she said tonelessly.

"I have your word on that?"

"Yes."

"Good." He glanced around. "I suppose it is too much to hope that you came here this morning with your chaperone."

Her sullen frown faded. She smiled triumphantly. "Matty is even now walking in your flower garden with Lord Thomas."

Malcolm's other brow rose to join its mate. "Is she?" he inquired with interest.

Phoebe looked to her left out the library window. Malcolm followed her glance. Lord Thomas and Matty's heads were tilted together confidingly. They were strolling about the townhouse grounds.

"I hope things work out between them," Phoebe said wistfully. "Matty is such a dear, and Lord Thomas seems like a very charming man."

"He is a good man as well, though a bit undisciplined. He has a tendency to play too deep at cards. I hope your cousin is more constant. My uncle could stand a steady woman in his life."

"She will be good for him, then, if they reach an understanding," Phoebe said sincerely. "Matty has had a great steadying influence on me."

Malcolm's lips twitched with amusement.

"Well," Phoebe amended with her own grin, "she would have had, had I given her the chance. At any rate, Matty has long wished to marry and have a family."

"Unlike you," Malcolm was unable to keep from muttering, "who thinks men are of no more value than apes."

"I beg your pardon?" When Phoebe jerked her head around to look at him, he cleared his throat.

"I said, 'she's a jewel,' " he replied lamely. "Who thinks men are just great."

"Oh." She turned back to the window.

Since he was watching Phoebe's face rather than the strolling couple, he saw her eyes fly open wide. A crimson blush stained her cheeks. Her hand flew up to cover her mouth.

"Good gracious!" she gasped.

Malcolm glanced back out the window.

Standing beneath a gnarled tree, beside a high stone wall that separated the Forbes townhouse from one of its neighbors, Lord Thomas had taken Matty into his arms and was kissing her with a passion that Malcolm hadn't, in his wildest dreams, suspected his uncle possessed. While it looked quite peculiar to see the short, pudgy man stretched as high as his spindly legs would take him, embracing the tall, large-boned woman, it also looked strangely *apropos*.

"Looks like that's settled," he murmured. "I cannot wait to see what their children look like."

For some reason he did not comprehend, but thought must be from happiness at seeing her cousin's future assured, Phoebe burst into tears. She made a soft mewling sound and turned toward him. He took her in his arms and held her close.

After a time she raised her head and smiled tremulously. "I apologize. I am not usually such a watering pot. I have ruined your coat."

"That is all right. I—" Malcolm's voice broke. "I can buy a new one." His heart was aching so badly at the thought that he would soon lose Phoebe, that he wished he could weep also. He would, once he was alone, and the devil take society's definition of manly equanimity. "I am sure you are just happy for Miss Stoat and my uncle. Your pleasure at their happiness does you great credit."

Though her eyes filled again, Phoebe nodded shakily. "Yes," she whimpered as tears once more began streaming down her cheeks. "Quite. I am very, very happy for her. For both of them."

She wept for another ten minutes, but managed to collect herself by the time Matty and Lord Thomas entered the house with their news. Neither Malcolm nor Phoebe mentioned that, after tomorrow, they would no longer be facing the same wonderful future as the older pair.

Shortly thereafter the two women returned to their home; Lord Thomas went to his club to spread his news; and Malcolm, forcibly pushing the heaviness in his heart to one side for later contemplation, removed to his library to consider many things, top among which was that night's nefarious activity.

22

A heavy fog obscured much of the city as Malcolm walked down the alley behind the London Metropolitan Museum. Midway through the street he paused and surveyed the museum's rear wall. High above his head a paltry ledge ran the length of the wall before disappearing around its corner.

He began moving again until he reached a vertical drainpipe that ran up the side of the museum. The pipe stopped at the bottom of the narrow ledge, and was bolted to the brick at three-foot intervals. Malcolm put out a hand and touched the slender cylinder. It was so cold his fingers immediately numbed. It was also, due to the fog, treacherously slick.

He grimaced as he gauged the distance he would have to climb up the fragile-looking pipe in order to reach the ledge. He could not even see the top of the building, which was shrouded in fog so thick it appeared that the heavens had descended to earth. If he managed to reach the ledge without falling, he hoped to be able to reach the roof from there.

He was unable to suppress an image of his fingers slipping on the wet metal pipe and his body plummeting to the street far below. Would he reach the ledge safely, or fulfill the amulet's curse this very night? It would be supremely ironic for him to die while trying to save others from the Eye of Horus's lethal curse.

From a black satchel tied to his waist, he removed worn black leather gloves and slid them over his hands. This was not the first time he had used these gloves, although it had been a long time. They had come in handy during several other covert engagements he'd experienced during his archaeological career. It had been years, however, since he had been witless enough to attempt such a dangerous endeavor. He had thought he'd gained wisdom with his years. Evidently, he had thought wrong.

Even now, he realized glumly, if it had not been for the possibility of Phoebe's getting hold of the amulet after his death, he would probably drop this absurd notion of sneaking into the museum like a cat burglar, and leave the amulet where it lay. His entire plan of obtaining and destroying the amulet had gotten entirely out of hand. Who knew but that the amulet, if left in the museum, would remain out of innocent hands for hundreds of years? Or forever?

Still studying the icy-cold metal drainpipe, he cursed silently. This was ridiculous. He was no longer a young man, and he was dangerously out of practice at this type of clandestine rendezvous. But it all came down to one thing: Phoebe. He had to protect her, and if that meant risking his life in foolish ways, then so be it. As long as he remembered that he was doomed, anyway, climbing the wall would not seem so utterly asinine.

A slight movement at the end of the alley made him stiffen and press his body against the rough wall. He was relieved that he'd worn all black clothing, as that would make him difficult to see. He relaxed again as a sack of bones in the shape of a black cat slid, wraithlike, through the fog before being swallowed up in swirling whiteness once more.

Pushing his spectacles up firmly onto his nose, he turned back to the task at hand. He grasped the metal drainpipe and began his slippery ascent. Pressing his thin-soled, low leather shoes against the rough brick, he found to his relief that the builders had not skimped when they'd applied mortar. Though the front of the museum looked smooth enough, back here the workers had apparently not bothered to scrape away the excess cement.

Up and up he went, higher and higher, until he grasped the ledge with his fingertips and swung himself onto the narrow precipice. He saw that the roof was, as he had hoped, a mere six feet above the ledge. Raising his arms, he gripped the edge of the roof with leather-clad fingers and hefted himself up, leaving the thick curtain of fog behind. So far, so good. The weather could not be more optimum; the air was crystal clear up here, and with the thick fog bank below no one would be able to see him from the street.

In the center of the museum's roof, the stained-glass cupola that topped the Egyptian Room gleamed in the moonlight. Malcolm moved forward, cautiously, until he stood at the edge of the glass dome. His mouth tightened with concentration as he placed a slippered foot onto one of the three-inch metal struts that radiated, spokelike, out from the center of the stained-glass window.

Step by slow step he inched toward the center of the cupola, leaning forward to maintain his balance as he climbed the dome. Twice his feet slipped and he fell forward, narrowly escaping disaster. At last he stood on the metal circle surrounding the dome's clear glass, three-foot-wide center.

Removing a hammer from his satchel, he knelt and tapped lightly against the clear glass. A single shard fell to the floor below, and he winced, holding his breath. Several minutes later, when he heard no alarms, he resumed his task.

Gripping the loosened glass chips to keep them from dropping to the Egyptian Room floor, he snapped them loose and tucked them into his satchel. Bit by bit he enlarged a space just big enough for his body to squeeze through.

Through discreet inquiry that afternoon, as well as a number of freely distributed guineas, he had learned that the new security system *probably* worked through a network of sensors positioned beneath a new floor constructed of marble and faux-marble tiles. The sensors, set up at night after the museum closed its doors to the public, were rumored to work through a system of weights and pulleys that perceived an intruder's weight when inadvertently stepped upon.

Long, narrow ropes attached to each unit purportedly jerked bells in the basement, alerting a night watchman whose sole task was sitting at a desk and listening for the tinkling alarms. Thus, if the glass shard that had fallen to the floor had struck one of the new security tiles, Malcolm knew he could have counted on spending a great deal of the rest of his life either in Newgate or Australia.

At last he replaced the hammer in his bag, withdrew a rope, and tied one end of it to the circular metal strut. After forming a seat with the other end of the rope, he placed it under his hips and drew it taut. Wrapping the excess hemp around his arm, he dropped to a sitting position on the rim of the circle and then, very, very slowly, began lowering himself into the Egyptian Room.

When he was a mere three feet off the ground, he began swinging his legs back and forth until he was sailing through the air like a child in a swing. As he neared the box containing the Eye he released more rope and jumped down to the top of the box. Not wanting to leave any more of this venture to chance, he had visited the museum that afternoon in order to make absolutely sure the amulet was there. He had also, to his great relief, seen young Officer O'Hara, looking hale and hearty and over his illness, standing guard outside the building. Hopefully the young officer would have a few more weeks of life before the curse struck him down.

For a few blood-curdling seconds Malcolm balanced on his toes, terrified the glass case would not support his weight. The panels groaned, but held. Breathing a sigh of relief, he knelt on the glass, once again removed his hammer from his satchel, and knocked a small hole in the top of the case. Again he froze, listening for alarms since he was not absolutely certain his contacts who'd told him about the floor security system had been correct, and that the new alarm was not really attached, somehow, to the display cases themselves.

He heard nothing but silence. It seemed almost too easy to pluck the Eye of Horus from its bed of white satin and drop both it and the hammer into his satchel. Seconds later he shimmied back up the rope and pulled himself out of the circular hole in the dome, breathing a sigh of relief that his long-unused skills at breaking into locked enclosures had not deserted him. A few minutes later he climbed back down the museum wall and walked swiftly down the alley toward the main street.

He had just left the alley and was turning onto the sidewalk in front of the museum when a slender figure slinked out of the shadows. Malcolm pivoted, instinctively reaching for his cane, only to remember he had left it at home, since he'd assumed it would be more of a hindrance than a help.

"Oi, mate," the figure whispered, stepping under one of the gaslights lining the road. The gleam of light on metal showed that the figure was carrying a knife, which it proceeded to wave back and forth, menacingly. "'And it over."

Malcolm forced himself to remain calm, knowing his only chance at besting the robber, since the thief was armed and Malcolm was not, was through trickery. "Hand what over?" he asked steadily. "Tell me what you want, and I will give it to you."

"The amulet. I want the amulet."

When the robber waved his knife again, Malcolm said smoothly, "All right. It's in my bag. I'll give it to you."

The robber nodded and waited, silently.

When Malcolm had loosened the satchel from his waist, he withdrew the amulet. "Here it is. What do you want me to do with it?"

The bandit shifted from side to side as if uncertain what to do next. "Set it down on the sidewalk, turn, and walk away."

"I'll do better than that. I'll toss it to you." Lifting his hand, Malcolm hurled the Eye straight up into the air. It flew backward, into the alley. He shook his head. "Damn. Sorry about that."

As the bandit ran forward to grab the amulet before it could smash into the ground, Malcolm lowered his head. Thrusting his skull into the robber's belly, he propelled the bandit backward into the museum's side wall. The bandit dropped the knife and let out a grunt as his head smacked into brick. He sank to the road. As he did, the kerchief covering his hair and face slipped.

For a moment, Malcolm's heart stopped beating. Then, burning-hot rage, surely hotter even than the flames of hell, roared through his body like a raging inferno.

"Phoebe!" he snarled. He dropped to his knees beside her motionless form on the wet street. "For God's sake, you imbecilic, impulsive, stupid woman! I could have killed you! My God! I would rather slice my own neck than hurt you. How could you be so utterly, completely brainless? What in the bloody hell are you doing here?"

"Ungh—" She wheezed, still suffering from his blow and unable to catch her breath.

"No! Don't tell me. I don't want to know. God, woman, I could kill you! But I won't. I will do precisely what I threatened to do if you came here tonight." Reaching out, he jerked her roughly toward him, bent her over his lap, and began slapping her breeched backside with sharp, yet controlled, blows.

"Malcolm!" Phoebe managed at last. Her arms and legs flailed. "Stop, please! You're hurting me!"

"I don't mean this to tickle, Phoebe. You broke your word."

"I didn't! Ow! I said I wouldn't come with you. Ouch! And I didn't. I came alone. Ow! Stop it, Malcolm!"

Lifting her to a kneeling position, he glared down at her. "You said you wouldn't come with *me,* so that makes everything all right? That is the most lame excuse I have ever heard."

"It is not an excuse," she said angrily. "I kept my

word. Not once did I say I would not come here tonight. As I already told you, I said I would not come *with you.*"

Gritting his teeth, Malcolm glared. "Oh, well that's just fine, then, isn't it? Are you aware that you could easily have been killed? What if I'd killed you? What would you have done then?"

Phoebe gazed up at Sir Malcolm's furious countenance, vaguely aware that his spectacles had fallen off in the scuffle. "Why, then I suppose I'd be dead and unable to do anything at all."

She was truly furious with him for spanking her. However, she realized with a large dose of astonishment, it was at the same time almost pleasant to have someone care enough about her welfare to think her digressions worth a spanking. Her own father had never bothered to punish her. He'd not even seemed aware of her existence, much less cared when she did something wrong. And she knew very well that coming here tonight had been very foolish.

She wondered, startled, why on earth she felt almost *happy* that Sir Malcolm had spanked her. Was it perhaps because she had come to see him as an authority figure, as someone she would not mind letting into her life? Not to take control, since she would never be completely willing to give up her independence, but perhaps to keep his hands on the reins for a time?

Independence sometimes became fatiguing, and, if truth be known, it was really very lonely. And while Sir Malcolm *had* overstepped the bounds in delivering a spanking—she was not a child, after all—he had still, in some strange way, proved supremely reliable because he had kept his word and done exactly as he'd said he would, especially since what he'd done had been utterly unthinkable. Her reasoning seemed outrageous in the extreme, even to her, but there it was.

To her relief, the baronet tipped his head back and began laughing. "God's precious blood, Phoebe. Every time I think I understand you, you surprise me again. You'd be dead eh? So you would."

Rising, he took her hands and helped her to her feet. She looked up at him uncertainly.

"I am sorry about that," he said then. "I had no right to punish you. No adult has the right to lay a hand on another." He added, thoughtfully, "You may strike me, now, if it will make you feel better."

The words were scarcely out of his mouth when she drew her hand back and slapped him hard across the face. He gaped at her, open-mouthed. Then he asked shakily, "Am I forgiven, then?"

Phoebe grinned and shook her hand. The blow had stung her as much as she expected it had hurt him. "Yes. Though I was angry at you for treating me like a child, now I feel much better. And I do not really blame you for spanking me, though if you do it again," she said warningly, "I shall never forgive you and shall hit you back with more than my hand."

"Don't worry." He grinned and rubbed his jaw. "You pack a mean right cross. But really, Phoebe, I do hope you will forgive me for overstepping the bounds of propriety. It is just that I was so worried about you, so horrified that you might have been hurt, that I lost control for a moment. It does not happen often." His gaze softened. "And then it happens only with people I care about deeply. I was forever scolding my younger brother, before he died."

Phoebe returned Malcolm's gaze. She believed he cared about her, but not in the way she wished. He did not want their betrothal to stand, and she simply could not humiliate herself further by begging him to go through with the marriage. She did not know how to respond, so she said nothing at all.

Both remembered the Eye of Horus at the same moment. They turned as one and began searching for it on the wet ground.

"Don't touch the amulet once we've located it," Sir Malcolm insisted. "Please?"

Phoebe was touched by his entreaty, but was torn by indecision. Though she still doubted the curse's veracity, the baronet obviously still believed in it. She gazed at him uncertainly. No, she decided abruptly. She would not touch it. How could she, when he was only asking because he believed the amulet would hurt her?

At that moment she thought she loved him more than ever. And far more than she had ever loved the Eye of Horus, superb artifact though it was.

He looked up when she did not respond. "Phoebe? I mean it. Please don't touch it." A smile tugged at his lips. "I know I have no right to tell you what to do, but I'm asking you to tell me, in precisely the right words, that you won't."

She gazed at him solemnly, fully aware that to give her promise would be tantamount to allowing the amulet's destruction. Nevertheless, she nodded. "I will not touch the amulet when we find it, Malcolm. I give you my word."

He stared at her, obviously finding it hard to believe she had capitulated. Finally he said huskily, as if speaking past deep emotion, "Thank you. I know what that promise cost you."

Then both turned and began seeking the amulet once again. They found it lying in a shallow puddle next to the museum wall. Sir Malcolm plucked it from the water and brushed it against his shirt. He glanced at it, and then at Phoebe, briefly.

Picking up a large stone, he laid the Eye on a level spot in the road and brought the rock down hard against the amulet. Several dull thuds later, the amulet had been turned into a pile of crushed jewels and a misshapen lump of gold.

Phoebe watched, sick at heart but certain Sir Malcolm was doing what he thought best. Then he turned, tucked the remaining bits of the amulet into his pocket, took her by the arm, and they walked to the front of the museum, with Sir Malcolm limping slightly.

There they hired a hansom cab and, holding tightly to each other, drove to the London docks, dismounted, and walked down a long pier to the water's edge. Drawing a deep breath, Sir Malcolm put back his arm and hurled the misshapen hunk of metal far out into the night-blackened sea. When he turned back he put his arm about Phoebe's shoulders and looked deep into her eyes.

"Thank you for trusting me, Phoebe," he said softly. He lowered his head and kissed her once, gently. "Although we were only pledged to marry for a short time, I could not have asked for a more superb fiancée."

Phoebe swallowed hard, blinking back tears. "Nor could I. You know, all my life I scoffed at the fairy tale of the gallant knight rescuing his maiden on a snow-white charger and carrying her away to his castle on the hill, and yet no maid could ever have had a more gallant knight than you, Sir Malcolm. With or without a white stallion or a castle. Thank you, from the bottom of my heart, for a truly grand adventure."

Sir Malcolm smiled down at her, his expression strangely melancholy. They climbed back into the cab and drove to Phoebe's townhouse, where he walked her to her gate. He kissed her again, tenderly, and turned to leave.

Suddenly, Phoebe grabbed his arm. "Wait. Please." She ran into the house, returning a few seconds later. "I . . . I forgot to give this back. It is yours." Thrusting something into his hand, she whirled about and disappeared into the townhouse.

Malcolm glanced down at the object. It was the slim leather volume of love poems he had loaned to her at the house party at The Meadows.

Putting the book in his pocket, he returned home. There, he removed the volume from his coat and laid it on his library desk, certain he would never open the book again, since to do so would only shatter his already fractured heart.

23

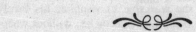

"Phoebe, you must eat something," Matty insisted anxiously. "You are beginning to look as thin as a ghost. I am so worried about you, dear."

Phoebe glanced vaguely at her cousin. "Thank you, but I am not hungry," she said wearily.

Matty frowned and clamped her hands down on her own thinning hips. "I have had enough of this moping about, Phoebe. All right, so your engagement to the baronet has ended. I do not know what happened between the two of you, but you've got to snap out of this brown study.

"It has been a week since you printed the retraction notice we drafted, and you haven't been out of the house since. You must go out or people will begin thinking that Sir Malcolm was the one who wished to end your betrothal. And if they begin believing that, you will never regain your good reputation."

Phoebe bit back a sob. Tears sprang to her eyes, and she brushed them away, furiously. "He *was* the one who wanted the retraction printed, Matty. I have told you all about it."

"So what? I do not want to see you tear yourself up any more than you already have about this dreadful occurrence, Phoebe. I, and so many others, love you far too much to watch you waste away because of it. I insist you sit down at that breakfast table and eat a good meal. Now.''

Too physically and emotionally exhausted to argue, Phoebe did as she was told. She had to admit, afterward, that she did feel somewhat stronger. While her heart still ached, she knew she would survive the end of her engagement to Sir Malcolm. Although she would always love him more than life, she was able to visualize his lovely hazel eyes, sparkling behind his spectacles, without weeping uncontrollably.

''Good,'' Matty said as Phoebe finished a third piece of toast. ''Now I want you to go upstairs and rest until this evening. I will not have you looking wan at my betrothal ball.''

''Oh, Matty,'' Phoebe said mournfully, shaking her head. Her hair, carefully dressed by Tribble, remained securely in place. ''I cannot rest.''

''You can and you will,'' Matty said firmly. ''I know you have not been sleeping, because I have seen candlelight under your bedchamber door every night for the last week. I left you alone then, because I knew you needed some time to yourself. But I can stand by and watch no longer. You are going upstairs, you are going to bed, and this evening you will put on your prettiest ball gown and dance the night away as if you hadn't a care in the world.''

Phoebe looked into Matty's worried face, and could not refuse. With Matty holding her elbow and propelling her forward like a sheepdog with a recalcitrant lamb, she went to her room, lay down across her bed, and was instantly asleep.

That evening, shortly after the betrothal ball for Miss Mathilde Stoat and Lord Thomas Creevey was to have begun, Sir Malcolm was just finishing a light repast before seeking an early bed. His trunk was packed, and his yacht, the *Lotus,* awaited his pleasure at the docks for his voyage to Zanzibar, on which he was to leave in the morning.

He finished his dinner and had decided to give in to a momentary lapse of self-control and go to his library, where he would undoubtedly spend the next several hours thinking about Phoebe, instead of to his bed, when he passed by the hall table on which Fobbs always left the daily pile of invitations. The pile was particularly deep, since Malcolm had not viewed the notes for the past week.

He paused to leaf lackadaisically through the stack, and had gone no further than halfway through it when he noticed a white envelope inscribed with Michael Dane, Lord Cullen's name.

Malcolm frowned. A letter from Michael? But Michael was supposed to have reached London in the morning, in order to leave on their voyage. Why would he send a letter in his stead?

Several other envelopes fell to the floor, unheeded, as Malcolm snatched up Michael's letter. He snapped the wax seal as he walked quickly down the hall to his library. As he seated himself at his desk, something small and shiny fell from his ink blotter to the thick aubusson carpet at his feet.

Bending to pick the object up, he recognized it as Phoebe's hairpin. His heart ached as he plucked it from the floor and set it on the desk atop the small leather volume of Byron's poems. His fingers brushed the leather volume tenderly. Suddenly he paused, and narrowed his eyes as he gazed at the book. Was something tucked between its pages?

Setting Lord Cullen's letter on his desk, he picked up the volume. It fell open immediately, exposing a dried spray of forget-me-nots.

Malcolm's chest constricted painfully. Why had Phoebe saved the flowers he'd put in her hair? His heart squeezed tighter. Sweet heaven. Surely she would not have done so unless she had felt more than friendship for him. Yet, he thought ruefully, touching the fragile petals gently, that did not mean she wanted to be married. And, as wonderful as wedding his darling girl would be, it did not mean he would marry her only to leave her a widow shortly thereafter.

Closing the book, he set it back on his desk, replaced

the gold hairpin on its cover, and picked up Lord Cullen's letter. He began to read.

Malcolm,

I write to you with most alarming news. Since arriving back in Egypt it has come to my attention that the Eye of Horus, which was sent to you in England as thanks for your discovery of Pharaoh Setet II's fabulous tomb, is a forgery. The genuine Eye was stolen from its packing crate on the Egyptian docks and was taken directly to a master jeweler in Cairo, who reproduced a copy. That copy was sent to you in the original amulet's place.

I have had the opportunity to observe this jeweler's work, and can honestly say that even I, who with all humility call myself, next to you, the best fraud-detector in the field of archaeology, could not differentiate between the man's creations and genuine artifacts.

Since the forgery was made, seven deaths, in addition to the thirteen you are already aware of, including that of the jeweler, have occurred. The other six have all been among top artifact collectors from both Europe and the East. All of these fatalities, in my opinion, have been due to the curse of the Eye of Horus.

It seems that each time the amulet's current owner dies, it is immediately resold to another collector, since there are more than enough men whose greed is stronger than their common sense. However, since the Egyptian officials believe the curse to be a mere flight of fancy, they are extremely embarrassed at having sent you a fake amulet in return for all your services and are actively seeking the Eye in order to ship it directly to you.

Malcolm, I pray you will come to Egypt immediately. We must find and destroy the amulet. We must not allow the curse to work its evil on English soil.

Rather than returning home to leave for our voyage to Zanzibar, I will remain in Egypt until I hear from you. Yrs.,

Michael Dane, Lord Cullen

Malcolm's hands trembled as he lay the letter down on his desk and stared blindly at his friend's sprawling script. In the back of his mind he remembered boasting to Phoebe of his expertise in detecting fraudulent artifacts, and flushed with chagrin.

But to think that the Eye was still rampaging through Egypt!

It was dreadful. It was horrible. It was . . .

A slow smile drifted over his face. Pushing up his spectacles in a decidedly resolute manner, he leapt to his feet, rushed to his bedchamber, and called for his valet. In a matter of minutes he was dressed in his finest evening clothes. Then, grabbing up his ebony cobra-handled cane, he ran out his back door, hurried to his garden, and cut a large bouquet of flowers. Turning toward his back door, he shouted loudly, "Fobbs! A white horse! I must have a white horse at once!"

The hideous butler thrust his head out the door, saw Sir Malcolm standing there in full evening dress, and smiled so widely it looked as if his bull-doggish face would split in two. "Immediately, sir!" he cried.

Ten minutes later Sir Malcolm, mounted upon a snow-white horse borrowed from a neighbor, galloped at full speed toward the Lawton townhouse, where his Uncle Thomas and Miss Mathilde Stoat were hosting their betrothal ball. And where his darling Phoebe waited.

Phoebe tried to look enthusiastic when Lord Peter Simmons asked her if she would like to waltz, but she could only sum up a token smile. She glided into his arms and across the floor with more grace than she had ever before possessed. But somehow, the music, which had always thrilled her to the marrow of her bones, failed to raise her spirits. To Phoebe's heartsick ears it sounded more like a funeral dirge than a celebratory dance.

Nearby, Lord Peter's twin, Lady Jane, waltzed past with a tall, thin young man whose hair was every bit as red as the twins', and who had nearly as many freckles as Jane herself. The two young people seemed blissfully unaware of anyone else as they moved across the ballroom floor. Phoebe was glad that they, and Matty and Lord Thomas, at least, had found a happy ending.

She was also glad that the betrothal ball was taking place in her own townhouse, since she would be able to escape to her bedchamber early. The ball had only been going for an hour, and already she was wondering if it was too soon to take her leave. Being around so many of Matty's smiling, well-wishing guests made Phoebe feel restless and irritable, and she had no desire to cast a pall over the celebration. Matty deserved better than that.

At Matty's insistence, Phoebe had donned a ball gown she'd ordered at the beginning of the Season but had not yet worn. Made of a blue silk that was so pale it seemed almost white until candlelight shone upon it at just the right angle, it was edged with sky-blue satin piping along the hem and sleeves. The neckline was very low, exposing a generous amount of Phoebe's bosom. Long white gloves and white kidskin slippers completed the ensemble.

Phoebe had offered no resistance when Matty had gone to Phoebe's jewelry chest and chosen a necklace and earrings of small star sapphires set in platinum to accent Phoebe's gown, nor when the older woman had instructed Tribble to thread a strand of small diamonds through Phoebe's golden hair. There was, Phoebe realized dimly as Lord Peter whirled her around the dance floor, not a hair out of place in the coiffure, a la Madonna, that the maid had laboriously constructed.

And yet, Phoebe thought, recalling her reflection in her bedchamber looking glass, no lovely clothing, no jewels, no expertly dressed hair could add any sparkle to her eyes. Her eyes looked almost dead—a perfect reflection of the state of her soul.

Though she knew, in time, she would recover from losing the love of her life, for now all she could do was mourn losing Sir Malcolm as if he had truly died, rather than just departed from her life at his own free will.

The waltz ended just as a flurry of motion near the ballroom entrance made Phoebe cast a dull glance in that direction. Immediately the grace she had been blessed with during the dance vanished, and she stomped hard on Lord Peter's slipper.

"Ouch!" he cried, then turned to see what had captured her attention. "Good God. Do you want me to throw him out, Phoebe?"

Phoebe could not answer. Her heart pounded so violently she thought it would leap out of her chest. Her hand flew up to her throat, and she stood motionless on the dance floor. The ball guests, seeing the baronet's approach, parted in a wave as if spread by the hand of Moses.

Phoebe stood alone in the center of the room. Tears sprang to her eyes and began sliding, unheeded, down her cheeks. She remained silent while Sir Malcolm handed his ebony cobra-handled cane to a footman and walked the long length of the dance floor to stand before her.

In his white-gloved hands he held a huge bouquet of vivid blue forget-me-nots. When he reached her side, he grinned nervously, the same delightful, boyish, crooked grin that had made Phoebe's heart pound from their very first conversation. Extending the flowers, he said nothing until she had accepted his token. Then, dropping to his knees, he gazed up at her.

Phoebe was faintly aware of the tears on her face, although they were not the same tears of heartbreak she had shed for the past week, but tears of joy that seemed to well up from the bottom of her heart.

Sir Malcolm pushed his spectacles up, firmly. Then he said gravely, "Phoebe. My darling, wonderful Miss Lawton. I lay my heart and my hand and all my worldly goods at your feet, and ask if you will make me the happiest man on earth.

"I do not have a castle on a hill or a snow-white stallion, but I have borrowed a snow-white mare that waits outside to carry you off to wherever you will. I am not much of a gallant knight, but if you will settle for a half-crippled bookworm who sometimes acts like an ape, I shall spend the rest of my life trying to make you happy and giving you as many adventures as your heart desires.''

Phoebe brushed ineffectively at her tears, and said brokenly, ''But you don't want to marry me, Malcolm. You said yourself you wanted our betrothal to last only until we had found and destroyed the amulet.''

He grinned again. ''Ah, there's the rub, my lovely partner in crime. We have *not* found the amulet.''

''What!''

''The amulet we destroyed was a fake.'' His grin faltered, and he flushed as he admitted his failure to detect the fraudulent Eye. His eyes clearly reflected his hope that she would not mock him for his mistake and remind him of his boastful words at the London Metropolitan Museum. ''The real Eye of Horus is still working its evil on the people of Egypt. Unless we go to Cairo immediately and seek out and destroy the genuine artifact, the Egyptian government will locate it and ship it to England. We cannot allow it to work its dastardly evil on British soil.''

Phoebe gazed at his face, so dear to her. Of course she would not chide him for his error. ''But you do not need me anymore, Malcolm,'' she said gently, her heart aching. ''If you are merely concerned about our partnership, you may forget about it. I simply do not have the will to continue with a sham betrothal. Anyway, look around us. Everyone here is taking in every word we utter. Our ruse would no longer fool any of them. Besides, you are to go to Zanzibar shortly.''

Sir Malcolm got to his feet. Reaching out, he grasped Phoebe's forearms. He shook her gently. ''Phoebe, you aren't listening to me. I want you to marry me. Really marry me. No more sham betrothals. No more pretending that I do not love you more than the sun loves the sky. My darling girl,'' he said, his voice breaking, ''I cannot live without you. Zanzibar be hanged.''

Phoebe gasped as an obvious fact occurred to her. "Malcolm! You did not touch the Eye of Horus until it reached the London docks! Does that mean you are not cursed? You no longer believe you are going to die? Is that what you are trying to tell me?"

"Yes," he shouted, lifting her into his arms and spinning her in a circle. "Why did you think I did not insist you marry me before?"

"I thought you simply did not want me."

"Not want you?" he asked disbelievingly. "My God, Phoebe, how could you ever have believed that? My dearest love, I feel as if I have been offered a new chance at life. And I want nothing more than to spend every moment of the time I have been given with you, whether it be thirty minutes or thirty years. Say you will marry me, Phoebe. Come to Egypt with me. I may not have a castle, but I will gladly give you the pyramids."

Lowering her brows, Phoebe pulled away gently. "Malcolm," she scolded, "do you not think you are behaving a bit impulsively? You realize that the amulet is dangerous, and yet you want to go vaulting off on an expedition to recover it?"

"Oh, yes. I am behaving quite impulsively," he agreed blissfully. "My self-restraint may go to the devil! Besides, you seem to have absorbed a good deal of my former cautious nature. I am sure you will temper my impetuosity."

Phoebe shook her head, uncertainly. "I do not know if this journey is such a good idea. If you touched the amulet, you would be cursed. I would not want to lose you after only just winning you. No, I will go nowhere unless you give me your word you will not touch the Eye of Horus. And that when we do find it, it will be destroyed immediately."

"Anything, my love, as long as you will say you are mine."

"Well," she said slowly. "I suppose someone had better go along to make sure you are properly careful." Then she smiled brilliantly. Reaching up, she blended his cowlick into his sandy-brown hair. "And I have always been yours, Malcolm. From the first day I read one of your articles in the *Times*."

Malcolm bent down and kissed her passionately. Then, as the orchestra struck up a sweeping waltz and the other guests set up a cheer and moved back onto the dance floor, he said, "One final waltz, Phoebe, and then I will carry you off on my borrowed charger. After I give you a quick tour of my artifact collection, we will leave on our journey this very night. The captain of my yacht can marry us beneath a sky filled with stars. That is," he added quickly, a frown creasing his brow, "if you trust me enough to commend your future into my safekeeping."

Phoebe smiled radiantly as all her fears about marriage and entrusting her future to a man vanished like clouds after a storm. Sir Malcolm was like no other man in the world, of that she was certain. He was hers, and she was his, and that was the way it would be until the end of time.

"I trust you, Malcolm," she answered sincerely. "With both my life, and my heart."

As Matty and Lord Thomas and Lady Jane and Lord Peter and all the other members of the ton looked on, the baronet put both hands around Phoebe's waist, swept her into the air, held her deliciously close to his solidly muscled chest, and whirled her about the dance floor until she was dizzy with life and love and happiness. When the dance ended, Phoebe realized that Tribble's carefully pinned coiffure had come undressed, and that her hair was cascading down her back in a wildly curling tangle.

They moved to the side of the ballroom, where Phoebe saw Matty standing beside the wall. The older woman beamed, weeping a little, and hugged both Phoebe and the baronet. "I knew everything would work out all right," she said moistly.

"Thank you, Matty," he answered, kissing her cheek. He quickly explained his plan to take Phoebe to his townhouse and then to Egypt, asking if Matty would mind overseeing the packing of Phoebe's trunks and the subsequent delivery of them to 102 Pritchard Place. Matty assented readily. Then he said, "Take care of Uncle Thomas, won't you?"

"And Bastet?" Phoebe inserted, remembering her cat.

"I will do both," Matty assured, sniffing. "You take care of yourselves."

"We shall."

They went outside amid the well-wishes of their friends. Sir Malcolm lifted Phoebe, still clasping the bouquet of forget-me-nots, onto the white mare's back. Swinging himself up behind her, he tucked his cane under one arm, settled his tall beaver hat jauntily onto the back of his head, pushed up his spectacles, and buried his face in her loose curls.

A surge of happiness stronger than anything Phoebe had ever felt swept through her. Snuggling into the warm curve of the baronet's shoulder, she murmured contentedly, "I love you, Malcolm. Even though you are a bit impulsive."

He hugged her tight. When his cheek brushed hers, she felt dampness on his skin. "And I love you, Phoebe. Even though you are a bit too sedate for my liking."

Together they rode off into the distance, each thinking that the future, while it would undoubtedly have its share of challenges, had never looked so bright.